Leonard Woolsey Bacon

A Life Worth Living

Memorials of Emily Bliss Gould, of Rome

Leonard Woolsey Bacon

A Life Worth Living
Memorials of Emily Bliss Gould, of Rome

ISBN/EAN: 9783744784535

Printed in Europe, USA, Canada, Australia, Japan

Cover: Foto ©Raphael Reischuk / pixelio.de

More available books at **www.hansebooks.com**

A Life Worth Living.

MEMORIALS OF

EMILY BLISS GOULD,

OF ROME.

BY

LEONARD WOOLSEY BACON.

NEW YORK:

ANSON D. F. RANDOLPH & CO.,

900 BROADWAY, COR. 20th STREET.

TO

MRS. EDGECUMBE EDWARDES,

AND

TO ALL THOSE CHRISTIAN WOMEN

OF

ITALY, GREAT BRITAIN, AND THE UNITED STATES
OF AMERICA,

WHO

HAVE AIDED, AND ARE STILL PROMOTING, THE CHARITABLE

WORKS BEGUN AT ROME

BY

EMILY BLISS GOULD,

THESE MEMORIALS ARE DEDICATED.

CONTENTS.

V.

1861—1865.

REDEEMING THE TIME:

VI.

1861—1866.

THE WALDENSES:

VII.

1866—1870.

THE FLORENCE ORPHANAGE:

VIII.

1859—1871.

CONTEMPORARY HISTORY:

I.

NEW YORK TO PARIS.

*Leave-taking—The Beginning of a Long Journal
—A Fortnight of Misery—Havre to Paris—The
First Zest of Travel.*

THE sailing of a young wife for her first visit from the New World to the Old is an every-day affair; but it is like a wedding or a funeral in this, that however common it may become, it can never be commonplace. There is so much in the occasion to touch the universal sympathy—not love alone, but the eagerness of hope, the lingering look behind, the relentings of heart toward those that are left, and, amid all the gayety and good cheer, the emerging into consciousness, from moment to moment, of that inevitable spectre of uncertainty which haunts the cabin of every departing ship.

Not many elements of personal interest were wanting when Emily Bliss, with her husband, Dr. James B. Gould, sailed from New York to Havre, in the summer of 1860. She was no longer a bride, for it was seven years since

(7)

her marriage to Dr. Gould, then surgeon in the United States Navy; and she was thirty-eight years of age. But she had not outlived, she never did outlive, the youthful beauty and grace by which she was distinguished in New York society. Her fine feminine wit and address were such as to fit her for an easy and unenvied leadership in whatever social circle she might enter. And to these attractive qualities were added a true dignity of Christian discipleship, and an "enthusiasm of humanity," which had endeared her to a multitude, not only of the high, but of the lowly. It is not necessary to say, then, that Mrs. Gould's "send-off," when she sailed for Havre, was an exceptional one. Of the multitude of handkerchiefs that waved from the crowd of friends upon the dock, as the steamer floated down the North River, not a few were wet with honest tears for the loss of a benefactress as well as of a friend. If the future could have been foreseen, the friends that lingered to watch the ship as she went dwindling through the Narrows might have spoken to each other the words of the weeping prophet: "Weep sore for her that goeth away; for she shall return no more, nor see her native country."

The story of the Atlantic voyage is a tale so manifold more than twice told that it might well be passed by, were it not that the grave distresses of the trip in Mrs. Gould's case had so much to do in determining the subsequent course of her life. But the story would be incomplete indeed if it failed to record the incidents upon which, in a considerable degree, the later action hinges.

It is almost impossible for me to describe our voyage from New York to Havre. It was a dreadful mixture of fever, foreign lingo, sea-sickness, ship-wrecks, frights, thirst and misery generally. We started with a fine sunshiny afternoon. Everybody seemed in good spirits. Our leave-taking was a levee. I did not know we had so many friends. I think there were full a hundred who came down to say good-bye. For myself, I kept up good courage until the ship parted her last cable, when I would have given anything to jump ashore again. We went down to tea with good appetites, after which I was very magnificent putting Carrie to bed. The next day was a lovely one too, and we all assembled for worship in the saloon. It was very sweet to direct our thoughts to the same Father who was watching the dear friends we had left and who holds the winds and waves in His hand.

The next day I disappeared from human view. For four days I never saw Mrs. R—— at all. For five successive nights I never closed my eyes. Tell me of the majestic magnificence of the sea, and the grandeur of being borne on its bosom. I insist that it is a beast—I am almost ready to say *the* beast. It has a thousand claws to shake you with, a tail three thousand miles long to pound you with, a monstrous broad back with which it runs under you to bump the breath out of your body; a great gaping mouth with which it is ever striving to swallow you. It is a treacherous, fierce, rioting, noisy, thumping, fight-ing villain. It has no crested waves, no moonlit

1*

beauty, no lovely sunrises, no anything good, but everything bad.

There was an angel on board in the shape of a chambermaid, who fed me on ice. Poor James took a dreadful cold, which saved my life, as it was caught from an open window without which I could not exist. At last, on Tuesday came the first light-house in view. This was the fifteenth of the month, we having left New York May 5, 1860. Soon afterward came The Lizard light-houses, lines of breakers, then The Needles, and at last the lovely Isle of Wight, with its verdure such as we never see, its cottages, its beautiful cultivation, and its sweet hedge-rows. It was like a lovely dream, that short glimpse of England, to sick and weary eyes. Here we parted with some pleasant fellow-passengers, and were soon steaming on toward Havre. We were obliged to lie by for the fog during the night, so that it was late in the afternoon when the bluff just off Havre rose on our sight. This slopes down to join a hill, up which creeps the old town. We floated past a queer old excrescence of stone with a several-storied tumor of wood on the top of it, called St. Francis' Tower, passed a series of long, low, quaint old houses, and were in the heart of the city.

Here were narrow streets, high pinched houses, be-capped women, be-red-trowsered men, and every-thing new and strange. Soon we were taken captive by magnificently attired *gendarmes*, and on deliver-ing our passports, allowed once more to tread dear mother earth. Here we entered a couple of car-riages and were driven to Frascati's. We were in

the hands of an immaculately got-up driver. On
arriving at the hotel he charged and we paid one
franc for his mustache, one for his white gloves, and
one for his elegant appearance generally — three
francs more than the other carriage being all that he
charged.

Frascati's is a queer old place. It is an immense
pile of buildings around a court. The grounds are
laid out with lovely flowers, trees, and shrubs. Then
there is a large clock-tower, piles of tiny turrets, a
theatre, a concert-room, etc. Beyond, one was at
sea again; Frascati's sea-baths being celebrated.
The interior is, first, a paved corridor with marble
stairs at each side; there is an office on one side, and
a little conciergerie on the other. Up one flight of
stairs the fat landlady proceeded and we went up by
the other. . . . .

We were all day getting our goods from the
custom - house, leaving in the afternoon for Rouen.
That lovely ride! It is too bad that I have forgotten so much of its beauty; for it is now nearly
two weeks since we saw it, and so much has occurred
in this time that the pictures are very much faded
from my mind. The railroad is hedged for miles.
Indeed, there are no fences to be seen excepting just
at the stations; these latter are situated each in its
own little garden, smiling with beauty. The hills
seem to roll *both ways*, unlike our own, and every
inch is covered with cultivation. The different
shades of green, meeting and crossing each other
in every direction; the flocks of sheep feeding on
the hill-sides, each with a black dog and a brown

boy to attend it ; the cows tethered carefully day by day so that there is lovely verdure before and blackness of brownness behind poor Moolly ; the trees so trimmed that the poplars look like long poles with green plumes in the dim distance above ; the plantations exquisitely green and leafy ; the châteaux so grand and extensive ; the mud or stone cottages of the peasants thatched with sloping roofs ; the villages with narrow, crooked streets, and odd, gabled houses ; all form a picture so novel and so lovely that we were in a fever of delight and excitement. It was a fête day, and the smiling peasants met us at each station. They looked very neat and very good-natured. The houses are the most interesting edifices I ever saw. They seem so squeezed that their eyes in the shape of windows are always popping out unexpectedly. They seem each to stand on tip-toe and elbow his neighbor to have a good peep at you, and look like an over-dressed lady with tier upon tier of gables, staircases, and windows peering one above the other.

Mrs. Gould was always an enthusiastic traveler. The many volumes of her journal, extending through fifteen years, show with what zealous and delighted study she devoted herself to gaining the utmost for her own improvement, from her frequent visits to the most interesting countries of Europe. And as time went on, and her own genuine and sincere instinct of appreciation became trained by large opportunities of comparison, and by the reading of the best masters in criticism, she gained a faculty of quick insight into works of art which makes her, in her later journals, a delightful guide to the sights best worth seeing in the great art-galleries of the world. But there is something in the rapture of first meeting with the great objects of art and history, in a mind well prepared for it by early culture, which is like "love's young dream." It never comes a second time; but while it stays it is a finer thing than criticism, and is even keener-sighted, in some respects, making observations which the practiced eye fails of just because it is practiced.

We shall be interested in reading a few more pages from the first volume of the journal; especially some of the commonplace pages, that show us what are the little things that "strike a stranger" just arrived. The wondering examination with which she takes inventory of the belongings of her first lodgings at Paris answers just the questions that some of us want to ask, but which old travelers in general quite forget to answer; and to others of us it brings up a pleasant reminiscence of our own first hour in a strange country. Withal, as we read from page to page, we shall be gradually getting better acquainted with the writer.

We have secured rooms at 236 Rue de Rivoli. We have a spacious parlor on the second floor. There are three square mirrors, one over the mantel which is decorated with a pair of bronze and gilt candelabra, and a bronze warrior leaning upon a gilt clock. Opposite the mantel is a pier-table, and over it a pier-glass. This stands between two curtained windows, one of which windows turns out to be a looking-glass. Under another square mirror is another pier-table with smaller candelabra. There are two crimson velvet sofas, four fauteuils, ordinary chairs *ad libitum*, a center-table, a large writing-table, two card-tables, and so forth. In the middle of the room is a very old-fashioned glass chandelier with gilt candlesticks. There are branches for candles in different parts of the room. . . . .

We have as yet seen but little. We spent an hour, one day, in the Salle de Napoléon at the Louvre. To me it was most affecting. There was his throne. There an arm-chair from his cabinet. We looked at the splendid crimson-and-gold and scarlet-and-gold coats, and the elegant white satin mantle embroidered with gold bees. Here were the cocked hats he wore on various occasions, the clothes that he wore at St. Helena, and locks of his hair and of his son's hair. But more interesting still were the little iron camp-bedstead which pillowed that great head, the folding-chair in which he sat and planned kingdoms and an empire, the desk at which he sat and consigned crowns to dust. Sad beyond description are the mementoes of the king of Rome—the gilt cradle, the little cups and saucers, the bows and arrows, and the rest of his toys. For this child the great father sacrificed his love and his honor, and brought down upon himself the wrath of God. And how was he punished in the child! An early, unhonored grave received the last hope of that proud parent. A life without one promise, a death without one hope!

Poor man! Almost a god, but when he attempted to be more than an instrument in the hands of his Maker, crushed like a moth!

. . . . Shall I ever forget our first drive to Neuilly the day after we arrived in Paris,—up the beautiful Rue de Rivoli with its uninterrupted two miles of arches? Here are the lovely gardens of the Tuilleries, with their exquisitely shaded walks, their clipped trees, their statues and fountains; then the Place de la Concorde, which can be compared to nothing American, and in the midst of it the obelisk of Luxor, inaugurated by poor Louis Philippe with so much ceremony; and then, the great groups of statuary at the entrance to the Champs Elysées. . . .

II.

SEEKING A COUNTRY.

*Through the Low Countries—A Rubens Night-
mare—Baden-Baden — Palace and Dungeon—
Switzerland—Alps! Alps!!—Bad News and
Back to Paris—Ecole Evangélique—First Day in
Italy—The Waldenses — Church and Schools—
Viva Italia!*

THERE is no occasion to transcribe from these
journals of the "grand tour," pleasantly, sometimes charmingly written as they are, more than
here and there a few lines, less for the sake of the subjects
spoken of than as illustrating the character of the writer.
To say nothing further of the six weeks' sight-seeing at
Paris, we may join company with the party once more as
they start for Belgium and Holland.

The country (from Paris to Douai) is not like
ma Normandie. There is nothing of that rolling
contour of the land. Now and then there is a pretty
vista with hills in the background, but not often.
We saw little but a fine, well-cultivated, level farming
country. As we advanced the flatness became still

(16)

more marked. In France we certainly see more women than men in the fields. But the women after all do not look unhappy. They grow very homely, however; and it does grate very much against all our ideas to see them so employed. I think that is one reason why women are so little respected here. The poorer classes are always bending their backs double, or, if in the cities, frowning over accounts, and looking sharper than razors.

At Douai we found a fête, and the people nearly wild with delight, while they were as big as elephants with pride. On our way to the hotel, we came near being swallowed alive, carriage, horses, and all, by a big, pursy, pop-eyed gendarme. He ran himself nearly to death chasing us, because our horses did not go on tip-toe in passing a French horn and drum which were making a noise in the square. I never shall forget his ludicrous, hard-boiled-looking eyes as he ran beside the wheels.

And so on to Brussels with its famous buildings and pictures, and Waterloo with its monuments, and Bruges with its belfry, and Ghent with its Cathedral and its Town Hall.

It was market-day at Ghent, and the city was full of peasant women with queer caps and hats shaped like our old-fashioned straws with ribbons plastered at the back, lappets projecting on either side, and odd, hooded cloaks, called *failles*. We saw far too little of this strange place. We were obliged to take a long drive to the railroad station for Antwerp.

Near the station we went into a funny little Dutch café, and took our dinner in the kitchen to avoid the smoke of the dining-room. It was as neat as wax, with brick floor and nicely scrubbed utensils. A tiny stove held a handful of coal, with two ovens under the cylinder to keep things hot when cooked, as only a place as big as the hand was exposed directly to the fire. What the tea was, I do not know. It had never seen China, and was dealt in a pepper-box.

And now came a ride through the Low Country. I never saw such richness of vegetation. It was like Rubens's coloring. The fields extended to the very edge of the road, from which they were fenced by iron rods. Each ear of grain was a type of grace, and the whole scene one of laughing beauty. We crossed the Scheldt soon after leaving this lovely patchwork of farms and hedges, but not before passing through a country still partly unredeemed from the ravages of the fiendish Alva.

. . . . I can scarcely bear to write of our visit to Antwerp. To me it is almost like a nightmare. I suffered dreadfully and in a most mortifying manner there. I think Rubens is partly to blame. It seems as if I never should forget his magnificent pictures, and I am hardly yet able to write an account of them without running the risk of a sleepless night.

Then follows page after page of detailed description of the pictures, as if the writer wished thus to transcribe them for her own memory, and to hold fast the intensity of these first impressions, that can never be renewed. It was her method of art study. She would transcribe thus the principal pictures of a great gallery into her note-book, grouping, coloring, and all, as diligently as the professional student who copies with easel and canvas. Let the few words spoken of the Descent from the Cross suffice for an example:

No picture ever affected me as this one did. I was haunted by it for days. The flesh-tints of the body exceed anything imaginable in power; the body itself presented to the eye could not affect the mind more powerfully. *Death* is written all over it, in the coloring, the position, and the apparent weight of the figure. The body is partly extended upon the cere-cloth in which it is to be wrapped. . . . . The whole picture is wonderful. Rubens seems two men. In his great works here there seems a true religious element. Those at Paris are the works of a panderer to the lower tastes of man.

The Hague detains the tourists many days with its quiet beauty.

The first thing we saw as we looked out upon the square this morning was a Dutch funeral. The hearse was preceded by two clergymen with huge cocked hats and long weepers, short breeches, and long silk stockings. The hearse-drivers wore a white band, and those walking in the procession all wore white cravats. This singular city has many features to remind one of old and young New York. We welcome back areas and stoops once more, and greet a front door without a conciergerie as if it were an old friend.

The brick houses trimmed with stone, the gables, the
seats on the door-steps, are like our own olden times.
The peddlers bear their baskets and boxes on yokes,
as I remember the milkmen did when I was a very
small child in our own city.

At Amsterdam; arriving at evening, the party started
to inspect the amphibious old town by twilight, and had
" a most absurd walk."

Both in Belgium and in Holland we have been
much admired; but I think I never was so popular in
my life as at Amsterdam.   James' whiskers and
mustache were exceedingly attractive; and C——'s
and my round hats were a Crystal Palace to the
people.   At last we met several peasant girls dressed
in bodices and skirts, half of black and half of red,
and wearing gold horseshoe-shaped ornaments, nar-
rowing at the back of the head, and growing wider
at the front, where there was a chasing of gold, being
further adorned with two round-headed shawl-pins, so
placed as to look as if the pin were driven bodily into
the skull.   The hair was combed straight back from
the face.   A little cap was put on apparently hind-
side-before.   At any rate, there was a square opening in front which showed the hair.   At the back
there was a hole for the hair to come through, and
the cap and hair were bound into a wad, and wound
round with a cotton string.   A little white handkerchief of muslin covered the dress, which was cut as
low behind as a fashionable lady with us sometimes
chooses to cut hers in front.   A white apron with a

narrow black string completed the costume. While
we were objects of admiration to a female attired in
this manner, who was going in one direction, and to
another woman coming in another, the two met with
such a good, solid Dutch bump, as nearly to knock
the breath out of the latter's body. Turning to look
back and scold, the poor thing was next assaulted
by a round-faced, big-stomached, gaping boy, who, I
think, finished her. For, just then, my attention was
called off to C——. A young peasant had set off
with her, bound to his triumphal car, and I did not
know but he would feed on her for supper. The fellow was pulling a hand-cart, and in a great hurry to
get home to his pipe. C——'s dress was caught in
the wheel, and her weight presenting no obstacle to
his perseverance, he dashed on and carried her with
him. It was vain for her to shout, *Attendez;* that
is probably the Dutch for " Hurry along:" and before we could come up with the procession, her dress
had been nearly torn off her back. We were by that
time the center of almost a mob, and were obliged to
take refuge in a shop to repair damages. Several of
our admirers, however, were lying in wait for us, and
followed us to our hotel.

But this unlucky beginning was followed by day after
day of great delight in the noble picture-galleries of Amsterdam, the impressions and recollections of which are
given, as usual, in full detail, in many pages of the journal.
Before leaving the city, however, they were persuaded to
spend their last hour in visiting one of its great sights.

We went to see the tomb of Admiral De Ruyter, an object of great admiration to our friends who live with the frogs. The recumbent statue of the Admiral represents a good-looking, big Hollander, who has had a very fine dinner, and lain down to digest it. In the act of patting his dear stomach, he has fallen asleep, and lies in that impressive attitude, an excellent specimen of Dutch serenity. It was impossible to help being amused. And yet the work is well executed; but the Dutch have no imagination. However, they are a good, honest, faithful, industrious people, serving God honestly; and I both like and respect them. All New Yorkers should go on pilgrimage to this, which is to many of us, more than any other, our mother-country. The aid and comfort they afforded our forefathers in their troubles with the step-mother country should never be forgotten; and in spite of the funny things they do, their ditches and their extreme simplicity, I would rather live in Holland than in many a fairer country. Its cleanliness too is a very great recommendation. The bridges and the boats are scrubbed as thoroughly as the floors of the rooms; and if it were not that the Rhine in Holland is rather unmanageable from its size, I am quite convinced that they would scrub that too.

The loyal New Yorker's just interest in heroic Amsterdam helps to explain, perhaps, how Mrs. Gould failed to be drawn by the charms of beautiful, historic Leyden — a holy city for pilgrims from New England. From Amster-

dam by Arnheim the party journeyed up the Rhine with
vast delight. And with fixed resolution to make it all her
own, and quite regardless of how many guide-books and
tourists' volumes contain it all in print, she fills her journal with full details of every day's sight-seeing. Those
who have tried it know what a proof of industrious per-
tinacity a sustained traveler's journal is, which not
only fills up the first volume, with no frequent hiatus, but
goes on to the next and the next in uninterrupted succession. We skip to

Baden-Baden. You poor journal! But what can
one do? I will, however, try to write a little of this
lovely spot, and thence perhaps "advance backward" to Heidelberg and the rest. Baden is situated
in the midst of charming scenery. Its houses nestle
in the narrow valley, or creep quietly up the hills.
They look down on a saucy, talkative little brook
which understands English and never ceases to prat-
tle about the mountains from which it has come, the
tall black fir-trees, the commencement of the Black
Forest, whose shadows are reflected in its waters, the
lovely harvest-fields and meadows it has enriched,
and the pretty little valley it has come to visit. The
best of the thing is that the tiny murmurer is dignified with the name of River, and calls itself the Oos.
From our window the view is lovely enough of a
sweet, smiling range of hills, covered with luxuriant
vegetation, and leading the eye up to what is called
the New Castle with Baden-Baden village at its feet,
and then over lovely forests to the Old Castle,

beyond which the tall trees meet the sky. *Das neue Schloss*, by the way, is not as new, for instance, as a Fifth Avenue castle. It was built in 1471. . . . . Contrasting with the life and light of the banquet-hall (in the new castle) with its larger than life-sized dukes that fill the panels, its frescoes on the ceiling, and its beautifully tesselated wood floors, were the dreadful dungeons to which we descended by a long, narrow, winding stair. Through grated windows perhaps the culprit took his last lingering look at the sweet hill-sides he had often climbed, the peaceful valley where he was born, or even the cottage that had sheltered his happy infancy. At last the light of day entirely faded from his view, as he was led deeper and deeper into the darkness of those dreadful caverns and found himself in a narrow vaulted chamber lit by lanterns (the places for them are pointed out) and in the presence of the judges whose hard stone benches may still be seen. The agony of that dreadful hour may be imagined by one who looks upon the frightful place where it was endured. Then came the examination by masked men with feigned voices, the leading to the chamber of torture, the application of the question. Released from the rack, he is unbound and led to kiss the image of the Virgin at a little distance. The poor wretch takes the first step to obey this order; it is his last on earth. He falls through a trap-door some ninety feet, upon a revolving wheel whose knives and lancets extinguish the last remnant of his miserable life. But if he be not adjudged to instant death, how much more miserable his fate! Trembling with fear, he is placed in a chair wound up to the top of the castle by a windlass and let down through a shaft in the tower to a horrible abode of darkness, where no ray of light or hope can ever enter. Against hard stone walls he may dash his brains if he will. It is his only privilege. No outlet can be seen or even felt, for the door is a solid mass of granite moving on a pivot. The shaft which served to convey air to these subterranean chambers runs the whole depth of the tower in which it was pierced, and there is no window in any of the dungeons communicating even with that. . . . .

And so up the Rhine again by Strasburg to Bâle, and thence for Schaffhausen.

We were at last in Switzerland. Our road lay through vine-covered hills and laden orchards. We are surrounded by mountains, and have constant views of the exquisite river. The towns we meet on this ride are hoary with age and romantically situated. Laufenberg is a specimen of them, situated on a range of crags overhanging the Rhine, which here turns and breaks in beautiful rapids. The houses are high and narrow, and have a squeezed appearance. On one side of the village is a gray old tower, and within it a young tree, standing proud in its young strength, and overlooking the scene from the midst of this ruin. We saw all this at a glance, and were then immediately swallowed up by a tunnel. The scenery, with the exception of these queer little villages,

2

reminds me of the Green Mountains and the Connecticut Valley.

Just after leaving Zurich, and coming out of the jaws of another long tunnel, the Alps, THE ALPS, rose before us. And as we advanced on the brow of a range of hills, looking down upon harvest-fields and Swiss villages, and meadows, with evergreens climbing the hill and wreathing it a crown of verdure as they climb,—looking far away from all this, over ranges of green mountains, and far-distant blue peaks, we see these snow Alps bending from their awful height, and calling us to look away from earth to heaven. But we soon lost them, much to my sorrow.

By way of Constance and its lake, they come really into the midst of the mountains.

Friday, August 4, 1860. . . . . . We left the boat at Rohrschach, and then the glories of the scene began. It was a ride of some four hours in the cars to Coire. The road was at first simply pretty, with views of the lake we had just left; vine-covered slopes, castle-crowned heights of ordinary beauty. But soon there was real Alpine scenery to delight us. The hills did not seem to rise in one single slope, but as if several were lifted from the ground side by side, and the green waves passed over each in succession. Then the splendid mountains towering far above us, while the little villages nestled their brown heads under the shadows. And when they stooped their great forms, how gloriously the gorges opened new gates to admit more distant views! The chalets looked like squirrels climbing a tree, as they showed far up the mountain sides. And how picturesque the peasants were with their red head-dresses, their blue bodices and skirts, their white sleeves and black aprons! And the herdsmen, with their cows and their kids, looked to us to-day, every one of them like a William Tell. Overlooking some gorge, or crowning some hill, are old castles, such as the Wartau, on the right bank of the Rhine, or the Schloss Gutburg, with a square tower and two or three bits of wall, around which nature is weaving a green robe. And farther down are the slender-spired churches and the white houses; the vineyards and golden orchards of the valley, while a mountain torrent or a ribbon-like rill, which owes its birth to the snows, or the Rhine itself in its pebbly bed is always to be seen. These mountains stand forth in their primitive naked-ness; those man has wreathed with vines, and these others are covered to the very summit with forest trees. Here is a long, long range of splendid Alps, wearing to-day a scarf of cloud-drift; and far above them, with a robe of snow, towers one of the mon-archs of Switzerland. Here are conical peaks, bare as the pyramids of Egypt, and reminding us of them; and here are sharp-pointed peaks, shooting upward. And here, almost under their shadow, we rest for the night at the Weisses Kreutz, where we find much better accommodation than we could have hoped for from appearances; have a comfortable meal in our own room, and hope for fine weather for the Via Mala to-morrow.

This was the beginning of " the regular Swiss round."
From the Splügen to Ragatz and Pfeffers, where they
found " greater wonders than ever." Thence to Zurich
and up the headwaters of the Rhine, and by Andermatt
to Lucerne, and over the Scheideck under the great peaks
to Interlaken, and to Visp, and Zermatt and the Monte
Rosa, whence by Martigny and Chamounix to Geneva.
And here a bitter piece of news to one of the party interrupted the course of the journey, and they all turned
back toward Paris, " with poor, dear, afflicted —— , to
see her thus far on her way to her desolate home. . . . .
Father and sister gone within a short month of each
other."

We left Geneva for Paris on Friday, October 12.
. . . . We were off after considerable humbug. We
could not sit down until we had bought our tickets,
and James could not remain with us after we had;
and he could not have the baggage checked without
showing the tickets; and he must not put us in the
cars, etc., etc. And we must get into the cars, and
he must leave us by Geneva time; and we must wait
and start by Paris time. At last, when all these little experiments and a few others had been tried on
us, the steam-whistle blew our brains out, and we
were off at almost lightning speed. How beautiful
Geneva lay this afternoon, with the long reaches of
snow on the Jura, as if nature were spreading out her
sheets for a general bleaching; with its lovely buildings and bridges; with the deep blue water of the
lake and the river; with the terraced range of the

Saline. Then we left it behind, but took its mountains with us as a background, and plunged into the country. Autumn has fairly come, and the foliage has turned jealous at her arrival, and the leaves begin to lie under the trees. The vine-leaves hang yellow and thin, and the purple clusters alone look warm. As to the Rhone, it has lost all the sweet hue which it had borrowed from the lake, and is cold, and gray, and rapid, and wintry, and desolate as the Tamina, reminding me very often of that chilled and rock-bound stream. It plays every part to-day that water can play. Sometimes it is a narrow, winding brook, madly impetuous indeed, but looking too insignificant to live long, and perfectly restrained by the high banks which inclose it ; and again it has spread out, as at Macon, into a lake, and seems destined to carry away the land which surrounds it. Suddenly the river contracts. We pass a singular-shaped mountain, rising sheer from its bank, and covered with dwarfed trees wearing their autumn crown, and are in Savoy. . . . .

With the struggling dawn we entered Paris, and taking a carriage, drove to the Westminster. How pretty the city looked in the early morning, and how familiar !

October 16th. I learned something more of the *Ecole Evangélique* for poor children of which E—— told me on Sunday. It seems that Mlle. Dumas, No. 18 Rue Neuve St. Geneviéve, has been the Elisabeth Fry of France. She has visited the prisons and tried to do the prisoners good. While making her visits to them, she found many who had abandoned or been taken from their children. ˙ One by one she sought out these little ones of sin and shame, and took them to her home. But more and more seemed to claim her sympathy. She spent her fortune, restricting herself to the simplest food and dress, giving up sugar and butter, etc.; and still the little ones continued to knock at the door of her heart. She was finally obliged to solicit aid, and has obtained it, so that she has now a school of five hundred children, and two houses have been taken and united by a chapel. They live very simply; have wine on Sundays, and on other days small-beer, or whatever two or three hops in water may be called; dress in blue cloth, etc. The *externes* pay a franc a month, and the boarders 300 francs a year. Three evangelical clergymen go out once a week to care for them.

Thursday, Nov. 1—*Turin.* Our first day in Italy. . . . . The little bits of Italian life that we have seen of course interest us exceedingly. In one street was a blind man with four little girls. The old man played the violin and the children the cithern, and all sang most sweetly. Between two arches, a gymnast was mounting by his feet stretched apart to their utmost distance. He descended at one time by a series of small leaps, at another by putting his hands in the place of one foot and so sliding down. I think he was in separate pieces and hung together only by his pantaloons. Another magician was balancing a poor little girl in every possible position on his toes. A "happy family" of cats, birds, monkeys, rats, etc., were on exhibition in another part of

our walk; and on all corners were men roasting
chestnuts. We were particularly pleased with the
soldiers, who look so like men and so little like ma-
chines. James pointed out to us the sharpshooters
with their little low hats decked with bunches of
cocks' feathers, and we longed to say "God speed
you" to every-one of them.

The Turin picture-gallery is not a famous one; but it is
pleasant to quote the concluding sentence from the several pages of journal which relate to it. "I enjoyed
the collection, although I believe I ought not. I am glad
I did, however, and I always mean to be glad in the like
case."

Turin, Sunday, Nov. 4th. The Government has
given the Vaudois a handsome church edifice, in
which they hold regular services. We went there
this morning. It is delightful to attend their simple
worship. On entering, every one stands a moment
with bowed head. The prayers, which are very simple and beautiful, are read, but this is optional, as
I was told by the pastor. The chapter and commandments are read by the clerk, who has a little
desk under the pulpit and who also leads the singing. There is an organ, but no choir. The men sit
on one side and the women on the other. The congregation stand during prayer, and sit during the
other services. After sermon and prayer, the Apostles' Creed is read, the Lord's Prayer is said, and the
Levitical and Apostolic Benedictions are pronounced.

The services being over, James thought well to speak to the clergyman, who seemed much gratified, and took us into a little vestry, where he removed his band and gown, and was very kind in giving us information with regard to his people. I have been exceedingly interested in an account of them by Monastier, published in 1848, which Mr. Bert was kind enough to lend me. I had never read, before, any account of the *Glorieuse Rentrée.* This was the return of the Vaudois from Switzerland, where they had been received, welcomed, and cared for. But they were anxious to return to their native valleys, and serve God in their own temples, and bring their children around their own hearth-stones again. Their kind hosts could not allow them to leave Switzerland, as they had promised the Duke of Savoy, when he opened the door to these persecuted ones, that they would not let them go back. Two or three unsuccessful attempts were made to escape, and the final one, which succeeded through unparalleled difficulties, is described at length, and is most interesting.

There has been another battle, and the city is illuminated. The palace and the public buildings connected with it are blazing with little lights in rows. The old castle has its façade decorated with flags of red, white, and green, surmounted with stars and crowns, and the king's cipher, and *Viva Italia.* The Hotel de Ville is ornamented in the same way, and the Senate House has a beautiful and novel decoration. Trees of evergreen are terminated with large masses of red and white flowers like fuchsias—

an exceedingly pretty device. Men are singing patriotic songs, and music and processions passing through
the streets. I am sorry they could not wait till
to-morrow.

Monday, Nov. 6th. We saw too much to-day, that is
certain. The first part of it was spent most delight-
fully. By appointment with Mr. Bert, we went to
visit the Vaudois institutions in the parsonage building. We saw first the rooms of the young men,
apprentices to various trades. The Vaudois in former
times being forbidden to practice any of these, on
account of their religion, the younger generation
would of course be unable to learn them at home.
Hence they are sent to Turin, where they are
boarded, lodged, and have their washing done at the
rate of only ten francs a month, for two years. If
during this period of probation they do well, all expenses cease for them during the remaining years of
their apprenticeship. Above is the hospital, where
the sick are cared for. Formerly, in Catholic hospitals
they were persecuted with constant endeavors to
turn them from their faith; the dying were not
spared from these importunities; and even the memory of the poor Christian was assailed, the priests
asserting that he had died in the "Catholic" faith.
A deaconess is in charge of these sick persons.
Next came the children. The boys, under the care
of their master, a Vaudois from the valleys, were
writing. The little fellows were taking great pains
with their penmanship, while the master was very
proud of them. The girls, who were in another
room, all rose when we entered and wished us good-

2*

morning. They too were writing at this hour; but their teacher called on them to lay aside their books and sing for us, which they did very sweetly. With their *Buon giorno* in our ears, we entered the Infant-class-room, where a large school of tiny boys and girls were gathered around their teacher, a remarkably pretty and bright young girl, who was teaching them their letters. . . . . There is a printing establishment and a library, and the room lent to the English for their services is used during the week for religious services, and for lectures on historical or scientific subjects. Thus these persecuted people, allowed at last to worship the God of their fathers with none to make them afraid, are engaged in every good work. I hope we may yet have an opportunity of becoming better acquainted with them in their homes.

Three things in the foregoing pages from Mrs. Gould's journal deserve to be noted as destined to have no small influence on the course of her subsequent life. First, her "love at first sight" for Italy, which grew, on longer acquaintance, into a true patriotic affection for the land that was to be her home, almost like the love she bore to the land of her birth. Second, her interest in the ancient Waldensian or Vaudois Church, of whose communion she afterward became a member, and to which she bequeathed as a legacy the dearest of all her possessions—the care of the Italo-American schools. Third, her sincere and tender interest in children, and especially in everything that could tend to the advancement and improvement of the children of the poor. How deep-seated and genuine and constitutional was this feeling in her mind; how little dependent on interesting or romantic circumstances; how little there was of sentimentality in it, and what absolute absence of cant; and under what a just title of inheritance she came by this trait of a noble woman : will appear in the course of this book, and particularly in the next chapter.

III.

RETROSPECTIVE.

*Recollections of Mrs. Gould's Parents—Emily's Forty
Children in the Sunday-school — Marriage to Dr.
James B. Gould—Declining Health—Aggravations
of the Voyage—Invigoration by Mountain Walks.*

WHAT sort of youth it was that ripened into
such beautiful and fruitful maturity ; under
what training those fine qualities were developed which won universal love and admiration in later
life ; by what title of spiritual inheritance these qualities
were possessed, are questions not in the least difficult or
obscure in the case of Mrs. Gould. The story of her
parentage and girlhood answers them plainly.

Emily Bliss was born in New York May 30, 1822. Her
father was Dr. James C. Bliss, an eminent and beloved
physician, of whom one who knew him well for fifty years
writes : "He was the purest and most noble-minded man
I ever knew. Every thought seemed to be governed by
an enlightened conscience. I believe that hundreds owed
their lives to his unselfish and benevolent care."

The same writer, a venerable lady still living, gives her recollections of Emily's mother, Maria Mumford Bliss, which go back to 1816—to the days when they were girls together in the old Garden Street Reformed Dutch Church, under the charge of Dr. James Matthews. It was in that year that she became a member of this church. She says of herself:

"I was very anxious and very ignorant; and Dr. Matthews introduced me to Miss Maria Mumford as one of his most efficient helpers. She was just the instructress I needed — spiritual, intelligent, well versed in the Scriptures, with a most cheerful and loving spirit—and she soon became to me as a dear sister. The next year the Sunday-school movement began. Mrs. Divie Bethune (if I mistake not) was the first to propose it. Miss Mumford and Mrs. Bethune were well known to each other, and Mrs. Bethune selected Miss Mumford as her secretary. Afterward Miss Mumford became [local] Secretary of the American Sunday-school Union. I can hardly give you too high an idea of the self-denying zeal with which the secretary performed her duties. The first Sunday-school was organized and opened in the lecture-room of the Dutch Church in Garden Street. Miss Mumford was superintendent of this school, in which I was a teacher, and the work done by her would astonish the young school teachers of our time. All correspondences, all new constitutions for country schools, were referred to her. She organized our Sabbath-school teachers' meeting, of which she was the leader; she arranged our juvenile tract societies; she was the head and front of all our female meetings. During a visit to friends of mine, in which she accompanied me, she organized three Sunday-schools and tract societies, sending them, on her return to the city, the needful books. One of these schools was in Dr. Johnson's church, at Newburg—even then a large town.

"In her last hours it was my privilege to be present with her, and never can I forget the solemn scene, when she addressed to each of those in the room her parting words of exhortation, and committed the little daughter, Emily, to the love of her Father in Heaven. Emily was nine years of age at that time."

To others as well as to this cherished friend and associate in good works this tranquil and beautiful death-bed scene was impressed forever upon the memory. But to none so deeply as to the little girl of nine years old who was brought from her bed, in her night-clothes, as the morning began to dawn, to receive the last blessing and farewell of her saintly mother. "Draw aside the curtain, Emily," said the dying woman. And when the little girl had let in the light to shine upon her mother's face, and had come back wondering and awe-struck to the bedside, she listened to these last words: "My darling child, look here upon your mother's face. Look well upon it, that you may never forget it, and never forget your mother's dying words." And then pausing a moment, she added, in a subdued voice: "Let the Lord Jesus Christ be your guide. Follow Him, for all your well-being for time and eternity depends on your devotion to Him." The lesson of that hour was never lost; for the child walked ever afterward in her mother's footsteps.*

Emily Bliss was hardly more than a child, when her dead mother's religious earnestness and strong affection for children, that reached out for the lowest and neediest, reappearing in the heart and life of the daughter, began to show itself in practical effort. She always fascinated children; and the sight of this child-teacher surrounded by her class of forty other children, is still remembered by some that saw it. She wrote afterward for the American Tract Society some reminiscences of this Sunday-school class, which were published in a thin volume of the small Sunday-school book pattern, entitled " Little Pilgrims." And one of the last published productions of her pen was a letter to the Sunday-school children of the United States in behalf of her Italian schools, from which we transcribe so much as speaks of this part of her life.

ROME, *December* 20, 1874.

MY DEAR CHILDREN :

Did you ever hear of Briareus ? If you never did, you will some day. He had a hundred hands and feet. I can not say I should like to have a hundred hands. It would be so very uncomfortable when they all got cold at once, and then it would be very tire-

* Chancellor Crosby's address at the Memorial service held in the Fourth Avenue Presbyterian church, New York, November 12, 1876.

some to put on so many gloves when one wanted to go out. But sometimes just one pair of hands does not seem enough. It will not write a letter to each one of you at a time, and that is what I should like to do. But as I can not, I wish each one of you would consider this letter as written to him or herself, and as you listen to it, make up your minds to answer it in some way.

Many years ago, when I was old enough to leave the Sunday-school, and go into the Bible-class, I asked my father to let me take an infant class. He thought I had better learn more myself; but you see, there were some little children that I loved so dearly, and I wanted to have them with me every Sunday. So my father consented to let me be a teacher instead of a scholar, and six little children, who were too young to read, came to me the next Sunday. My dear little girls! How I loved them! By-and-by my class grew too large to meet in the Sunday-school room, and we had to go up into the gallery of the church, and there forty little boys and girls met every Sunday. How often I think of them; of dear little Carrie, whom God wanted in heaven, and who soon left us, in her Saviour's arms, safe forever with Him; of Bobbie, a poor little Irish boy. Poor Bobbie! One of his shoes was so bad that he could not keep it on any longer, but he wore the best one; and on the other poor, cold little foot, his father let him wear one of his boots. There was Bella too, who was not a very good little girl. She used to get angry sometimes, and push, and even strike. Then I used to say, "Come, let us sing something." All the children stood up when I said that, excepting Bella. But before the first verse was over Bella got up too. The angry color in her cheeks went away, the naughty little hands were still, and very soon I began to hear her clear little voice with the rest. When we sing about Jesus we can not keep angry, can we? Well! I can not tell you about all my little children. They are all grown up now, excepting those that the dear Father in heaven took to live with Him. I taught them something, but they taught me much more: to love children dearly, to make them love me, to know how to tell them of Him who died for them. That infant class was the school in which God put me to make me ready for a work here.

Beside the best opportunities of education that New York afforded, Emily enjoyed the benefits of some years' residence in the family of M. Picot, principal of a noted French school in Philadelphia. The facility which she there gained in the use of the French language was destined to be of the greatest value both to herself and to others.

On the 22d of September, 1853, Emily Bliss was married to Dr. James B. Gould, Surgeon in the United States Navy. The next year her husband resigned his commission, and settled at New York in the practice of medicine and surgery in partnership with Dr. Bliss. But in May, 1860, the failure of Mrs. Gould's health required that voyage to Europe which is related in the first chapter, and from which she never returned alive.

Those inconsiderate people who are accustomed to think
of sea-sickness as never anything more than a pretty severe
practical joke, are quite incapable of appreciating the pro-
tracted anguish, permanently damaging the health and en-
dangering or actually shortening the life, to which some
are subjected by it. To these inappreciative people it
will doubtless seem very absurd that the distress and danger of a sea voyage should be a grave consideration in de-
ciding important questions. But in fact there have been
not a few cases in which the course of important lives has
been modified, and wisely modified, by this consideration.
And Mrs. Gould's must be counted among them. Those
who follow this story to the end will find evidence enough
that she was not of the number of those Americans " with
souls so dead," who willingly spend their lives abroad from
sheer lack of interest in their own home and country. It
is a pleasure to relieve her memory of this reproach by
counting her among those involuntary exiles of necessity
and duty, whose patriotic love and pride only grows
stronger by years of absence. It was with a serious meaning, and not with a mere playful aptitude of quotation,
that she was wont to cite, among the comforting promises
connected with the New Jerusalem, the assurance that
there shall be " no more sea."

A recurring hay-fever had irritated and weakened her
system to an alarming degree. Embarking in this unfa-
vorable condition, " she suffered exceedingly on the passage, and arrived in Paris worn out with fever and want
of sleep." [The quotations are from a letter of Dr.

Gould, of the time]. " Our rooms are opposite the gardens of the Tuileries—a beautiful situation, but with too much vegetation near it for her health. Still, with all these drawbacks, she enjoys everything with the zest of a child, or, rather, of an intelligent, educated, and enthusiastic woman. Nothing escapes her notice or appreciation. She speaks the language with the utmost fluency and correctness, the result of early training. . . . . It will be better for her to get the bracing air of Switzerland, before returning to the more highly cultivated regions, where she would be more liable to be troubled with her fever."

The hopes of her improvement in Switzerland were fairly realized. She writes to a friend from Chamounix :

You know, I think, how much my fever is mitigated by exercise in the open air. When we began mountain travel, however, it was much increased by the antics of the horses (if they are really the same animals which we knew by that name in America). They snort defiance at all attempts to guide them ; persist in surveying the depths below, on the very edges of unfathomable precipices ; never go on when you wish them to, and always stop when you are in a hurry. They understand neither French, English, nor German, and are obedient only to certain frightful sounds emitted by the guides, and disagreeably suggestive of the agonies of sea-sickness.

With some difficulty I persuaded James to allow me to try walking where carriages could not be taken, and the experiment has proved wonderfully successful, my health having constantly improved ever since

I commenced taking long walks.   So I left Martigny early Thursday, September 27th, for the ascent of the Tête Noire, with my alpenstock as my only companion, preceding the others by about an hour.

. . . . This torrent of the Trient is a very wonderful river. Noisy and rapid as it is now, I saw it at Martigny imprisoned in rocky walls a thousand feet high. It reminds me of the impetuosity and heedlessness of a youth who thinks the world before him is for him to conquer, and bursts through the restraints of home to throw himself into life. This young river opposes itself to all the obstacles in its course, sweeps down the huge boulders that would stay its waves, but is caught and imprisoned for twelve or fifteen miles between adamantine walls, chafes and rages in vain against the stony barrier on either side, and when, with waters that never reflected a sunbeam or a waving tree, a smiling field, or a hamlet, it finds its way at last out of its prison-house, it is plunged into the Rhone, and its existence blotted out forever.

IV.

"O ROME, MY COUNTRY!"

To Milan — The Plain of Lombardy — Milan Cathedral — The "Last Supper" — Genoa: Strange Sights and Queer People — Panorama of "La Superba" — Garibaldians — Florence — The Glory of the Boboli Gardens — To Rome by Siena — Home at Last.

BEING such as she is shown to be in these extracts, it is as obvious that Mrs. Gould, in choosing a residence, will be drawn toward Italy and Rome, as it is in the case of some other persons, that they will settle in Paris. The fine verse of Childe Harold,

"O Rome, my country, city of the soul!"

only translates what is a proverb in other languages than English, and expresses a sentiment common to poetic and thoughtful minds, even of those who never have trodden the classic peninsula, nor seen the Eternal City.

It is not necessary to follow in detail the well-beaten route of tourists toward Rome—by Milan, Verona, Venice, back again to Genoa, and so by Leghorn and Pisa to Florence. At every stopping place, Mrs. Gould went through

(45)

with the regular round of sights, writing them up diligently in her journal, and in particular " doing " the picture-galleries with the ardent zeal of the cultivated American tourist, who combines preparation of mind with absolutely unslaked zest of appetite. The delighted descriptions of the paintings and statues that she most enjoyed, fill page after page of her journals, and overflow from volume to volume. But we can only touch here and there, almost at random, a bit of description that seems characteristic of the writer or of the country that she loved only next to her own.

Tuesday, Nov. 7th. We left Turin this morning at 8.50 for Milan, in the express train, which brought us to our journey's end at half-past twelve. The plain through which Victor Emanuel's railroad runs, is one of great fertility and beauty. We are no longer confined to meadows and pasture-fields as in Switzerland, but there are rich gardens, furrows, and hillocks that tell of abundant grain and vegetables, while the grass is of the deepest hue, and not choked with weeds. The absence of fences is very striking in so extensive a plain. The trees are many and old. Mulberry-trees are scattered here and there, the raising of the silkworm being an important industry. The trees are kept low, and at a distance resemble large water-willows. As soon as we had crossed the mountains, we began to see little bits of the picturesque, that remind one of the childish ideas we all form of this land. I am surprised to find how entirely brick is substituted for stone in the buildings.

Certainly the former would seem to be much the less capable of producing any impression of the picturesque upon the mind. But the houses are stuccoed; they have pointed windows; there are queer swallow-nest appendages to them; the roofs abound in strange windows, or are, so to speak, terraced; or, if the building is an irremediably straight up and down thing, the chimneys at least indulge in all sorts of fantasies, and are rows of little columns supporting a tiny roof, or little Gothic shrines, or something or other to please the eye and prevent monotony. Just so with the people's dress. They delight in red handkerchiefs upon their heads. The men put on, perhaps, a blue cap with a red tassel. The everlasting browns and grays one sees at home are at least accompanied with warmer hues, just as the brown and shriveled skins are lighted up with dark, bright eyes and crimsoned cheeks. The old women we met coming from town as we were on the road to the *Superga* would, any one of them, have been an effective figure in a picture. First, was the droll, dignified little long-eared donkey, the very embodiment of Italian independence. He was decorated with two heaps of empty baskets, one on either side, and between them was packed Gaffer with a red handkerchief on her head, a blue bodice, and a gray gown, her black eyes sparkling, and her brown face lighted up with a pleasant smile. And the *dolce far niente !* All that we met driving carts, I believe, without exception, were lying at full length therein, leaving the driving to the animal who is generally supposed to be, not the driver, but the drivee. We observed the cattle, as in Switzerland. The oxen

are very fine. Those we saw about Turin were splendid creatures of a dun color, large and well-built. Each
one has a little cloth on its back, about as large as
I suppose it would require for a pocket-handker-
chief. . . . .

Wednesday, Nov. 8th. I did not feel much like rising this morning, but the Duomo refusing to come to
me, there was nothing but for me to go and pay my
respects to it. It is to me the most magnificent creation of the genius of man that I have ever seen. The
outside, from the ground, does not strike me as did
the cathedral of Cologne. But the interior is magnificent beyond anything I have ever imagined. The
vastness of the building can be comprehended, as I
suppose that of St. Peter's can not. Standing at one
end of the nave and looking toward the high altar,
the view is superb. . . . . But fine as is the interior,
it is nothing to the exterior, as surveyed from the
roof. This is a combination of sublimity and beauty
-—sublimity in vastness and strength, and beauty in
finish and detail. The pinnacles are each a splendid
Gothic monument, exquisitely sculptured and adorned
with statues of perfect workmanship. It has a religious character which has before seemed to me to be
wanting in such edifices. It seems a vast temple
always filled with God's worship, in which the archi-
tect had striven to lift the mind from the work of his
own hands to the great Being in whose honor he
built. The statues seem to embody the communion
of saints, and, so far from requiring worship, to be
themselves setting the example of fervent prayer, or
by their attitude to point us upward far above the

loftiest of these pinnacles. . . . . To-day, not being
well, I have not studied this exquisite creation as I
hope to do ; and I must leave it after we have paid
a little visit to the tomb of St. Charles Borromeo.
This is under the high altar. The little chapel is partly
lighted from an opening in the floor of the cathedral ;
but twelve candles are also kept burning on the
shrine. The sarcophagus is of crystal and silver.
The silver covering was removed, and we stepped up
to look at what could be done by man for the honor
of a fellow mortal. Clothed in rich robes, with a
golden crozier studded with diamonds by his side,
a gold cross sparkling with the same precious gems,
and the most magnificent emerald cross I ever saw,
lay a blackened, grinning skeleton. And this is all
that is left of this great saint, for saint he doubtless
was, and when his spiritual body shall be seen, it will
have all the beauty and glory wanting now, while the
jewels and gold that are lavished here will take their
proper place as dross for the fire. . . . .

Thursday, Nov. 9th. To-day we have seen a sight
such as we shall never see again when we have bid-
den our final farewell to Milan. In the church of Sta.
Maria delle Grazie, or rather in the refectory of the
adjoining convent, is the "Last Supper" of Leonardo
da Vinci. I was going to say the immortal picture,
but, alas ! it is fast passing away, and in a few years
will have ceased to exist. The picture is painted on
the wall, and has been ruined by the elements. It
has been flooded several times, and the room has
been made a stable for horses and a store-room for
forage. The St. John has the face so disfigured that

3

I could not tell anything about the beauty of it ; but
the figure is wonderful.   It is almost angelic, but
withal there is in it true human suffering and shrinking.   The other apostles have, generally, as they
should have, hard, rude, strongly-marked faces.   The
painter has not forgotten that they were of the common people.   St. Philip only has his softened by the
love for his divine Master, which he seems to be expressing.   One could imagine that his emotions were
too deep for utterance, and there seems an involuntary clutching of the heart, as if its action had been
impaired by the intensity of love and sorrow.   The
others, either incredulous or angry, have a more stern
and harsh expression than their faces would ordinarily wear.   All this is true to nature.   St. Thomas,
with uplifted hand and forefinger, seems carried away
with his righteous indignation.   St. Peter has unwit-
tingly seized a knife with one hand, while the other
rudely grasps the shoulder of the shrinking and loving beloved disciple.   The attitude of this latter is a
volume of loveliness.   It expresses grief so great
that the swaying body has yielded to the hand laid
upon it, and might be hurled to the ground without
thinking or caring.   It is abandoned to the agony of
the afflicted spirit.   But the figure and face of the
Saviour !   " Did e'er such love and sorrow meet ? "
It is the realization of the Man of Sorrows.   It is
He who consented to die.   It is the bending to par-
take of the cup of agony, each drop of which was
known to the divine Sufferer.   The sweet, loving face
bears the expression of the deep sorrow that weighed
upon the spirit.   And the love and pity, too, in that

countenance, with calm, fixed determination, the voluntary surrender of Himself to the shame and the
agony! Wonderful inspiration! It is said that Leonardo saw this face in a vision. One thing is certain :
he understood in his heart the blessed Gospel whose
King he has depicted. Other faces of Jesus that we
see have an effeminate aspect ; this has not. Others
are human only ; this is divine. There is no look
toward the betrayer — no mere suffering — no mere
resignation. All these are expressed, but they are
glorified. . . . . I think Mrs. Browning must have
had this picture in her mind when, in her poem upon
" Cowper's Grave," she speaks of the poet waking
from the sleep of death

> " Beneath those *deep, pathetic* eyes,
> Which closed in death to save him."

Farewell, for the present, lovely vision of divine
beauty !

We resume the extracts from the journal, at Milan,
again, after the party has returned thither on the way to
Genoa, after a visit to Venice and Verona.

Genoa, Nov. 21st. We left the Grande Bretagne at
Milan this morning a little before eight o'clock, to
take the cars for Genoa. I groaned in spirit at being
obliged to rise so early, but I must confess that the
splendid mountain views almost repaid me for the
effort. Monte Rosa was a resplendent bride. No!
that will not do. The figure should be masculine.
It is the Frost-King himself, who, having powdered

the earth and stiffened the streams, lies resting himself after his labors.   May he forget to rise to-morrow morning !   We had not lost the snow-peaks before we began to approach the Apennines.   At last
they bade us good-bye for the winter and passed from
our sight, and we crept along the spurs of the Apennines.   They are beautifully broken, though appearing from Milan like a long straight line of unbroken
elevations.   The country near Genoa is beautifully
undulating, and the hills crowned with noble fortifications.   As soon as we had passed the great tunnel
through the Apennines and issued on their southern
side, we felt a change in the temperature.   Just before we reached the town, we had the first view of
the Mediterranean.   Soon after, we had arrived at
" La Superba," and were driven to the Hotel de la
Ville, on the quay.

This struck us as more absurd than any hotel we
have been in yet.   We entered by a most extraordinary cellar-like arrangement, under the queerest
and ugliest old arches that we have yet encountered.
On one side the entrance is the stable, and on the
other a blacksmith's shop, the noise whereof is inces-
sant and absurd.   And the old Vulcans—there they
are penned up in this little corner of an old palace,
going as hard as they can go.   A little further on,
under the same arches, is a great kitchen, where vast
cauldrons of soup are always simmering, and an immense pasty, large enough to feed the ship's company of a man-of-war, is displayed, to tempt Jack
Tar and his friends.

Thursday, November 22d.   There never was anything queerer than the street we live on ; and the people are all alive too. Long trains of donkeys, each with a basket on his nose and a bunch of bags on his back ; groups of men talking and gesticulating ; ladies with a scarf of clear white muslin pinned upon the head ; servants with the same shaped head-dress, but in bright calicoes, whereon are depicted birds and beasts, flowers and fruits, and objects generally ; unfortunate chickens surveying the prospect from baskets carried on men's heads. Such slow, poky, good-natured, noisy, gesticulating, gaping, thoroughly lazy people I never saw as those we see in the streets. They are out of doors all the time. They are moving about, but *such* motion. The hour-hand of a clock is faster.

Monday, November 26th. It is still too unpleasant for us to venture out to sea, and we are still ruining ourselves and making the shopkeepers happy in Genoa. We have been able to take one walk, without which I feel that I should have known nothing of the beauty of the town. We went up to the entrance of the Marquis di Negro's grounds. They are built up like a fortification, and exquisitely laid out. I wish I could have a picture of the scene we saw from them : the heights on which Genoa is built ; the Apennines soft and hazy, and some of them just powdered with snow ; the moles, each with its light-house—the one which winks at us all night standing high and proud on a great ledge of rocks ; Genoa, with her palaces, towers, arches, terraces ; the harbor, with its dismasted or sailless ships clinging close to the shore ; the blue Mediterranean frolicking wildly

in the distance and tossing about a solitary sail, and
trying its strength against the sturdy walls of the light-
house.   The infinite variety of the architecture is so
interesting and so novel. The gardens up in the third
story, the long lines of arches, the courts, the statues,
the frescoes, the bridges over streets, the stairs leading up the hill, the roofs made promenades, the thousand bits of light and shade and warmth of coloring
and coolness of architecture are enchanting. And the
people help to set it all off—they are so funny, and
their ways so absurd to us.   The caps the men wear,
of plain red or blue, or the shopkeepers, of black
velvet embroidered in bright colors; the veils of
which I have spoken; the everlasting jabbering and
gesticulating; the doing of everything in the open
air.   Not one of the little shops on the quay has a
window; the whole front is open all day and boarded
up at night.   The women carry about a little affair,
about the shape and size of a slop-bowl on a tea-tray.
It has a handle over the top, and constitutes their
stove.   Sometimes it sits upon them, and sometimes
they sit upon it; sometimes it warms their hands,
and sometimes their feet.   The waiters in this hotel
have a copper pan, like a deep frying-pan without a
handle, around which they sit and doze in the evenings.   They do not mind the smell of the charcoal
at all.   In the stores, one of these is on the counter,
and the inevitable cat has a station beside it.   Besides the basket-nosed and parrot-toed donkeys (for
their shoes project in the most absurd way, reminding one of gigantic parrot's claws), there is under our
arches a great scurrying of men, with baskets on

their heads, who are forever shouting good-humoredly
to you to get out of their way. The whole aspect of
everything is very odd, and I wish I could take some
of my friends at home on the walks we have taken.

November 28*th*. We were much interested in a gentleman and three young Garibaldians, his son and two
nephews, who breakfasted with us. Of the young
creatures it might almost be said that their mother's
milk was still warm upon their lips. They wore the
Garibaldi red shirt and necktie, blue pants, and broad,
blue belt, checked lilac-and-white undershirt. They
were beautiful, bright, beardless boys, evidently full
of life and hope, and gentle and modest as women.
Of such stuff as this—this father and these children—
is Garibaldi's army constituted. Such lovely boys as
these lie stiff and stark under their own native sky,
after every battle with the hated foreigner. And
their mothers, their poor mothers, send them and
watch and wait and pray for their return. These go
home to their mother's embrace; but, alas! how many
mothers in Italy to-day raise their empty arms to heav-
en against the tyrant! It is five months since these
children have been home. One of them was wounded,
and all were taken prisoners. Two hundred and fifty
such fought and resisted five thousand Austrians, and
saved the battle for Garibaldi. The enthusiasm of
the father is wonderful. He worships Garibaldi!

The party had two months of delight and hard study at
Florence. But out of many pages of description, let us
be content with these few lines about an afternoon in the
Boboli Gardens:

I never before had had the least idea of the extent
and beauty of them. The great walls of verdure,
which consist of trees allowed to grow almost to the
natural height, and then trimmed evenly at the top;
the variety and beauty of the statues, the fountains,
the terraces, the arches, the views from the hills,
make it enchanting. Some of the ancient statuary
is very beautiful, and some of the modern quite vies
with it. I remember the group of a man pressing the
juice of grapes into an enormous tub which a little
boy is trying to lift. There is a lake containing an
island, all artificial and surrounded by statues. Some
of these are very odd, and are contrived with water-
pipes so that they can be made to play as fountains.
Many of the walks are cut through arches of foliage,
and, as you look up through the long, green vista,
you see a statue at the end. And from the hill-tops,
what views! Only to look down on the grounds
themselves, where amphitheatre extends beyond amphitheatre, and walk succeeds walk, and one arched
vista leads into another, and statues and pyramids
and fountains come out anew at every turn! On a
hill, just back of the palace, we looked down on the
Pitti, with its three sides, its grounds, its fountain
and statues, the Egyptian obelisk, a rockery not far
from the palace, and walls of verdure that would fain
inclose it and us, but beyond which still stretch in
every direction enchanting walks and lovely views,
luring us on. And on we went, and were entrapped
at last by a " cove," who conducted us up to the old
walls, at which we looked, as they did at us, but up to
which no steps lead. Finally the *uomo* presented a

ladder, up which we gathered courage to mount in turn, and surveyed the prospect. It was worth mounting even the rounds of a ladder. Florence on both sides of the river, with her bridges and her buildings rising from the plain ; Fiesole leaving her to climb the hill ; the Cathedral, and the tall, sky-piercing Campanile, with the modest Baptistery just showing its head ; about us this exquisite garden and these walls of greenery ; beyond, the rugged Apennines, purpled by the glory of departing day ; and the more distant mountains with their old white heads lifted so far above us. We all confess that we have, as yet, seen nothing at all approaching to these grounds in beauty, extent, or variety of scenery.

It is reluctantly enough that we leave Florence, the scene, as it was to be, of some of Mrs. Gould's best charitable labors, with such scanty extracts from the many pages of intelligent, enthusiastic description that are found in this part of her journal. The pleasant society that welcomed her there, the picturesque beauty and historic dignity of the city, the glory of its architecture, the boundless treasures of art in the great galleries, and (not the least) the religious comfort which she found in the worship and fellowship of the Italian Protestant Church, made these two months at Florence a delightful part of a happy life. But, after all, it was not home, and we may rightly be, as she began to be, impatient to push forward to her "city of habitation."

They bade a reluctant, and not at all a final farewell to Florence early in the morning of January 30th, for Rome

3*

by way of Siena. The most interesting part of the story of this trip is the latter part, describing the drive from Siena to Rome.

Siena showed beautifully as we drove away from it, and it rose upon its hill sending its towers and walls and roofs heavenward, with its campaniles shining white in the sunlight. We had a delightful journey. It is true the hills are barren, but the valleys and fields smile with verdure and cultivation, and the hills as they stretched in the distance were made glorious by the bright tints of a cloudless day. There were many towers crowning the heights, reminding us of Rhine scenery, and old tales and old songs. The architecture to-day is different from the dark, solid Florentine architecture; it is so much less massive, so straggling—a wall running in one direction and then starting up into a tower, and then running down in another direction and producing a shed, and turning and twisting and throwing up points and peaks at its own sweet will. The mulberry orchards seemed endless; the olives shaded off the slopes; the vines gave promise for the year. But the hills were the charm—a sea of hills; hills of chalk and clay hills; hills of green and purple hills; billows on billows of green hills, and farther away the gray hills, all surging around us as if the world was one ocean of newly created land, not yet settled in its appointed bounds.

Rome, February 4th. We reached the Eternal City about half-past four o'clock on Saturday afternoon. James walked out on the Campagna to meet us, and we were all in a great excitement. St. Peter's had been visible for some time, its great dome swelling like a huge bubble in the gray atmosphere. Then we saw the castle of Sant' Angelo, and after awhile the city dimly showed itself. Those who had been there before were very busy pointing out to us verdant ones the various objects of interest that were in sight. . . . . I am so excited at really reaching Rome that I sleep very little, and when I do, am visiting old ruins in my sleep. I have been once to St. Peter's just to get a general view of it, and have wandered among the ruins of the Coliseum, the Forum, and the triumphal arches and temples which cluster so closely together on and near the Aventine, Capitoline, and Cœlian hills. It is in vain to try to describe, as yet, these magnificent sights.

In Rome Dr. Gould recommenced the practice of his profession; and this city was the home of himself and wife for fifteen years; the summers (during which Rome is deserted by all foreigners and by such of her own people as are able to leave) being spent either in travel, or in the hills near Rome and Florence.

V.

1861–1865.

REDEEMING THE TIME.

*Evil Days at Rome—Literature, Art, and Society
—Journal at Rome—A Wealthy Madonna—
Churches and Ruins—The Cardinal and the
Lambs at St. Agnes'—Feet-washings—St. Peter's
Illuminated—Excursions: 1. To Subiaco and its
Convent; 2. To Valombrosa; 3. To the Painted
Tomb of Veii.*

DELIGHTFUL Bengel, who, alone of commenta-
tors, knows how to say nothing where nothing is
necessary and to stop when he has got through,
gives us to understand that we are apt to put a mistaken
interpretation on that text, "See that ye walk circumspectly,
not as fools, but as wise, *redeeming the time,* because the days
are evil." Instead of an exhortation to activity, it is rather
a dissuasive from too much eagerness to work in unfavor-
able times, and a counsel to manage circumspectly, that
is, with a regard to circumstances, and let work wait, sometimes, for better and more hopeful days.

Thus Mrs. Gould, finding herself placed, at Rome, in
evil days—the wretchedly evil days just before the emancipation of the city, while the Papal Government was fast

filling up the measure of its iniquities—"redeemed the
time." On the side of the oppressor there was power—
the power of French bayonets and cannon. But on the
side of the oppressed there was omnipotence, slowly preparing the complete and hopeless overthrow of the tyranny.
"He that believeth shall not make haste."

Accordingly she worked with her might at what her
hand found to do, not at things which she did not find.
No ambitious school-girl ever worked harder at her lessons than Mrs. Gould did to get the utmost of personal
culture from the peculiar opportunities that surrounded
her. Her endless note-books, written always with beautiful penmanship, and in a literary style which (for such
rough work, intended only for her own eye) is astonish-
ingly correct and even elegant, are filled with descriptions of objects of nature and art, and monuments of history, and with careful analyses of books of archæology
and art-criticism; also with plans and rough drafts of
tales and magazine articles, some of which were afterward
published, from time to time. At the same time she came
to be a leader in the foreign society of Rome and Florence,
especially the American and English society; and the
grace and wit of her conversation kept winning friends to
her that were invaluable afterward when the evil days
were past, and the happy days come when she had great
burdens of charitable work to bear, and needed friends to
help her. At Rome, in the earlier days, there was comparatively little that she could do of Christian work, except in the circle of her American and English friends.

There was a little American church within the walls, that
dated from as far back as the Republic of '48, and which
was the center of a beautiful fellowship for all Christian
people and ministers, until by and by it was placed on an
exclusive footing.   Among the worshipers at this church,
and among the sick strangers whom her husband's profession brought to her knowledge, were opportunities of a
Christian woman's ministry which were not neglected.
Also in her many personal relations with Italians, both
of high rank and of low, there was a growing influence,
the value of which was beautifully to manifest itself by
and by.   But for the present " the days were evil," and in
her active studies and enthusiastic enjoyment in nature,
art, history, and society, and such comparatively indiffer-
ent matters, Mrs. Gould was "gaining the time "* for
the distinctively charitable and religious work which she
loved, and the zeal of which finally consumed her.   In
her journals and ordinary letters she certainly does not
appear at all as the typical heroine of religious biography.
There are almost no reflections recorded on her spiritual
condition.   In fact, there are almost no reflections on
herself at all.   The absence of them, her whole life long,
is remarkable and delightful.   It might save us the effort
of making our own estimate of her if we could transcribe
from time to time some pages of self-examination and self-
estimate.   But self-examination (in the prevailing sense of

---

* When Nebuchadnezzar says to the Chaldeans (Dan. ii. 8), " I know that ye
would *gain the time*," the literal translation (see margin) is " buy the time," and
the Greek word used in the Septuagint version is the same that in Ephesians v. 16
is translated, " redeem the time."   See Bengel *in loc.*

the word) was not her habitual way of serving God. Let
the absence of quotable talk about herself be judged according to each reader's judgment, whether favorably or
unfavorably. It is a fact, and too characteristic a fact not
to be noted.

This is a censorious world; and when seriously and
earnestly conscientious people allow themselves to over-
step the boundary-line of duty, probably it is as often on
the side of censoriousness as on any other—this sin does
look so much like some of the most respectable virtues,
and, judiciously indulged, gives a pleasant thrill of self-
esteem that seems almost like the satisfaction of a good
conscience. I can not but think how easily some who
regarded Mrs. Gould's manner of life from the outside,
and marked her vivacity and brilliancy in society, and her
keen enjoyment of the infinitely varied delights of life in
Rome, may have been led to lament over her as a frivolous
and worldly person, with no appreciation of the great end
of life. But it would have been a mistake.

It is not impossible to construct an agreeable addition
to the literature of the Grand Tour out of Mrs. Gould's
journals. But that is not the object of this volume, and
a very few pages, taken almost at random, suffice to give
an idea of the course of her life at Rome.

. . . . On New Year's Day we received about
twenty-five calls, and the evening we spent very
pleasantly at Mr. E.'s. Since then we have done no
sight-seeing, and have been as dissipated as possible.
We have spent every evening out. I am taking Italian

lessons twice a week. The weather has been cold, so that we have kept away from the galleries. We are reading a good deal. I hope to do some sight-seeing next week and get up my journal, which is much neglected. The Church of St. Agostino, which we have lately seen, has some fine works of art, but we could not examine them because the church is under repairs. We visited, however, the famous Madonna by Jacopo da Sansovino, which is a respectable work of art. But it is not its merit as a work of art that makes it famous now. Like the Bambino of the Ara Cœli, it is a " medical person," and its fees have enriched it to such a degree that it is the envy of all its brother practitioners. The figure is per-fectly covered with jewelry; the neck being encircled with many strings of pearls, the breast blazing with diamonds; a diamond frontlet sparkles upon its brow; its coronet is set thick with jewels; there are diamond rings upon its fingers, three diamond earrings in each ear, bracelets all the way up its arms, etc. The child has three watches on one of its feet, and is equally covered with gems. Beside the altar, and upon the nearest piers, are cases such as we see in the jewelers' stores, which are filled with jewelry of every descrip-tion. There are literally hundreds, and I am not sure that there are not thousands, of rings, pins, bracelets, necklaces, etc., etc. By the way, I do not know how this Madonna came to be miraculous, as St. Luke seems to have had nothing to do with get-ting her up. The Bambino is a foundling, which was dropped at the convent door one night, and has been very well cared for by the good friars. An angel brought it down, rang the bell of the convent, and then went home again. . . . .

Monday, Jan. 6th. Started for a walk in the direction of the Church of Santa Maria degli Angeli. The church was not open, and I wandered about the ruins of these wonderful Baths of Diocletian. It seems almost a shame to call these or the vast buildings of Caracalla by the name of baths. There was so much that was splendid beside the mere halls for bathing. There is among these ruins another *cella*, or whatever one chooses to call a building such as that which Michael Angelo turned into a church. There are also immense arches, great piers of brick-work, and a semicircular theatre (?) of great size. The pile actually covered an area a mile in circuit. It is now applied to the basest uses ; but there is something left of its original nobleness even in its decay. Flowers and moss climb and cling to its rugged sides, which still tower above the pigmy buildings constructed in its inclosure. . . . .

We have seen beautiful frescoes at the Church of St. Andrea della Valle. The four evangelists, though not Domenichino's happiest efforts, are not unworthy of him. The choir is adorned with frescoes representing the life and death of St. Andrew, powerfully rendered. This church occupies the site of the ancient Curia ; on this spot great Cæsar fell. Before I forget it, I must mention that we came upon a new ruin in our peregrinations to-day—that of the old theatre of Balbus. It was little—only two great towering and projecting masses of brick-work—but we delighted to find it, and then by the map and Mur-

ray to study out its history. But Rome is full of
little and big bits of antiquity which burst upon the
sight of the traveler at almost every turn. Now it
is a mass of ancient masonry; at another corner is a
huge marble foot, left by the great body to which it
belonged in the flight of the latter. Now it is a recumbent figure almost smoothed by time; now it is
a marble basin, part of an ancient fountain, and not
yet forsaken by the water. Now it is an exquisitely
sculptured doorway; anon, a column beautifully decorated, supporting a modern dirty brick wall; again
it is bits of bas-relief, heads, arms, legs, and inscriptions, dug up and transferred to the front of a house.
. . . . The drive to the Church of St. Agnes without the walls is pleasant, like all the drives outside
the gates of Rome. We visited the church last year,
but it is well worth more than one visit. It is said
to have been built by Constantine at the request of
his daughter, on the spot where the body of the saint
was found. It is completely subterranean, so that it
is reached by descending several flights of marble
steps. In the walls of this staircase are imbedded
inscriptions taken from the ancient cemetery. These
are like those from the catacombs which adorn the
walls of the Vatican gallery. . . . . The services were
of the usual style. I had a position which enabled
me to witness them to the best advantage. The bal-
dacchino was wreathed with flowers; and the statue
of St. Agnes was placed upon the altar, and appeared
to divide the adoration with the officiating cardinal.
This latter entered in plain garments, and was dressed
at the altar even to his dark violet gloves with the

ring on the outside. Then after a while he was all undressed again, and such an amount of hand-washing, donning of aprons, kissing the altar, the cardinal's ring, silver plates, napkins and books, I never saw before. Then the cardinal kissed the bishop, and the bishop the deacon, who flew and embraced a priestling, whereupon each priestling embraced his neighbor. As soon as mass was ended, the lambs were brought on. The little creatures had been washed with the greatest care, so that their fleece was as white as the driven snow. This was tied up with little knots of red ribbon about half an inch apart, and a garland of roses was placed on the head. They were, of course, tied, and were laid each on a crimson cushion. It was really a very pretty sight. The cardinal and the lambs now held an argument. The cardinal bowed and kissed the altar. " Ba! " said the lamb. " *Oremus*," said the cardinal. " Ba-a ! " said the lamb. The cardinal referred the matter to St. Agnes herself. " Ba-a-a ! " said the lamb. The cardinal shook what appeared to be a rattle at the lamb. " Ba-a-a-a ! " replied the insulted quadruped. The cardinal tried incensing his opponent. " Ba-a-a-a ! " said the lamb. Then the cardinal, as a last resort, fell to blessing the lamb and consigning his wool to the making of pontifical vestments forever. " Ba-a-a-a-a-a !!! " said the lamb. And the cardinal gave it up, and let the lamb have it all his own way ; and we went on to the Church of St. Constantia.

Out of many pages descriptive of the ceremonies and festivities of Holy Week we select a few. The washing

of the feet of poor pilgrims by Roman ladies of rank, is
one of the sights which strangers are sometimes invited
to witness.

We entered a room with clean brick floors furnished
with chairs and benches, and hung with small common prints and crosses. Here we could look into a
long dining-room with the tables spread with a not
over-nice table-cloth, and set with plates, pitchers,
bowls, and napkins. After we had reached the gate
which shut off the dining-room, it was opened, and
we swept down-stairs. And now we entered a small,
low room with seats against the walls, on which sat
the women, beggars from the Campagna, unwashed,
uncombed, each with her feet in a tub of water. Before each stood a Sorella in her uniform, consisting
of a full apron of Turkey red with a full front and
straps crossing behind, and a little white pinafore
over this. Underneath were magnificent silks and
velvet trimmings; diamonds sparkled in the ears;
gold daggers stabbed the elegantly dressed hair, and
rich laces peeped from beneath the garb of humility.
The cardinal and his satellites spoke. Beggar and
princess made the sign of the cross, and the scrub-
bing began. It was too much. Such blackness of
darkness and such odors! We rushed up-stairs. Our
party had been kindly taken in charge by one of the
sorelle, who is a Princess B——, who chatted with us
most pleasantly, and finally led us to the dormitory,
a long room containing more than a hundred comfortable beds. I thought how sweetly the poor
things would sleep, some of whom, as the *principessa*

told us, had never slept in a bed before. We got back to the refectory in time to see the soup brought on. Already plates of fish, great quantities of bread, plates of salad and fruit had been set forth. The pitchers were filled with wine. The Countess Altieri presided at the soup tureen, and a long line of *sorelle* was formed, who passed the bowls of soup from hand to hand. Meanwhile the pilgrims came up and were placed at table. Grace was said and the sign of the cross made, and then the repast began. I scarcely ever enjoyed one more. To see the poor creatures take in the soup, put out their tongues and lap it, to see their eager looks, their great, dark eyes brighten, their pure enjoyment, was a perfect feast. How they *did* eat, and also how they *did* drink! The wine was poured into little bowls, and they emptied one at a draught, without once stopping to swallow. They were generally young or middle-aged; some were children, and one was a pretty little black-eyed baby—a dear little dirty thing, the perfect picture of comfort. The fragments were made up into bundles for them, and when all had finished, the young girls formed a line in the passage leading to the dormitory, and sang a litany while the pilgrims passed through and went to their comfortable beds.

We skip the full and interesting account of the Easter ceremonies in St. Peter's Church, and come to the description of the illumination of St. Peter's. Perhaps it has never been better described than in these private pages.

We saw it most advantageously; first from the

Piazza, where it showed best, I thought; then going
to Mr. Rogers', where we stopped for a few minutes
to take a dish of tea and another of gossip, and to
look from their windows and balcony; and finally
from the Pincio, where it seemed like a new creation,
or an unveiling of some of the splendors of heaven.
It would be impossible to give a description of this
gorgeous scene that could convey to one who had not
seen it even a faint idea of its glories.   The church is
so illuminated as to resemble a church of fire: the pi-
lasters, capitals, frieze, all distinctly marked out.   The
cross points upward, a faint cross of silver.   The sil-
vered lantern surmounts a dome whose lines are of
shining silver, and between these lines are glimmer-
ing crowns of pale beauty.   To this beautiful structure conduct two lines of light suspended from the
colonnade.   The shadows that fall rich and full from
the splendid columns, from the great galleries, from the
doors and all the unilluminated parts of the church
and its surroundings make the light the more beautiful and brilliant.   The Piazza is crowded with car-
riages and spectators on foot.   The band plays en-
livening music.   Bells ring and guns are fired, and
everything seems to enhance the charms of the spectacle.   But long before we are wearied with gazing,
a ball of fire is seen on the summit of the dome; it
mounts to the top of the cross, and presto! thousands
of flames burst from lantern and dome, capital and
pilaster, bell-tower and window.   The façade, the
colonnade, are burning with brightness.   The statues
start in an instant into full view like armed men.
The long lines stream down the church and into the

Piazza. The pillars cast long shadows and long streams of light beside them. The enchantment is complete. There never was anything lovelier than the appearance of the dome. Each crown was surrounded with lines of gold that flashed most gloriously, paling the silver lights, it is true, but by no means extinguishing them ; and the whole dome was like a great illuminated globe set in the heavens and shining sharp and full against the clear blue sky. The city for a long distance caught and reflected the glorious light. The absence of the moon made it all the more splendid — the brightness streaming full and clear from the great basilica, and where it died away the night lay dark and deep.

To this period belongs some of the best of Mrs. Gould's literary work. A series of six articles in " Hours at Home," entitled " Rambles among the Italian Hills," is so nearly of the nature of autobiography that it is right to quote at length some passages relating to the less common excursions from Rome and Florence.

The first describes an excursion by Tivoli and Vico Varo (shrine of a famous winking Madonna) to a convent of St. Benedict on a cliff in the Apennines. The first halt was at Vico Varo, in an extraordinary inn, the appearance of which inspired no confidence in the cook ; " so I called for eggs and wine and speedily manufactured a concoction which made the rest of the party extremely ill, while I slept placidly until they recovered."

As the shades of the afternoon were beginning to

fall, we left Vico Varo, and wound down the hill toward the Anio. How lovely were the scenes! The
hill we descended is crowned by the white walls of
the convent of Cosmiato and its church-towers, shining pure and lovely amid surrounding verdure. The
cliff is pierced with caves and galleries. Long fingers
of the curious travertine formation hang over them, or
pry into their depths. Some of these are sacred places,
sacred to the memory of Saint Benedict. Just beneath the hill is a mill, with its little flume pouring
into the river; and rising above the latter are portions of the pier, and part of one of the arches of a
ruined bridge, over which the feet of Bassus and his
contemporaries passed. Our path went up and down,
and around and about, winding at its will with the
winding river in a way rather aggravating to people
who are aiming at an eagle's nest on the opposite
side of the stream and far above its waters. It is
stony too, and unkind to tender feet, but all ablaze
with lovely flowers that smile to win us to pluck
them, and blush as we pass them by in their young
beauty. At last the road came to a sudden end by
dipping into the river, and there was nothing for us
to do but to follow its example and ford the stream
too. This we accomplished without much trouble.
And now the hill Difficulty apparently rising above
us, the pilgrims suspended their progress a little, to
rest and feast upon hard-boiled eggs and dry bread.
In this repast we were assisted by a darling little
gipsy of a girl and her boy companion. They were
both in costume. Little Gitana wore a short, narrow
skirt, leathern sandals bound with thongs over the

instep, a white chemise gathered into the throat, and made with long sleeves, a blue bodice into which was thrust her painted distaff, and a heavy yellow and white woolen head-dress, laid upon the head so as to hang in folds behind and at the sides. When we arose to go up the mountain, we bade her good-bye. But she rose too, and calling "Sta! Sta!" prepared to accompany us. In answer to her call, there came rushing tumultuously up the other side of the slope a little black pig. He and his little mistress were evidently on the very best of terms, for he put up his head for a caress, and followed close at her heels like a dog. So our party was now increased by a most lovely little girl, and her most extraordinary and amusing pet. Gitana took possession of my bag and water-proof cloak, and put them both on her head without their interfering with her turning in every direction, gesticulating in a most animated way as she talked to us, and even stooping to drink at a fountain on the road. By and by another young girl joined us. Then came a man and woman driving a donkey loaded with sticks, a shepherd-boy with his flock, a drove of pigs with their guardian. Then came more girls, and so on until we formed a large procession. There were ten or fifteen young girls, any one of whom would have been an exquisite model for our artist friends in Rome. They all had the same distinctive characteristic features as our first young acquaintance. All had rich, brown complexions, rosy cheeks and lips, dark eyes, with a *soupçon* of the Eastern almond shape, long, drooping eyelashes, and masses of black hair. They have a right

4

to their Eastern looks, as they are partly of Eastern descent. Saracenesca, the village which they inhabit, and where we were intending to pass the night, was originally settled by a colony of Saracens. In one of their incursions they were defeated in the plain be- low, and the survivors succeeded in scaling an ap- parently inaccessible crag. Here they were safe from their enemies, for no foot save that of the wild goat and their own could reach their place of shelter. After a while they and the inhabitants of the plain made peace with each other. The Saracens gradually mingled with the Italians, adopted their religion, in- termarried with them, and their children, retaining much of the wild beauty and grace of their fathers, still inhabit the old nest. They are a simple, honest people. Of the latter trait we had ample proof on our return to Rome. One of our party lost a ring, valued more from its association than from anything else. Of course, we never hoped to see it again, unless it had been dropped in the house where we spent the night. But the next day, a boy returning from his work in the valley below saw something glittering on the rock. It was the ring. The child carried it to his father, and the father at once took it to the priest, and the priest sent a messenger to Rome to return the ring to its owner. But on our journey, I think I was more struck with their powers of dis- cernment than with anything else about them. I certainly met with such warm admiration that I think I never can be easily put down again. It is sad that my present residence is the palace of truth, because I consequently feel obliged to confess that the dress received, if possible, more attention than the person. My new friends felt of my skirt, smoothed the embroidery of my jacket, took hold of my hands to examine my undersleeves and gloves, and their admiration of my hat and veil was intense. As the way was long and weary, they offered to carry me. This, of course, I could not permit; and then they proposed to unload the donkey and mount me instead of the sticks. But I have a great horror of all ridable animals, and there was neither saddle nor bridle. The sticks were therefore undisturbed. Finally, however, I consented to try a decidedly ignominious mode of conveyance, and hang myself to the donkey's handle. Then the scene became too ludicrous, and sometimes I swung to and fro, too weak with laughter to be able to keep my footing, but grasping the creature's tail with all my might, while he pulled and grunted as if he did not seem to see it in that funny light. When we laughed, our friends laughed too, and the rocks rang again that sweet afternoon with most genuine mirth.

But it did seem as if we should never arrive at our journey's end. We climbed, and wound, and wound and climbed again, and still Saracenesca calmly looked down upon us from an apparently inaccessible height, reminding one in the distance of the Tower of Babel as seen in the old-fashioned picture-books. It looks, even when one approaches quite near it, as if it must have been built from above, by the aid, perhaps, of a smart shower of meteoric stones, or, at any rate, by the united efforts of a colony of eagles. More villagers met us as we continued our journey, and our little Gitana told, over and over again, the story of our coming down the hills, crossing the river, etc. Each one pressed to have a nearer view of the strangers, and claimed a word or a smile, while every word or act of theirs was a caress or a term of endearment. " Little dove ! " " Little darling ! " " Precious one ! " etc., rolled off their tongues in their own soft language. Hence we view how far one must sometimes go from home, and how long one may sometimes live, without being properly appreciated.

At last we arrived at a sort of *cordonata* path, or Via Dolorosa, leading direct to the village. Here the procession paused, and arranging themselves in a semicircle, all crossed themselves and repeated a short prayer. I am sorry to say that the sweet poem of rural life and beauty lost a canto when we began to ascend into the town itself. This was so very, very dirty that we could think of nothing but an infinite succession of piggeries. There are no streets in Saracenesca. A certain portion of the living rock which caps the mountain is left between the houses, and that is all. The houses seem to consist of little else than four covered walls and a chimney. I was glad to see, the next morning, smoke issuing from most of the chimneys. Everybody stood outside the doors looking at us, and on exhibition was the most beautiful baby I ever saw in my life — a little creature of perhaps ten months old. We all had but one opinion on the subject. The baby had been a peach in the other life. The skin had the downiness and softness of the fruit, and the deep coloring of the cheeks and lips answered to that of the peach.

It raised its great dark eyes, with their long lashes, and looked as fearlessly and wonderingly at the strangers as if it had been a bird for the first time beholding a man. Well, we resigned the baby, and passed the groups of beautiful children, and climbed up, still up, the winding steep to the very summit, where is the abode of the priest. He came in, and then our friends delivered us into his hands, full of kind wishes, never having sought reward by word or look. Those who aided us were satisfied with a very moderate remembrance, and those who had not gave us just as beaming smiles and as kind good-nights as their more fortunate friends. The priest is a young man, seemingly as guileless as the flock he leads. His mother, and the assistant priest, who is also the schoolmaster, form the family. We were welcomed as if we were dear friends, and I had soon made myself at home, and undertaken an expedition into the kitchen. There, I went into a committee of ways and means with regard to our supper, of which we stood greatly in need, made a cup of tea, and rescued a pigeon which was being thrown headlong into the pot of boiling water, and soon had the pleasure of seeing it revolving around a spit in front of the comfortable wood fire. Presently the church-bell sounded, and soon after, the sweet tones of the choristers fell upon our ears. By this time it was entirely dark, and when we entered the church, the scene was very impressive. The only light was that of the candles of the chapel, at whose altar the assistant priest was kneeling. The priest had gone into the choir, to lead the music himself, and the responses came up chanted in the wild tones of the villagers, the companions of our journey, who were kneeling on the floor of the church. The services closed by a prayer, written in Italian, in a simple style, suited to the understanding of the worshipers, begging for a blessing on their labors in the Campagna that day, and for protection during the night. Then the congregation arose, crossed themselves, and silently left the church. I never attended a Catholic service where there seemed so much simplicity and sincerity. And now came our supper, which was excellent. We made a beaten-up egg do the part of milk in the tea, for they never have any milk or butter in these little villages. And as this was the Pilgrim's Progress, I felt as if conducted to a fair chamber called Peace when the priest's mother and the maid conducted me to my room, and lavished every possible kindness and attention upon me. The stillness of night hushed us to sleep, which lasted until a little before day. Then the sweet tones of the church-bell, repeated and deepened by the echoes of the mountain, fell upon the ear. A second peal was soon followed by the voices of the choristers at their early morning worship. These hushed, I fell asleep again, and long before we had breakfasted, the simple villagers had wound down the steep to their labor in the valley below.

At last, the time came for us to start again on our journey. The priest first took us up to the fortress, whence the view is decidedly Swiss. We are among the very highest of this spur of the Apennines, twenty-five hundred feet above the river, and the

Campagna with its hills lies at our feet. We took a
bird's-eye view of it, and then bade our kind hosts
farewell. In villages where there is no inn, it is customary to be received at the house of the priest, and
on leaving to give them a family donation of the
same amount as the bill at a country inn. This we
understood, and I believe satisfied our entertainers
fully, who wished us God-speed very heartily as we
left them.

A council of war had been held, and a donkey
taken for me; but as there was no woman's saddle, I
handed it over to the gentlemen, and proceeded on
foot to our first resting-place. This was at Antigone,
which we reached by a very sweet walk. Here we
clambered again up step and steep to procure a
breakfast. This was promised us at the house of the
doctor, and we were invited to walk into the doctor's
parlor. It is not improper to state that the furniture
of this saloon was slightly unique. A large collection
of logs stood in one corner of the room. The center-
table was adorned with a straw bed, and other extraordinary articles were to be found in extraordinary
places. But the doctor received us with great hospi-
tality, even sacrificing in our honor the life of one of
his oldest friends. The principal dish on the table
was a very ancient and venerable cock, who was
served up comb and all. He had been cooked, but
he positively refused to be carved, and of course de-
clined to be eaten. However, we had good bread
and ricolta, with Bologna sausage, and, hungry as we
were, it was angels' food. The doctor had the goodness, also, in addition to the bird's comb, to present

us with his bill, which being attended to, the cloaks
and coats of the party were put upon the donkey. I
mounted thereon, and collaring the unhappy guide
with both hands, rode in triumph out of Antigone.

My donkey was a young one, and foolishness was
bound up in his heart. It was very difficult to keep
him in the path, and he entered into earnest conversation with his brethren at work in the distant fields,
trying to carry me off for a frolic with them, and
rubbing his nose coaxingly against his master for permission to go. Still, on the whole, we had a charming ride, and before we reached Subiaco, the beauty
of the scenery was greatly enhanced. We had the
same cultivation—the great fields of grain, the vine-
yards, the blooming hedges, the olive-groves on the
hill-sides. In addition to all this, we had the village
of Subiaco stretching up the hill, and churches and
convents still higher on the slopes hung above the
town, from whose towers the Ave Maria, repeated
from one chime to another, was sounding in our ears.
We have been greatly saddened to-day, however, by
the poverty of the people whom we have met, and
this in the midst of a land smiling like the Garden of
Eden. Little children, bending under the loads of
sticks they were carrying on their heads; women with
scarcely a vestige of womanhood to be seen about
them; men sickly and pale for the want of good
food, toiling for a mere subsistence. As we approached Antigone, a miserable acolyte came out of
a little chapel by the roadside, and begged. He was
still a young man, but all youth and life seemed
crushed out of him. He was dressed in a coarse,

black cotton gown, and his face and hands were only one degree less black than his dress. His whole appearance was like one who had never eaten a good meal, or been washed, or smiled, or been smiled upon in all his miserable life. God help the poor sheep wandering over these hills, for surely the shepherds act the wolf's part! . . . .

The convent of San Benedetto, to which we climbed next morning, is one of those strange, wild, beautiful, fanciful creations never seen out of Italy, and almost impossible to describe. It is said that Saint Benedict retired to a cave in the travertine cliff overhanging the town when a boy of fourteen. So secluded was he from the world that his food was let down to him in a basket, while he spent his time in meditation and prayer, and was, I hope, careful to offer an occasional thanksgiving that he had not yet become mad. Over and under and around his dwelling, the series of chapels we visited has been erected with consummate skill and taste, and with them a convent is connected. I never realized more fully the piety of many of the painters of the middle ages than I did while examining the frescoes with which the chapels are decorated. In those early days, good men painted a religious picture as one now writes a religious book, mingling prayers with their labors, and leaving behind them, as in this instance, the sweet impress of their sweet spirits. Did one wish to soften the heart encased in selfishness and worldliness? He brought before the eye the picture of the Man of Sorrows. He painted the cruel mocking and scourging, the shame and agony of the cross. He

4*

depicted the brow contracted with anguish, the lips saying, "Father, forgive them," the bowed head, and the dead Christ. Was there a Rachel weeping for her children, who would not be comforted because they were not? He bade her look upon that most loving and most sorrowing mother, who unclasped her tender arms from about her babe that he might go forth to a life of toil and pain, and a death of agony. He bade her be strong in faith as he held before her that mother and Son meeting again in glory, with no pain, nor sorrow, nor parting for them more. Were there lambs of the flock whose tender feet were wounded as they essayed to tread the narrow path? He showed them the Good Shepherd, ever going before them and leading them, and ready to gather them in his arms, and in his own time receive them into his bosom. He preached patience under trial here as he dipped his pencil in gold and brilliant colors, and painted the New Jerusalem. He opened its gates before them, and they beheld its beauty. He showed them the tree of life, and reminded them that they should eat of its fruits and rest beneath its shadow. To those bereft of human sympathy, he brought to view the innumerable company and church of the first-born. He showed them the patriarchs and prophets of old. He bade them look upon and listen to the beloved and loving disciple; and if he comforted maid and matron with the thought that the gentle Agnes or the lovely Cecilia ministered to them on earth or prayed for them in heaven, it was a pardonable error. But error, however small and venial at first, will grow, and strengthen as it grows. Like a weed, graceful and pretty, charming the eye with its bright coloring, and perhaps refreshing the senses with its odor, it increases its strength and size, and finally crushes out the good seed, takes its place, and flaunts its ugly stalk and poisonous fruit as the true harvest.

I am fully aware that I am not describing the church of San Benedetto all this time, and perhaps I may as well admit that I shall not be able to do so by direct attack. The lower chapel, in which the saint lived, has been left as it was, and is merely a strange weird grotto in the travertine cliff. Up and down the stairs leading to this, the peasants were continually passing. It is a *scala santa*, and so they mounted it upon their knees. Above this chapel is another, from which you look down upon the others. It is beautifully adorned with frescoes, and lighted by a single painted window, representing San Benedetto in the dress of his order. Beside the *scala santa* is another grotto in the travertine. In this is a statue of the saint at prayer, and the basket from which he was fed is to be seen near him. Opposite this is the choir, where service is generally held, but closed this festa day, when the other chapels are open. In short, San Benedetto seemed to me a great kaleidoscope, full of sweet, strange, variable pictures ; and now they waver and dance before my eye, and will not be fixed upon paper.

The next excursion is from Florence to the famous Benedictine monastery of Miltonic Valombrosa.

I think I do not particularly object to cooking. I

have had some little experience in the divine art, and it was rather pleasant. I shall never forget my first attempt. It was at broiling a mackerel for my father one dreadful day when we were moving, and everybody else was at the old house, and I at the new. How I labored over that fish ! I washed him as carefully as if he had been a baby, and laid him daintily on the gridiron. Then he spluttered, and I buttered him fiercely, and turned him over. Then he frizzled, and I buttered him again, and gave him another turn. Then he hissed, and I repeated the operation, and so we fought until I finally conquered, and reduced him to silence and rags. When he came upon the table, he presented a very extraordinary appearance, I must confess ; but my father looked at him with loving eyes, and declared that he had never eaten a better fish in his life. Seasoned with the sauce of affection, he became a dainty morsel. Some others of the family hinted that half a pound of butter was rather a liberal allowance for one fish, but the resolution was immediately laid upon the table, and my triumph was complete.

And shall I ever forget a second experience, when I had attained to the glory of a house of my own, and a little misunderstanding had occurred between myself and one or two members of the kitchen cabinet, causing a division of the house, by which I retained the small portion inside the walls for myself. Of course I need not mention to experienced city housekeepers that the same day a carriage-load of friends drove up to the door to make us a visit. My forces at the time consisted of a seamstress, who knew of the kitchen but from vague hearsay, and of a boy who was acquainted with it only as the place of deposit for the crockery which he was accustomed to break on its descent from the dining-room. However, our friends were met with a warm welcome, and the maid and myself, transmuting the youth above mentioned into a Gibeonite, descended into the lower regions. Then and there, with the aid of Mrs. Cornelius, the kindest " young housekeeper's friend " that ever discussed the mode of cooking a hare, did I perpetrate a dinner that drew down the warm encomiums of our friends, and also nearly brought down the house, as I was gravely asked where I had procured my cook.

But although I do not object to cooking, I have my prejudices against being cooked. And one fine day this summer Florence was converted into an enormous kitchen-range, wherein everybody was either frying, boiling, or roasting. Our household envied St. Lawrence, for that we had no kind Christian soul to turn us over when one side was done. So we finally decided that the bar of the gridiron known as the Via Maggio should know us no more for the present, and forthwith turned our longing eyes and willing feet toward the green shades of Valombrosa. With Antonio di Pelago as our charioteer, we were soon driving outside the Porta alla Croce, and hoping that the hill-sides would afford us the cool breezes for which we panted. Soon the envious walls near Florence had disappeared, and we had glimpses of pretty fertile country villas, and their olive-yards and gardens smiling upon the hills,

their verdure and loveliness extending to our long
line of curving road. For the road bends and
sweeps greatly, to follow in some degree the many
sweeps and curves of the Arno. The workmen
were digging clay and making brick beside its
shrunken waters. Their costume, or rather the
want thereof, was very remarkable. Among other
little eccentricities, they dispense with everything in
the shape of an upper garment, and display a charmingly well-tanned specimen of bear skin. As to the
country people whom we passed, the superhuman
exertions of every one of them alarmed us with the
idea that they must surely rupture a blood-vessel before night. Spread out at full length in their carts,
the shafts of which were attached to the backs of
their steeds, and the reins left at home, they were
drawn along at the pace the steeds chose to assume.
But when we rattled by them, they actually opened
their eyes, and in one or two instances went so far as
to raise their heads.

The villages near Florence present little else to the
eye but long ranges of wall, broken into the requisite
number of doors and windows. But those nearer the
end of our journey were much more pleasing; each
adorned with a tall slender campanile, and watched
over by a neighborly castle. And then the luxuriant
vegetation, the grapes struggling into ripeness, each
bunch a fair picture in which tints of soft green and
imperial purple struggle for the mastery—the pear-
tree and the loaded fig! The olive and the mulberry
rise above the fields of grain and gardens of vegetables, tier upon tier of fruitfulness climbing up toward

the loving, cloudless sky. Clematis and blackberry bushes struggle all over the hedges and mingle their colors in pleasing variety. Before us, walling in the vast garden, rise the mountains of Valombrosa. They darken and recede as we approach them, under the shade of evening's gray mantle. A steep pitch, a few more twists and turns, and our driver bids us " Buon Arrivato," while the whole Antonine family rush out with lights and warm welcomes to the " Hotel del Buon Cuore." Here we set up our tents in the village of Pelago, kindly cared for by the inhabitants of the aforesaid " good heart." But the heart was great even here, and Valombrosa lay before us. its white convent winking in the sunlight, an invitation to come up higher. So we scrambled down the hill upon which Pelago has seated herself, crossed a small stream, which the thirsty sun had emptied in his summer travels, and commenced our climb of the heights above us. Vegetation was very rife. The sweet children of the spring-time had nearly all disappeared, and Flora had given place to her bountiful sister Ceres. Amid her domain, we climbed for a long distance, and then entered a lovely chestnut forest, which in its turn gave way to a magnificent forest of pines. The long rows of trees that stretched in every direction about us, sent long rows of sunlight from beside them, which crossed and intertwined with the windings of the forest. And wherever there was a small clearing, great globes of light danced in our path, while the grave pines looked down and shook their heads the while. And still we clambered, now chasing the young shadows under the trees ; now

mounted on our steady, sensible old mules, and jog-
ging in the road, until the long rows of light grew
dim, and the shadows grew larger and chased them
away, and the mountain top was nearly reached.
Suddenly we emerged upon a beautiful, lately-shorn
meadow, and the white convent building closed it in.
We were conducted to a building apart, for the foot
of woman must not tread these holy courts. The
door of the "Forestiera" was opened by a lay brother; we dismounted, and ourselves and our belongings
were carried in. Then ensued a tragic scene. The
"Padre Decano," whose office it is to attend to the
comfort of strangers, presented himself, and informed
us that the Paradise we had just entered closed its
doors the next day. The great festa of the year for
Valombrosa is the Feast of Assumption, and we had
arrived on its vigil. The gentlemen could be accom-
modated in the convent, but such crowds would wish
to be admitted to the rooms set apart for the enslaved
sex to which we belonged, that the rules required
them to be closed entirely. In vain did we plead and
beg for an exception in our favor. At last I was advised to try the sick-dodge, which had at least the
merit of truth to recommend it. So I adopted fainter
tones. I slowly remarked that Pelago was to me the
valley of the shadow, sadly mentioned that Pelago
air I had found a slow but very sure poison, and
gaspingly stated that I had left America in quest of
health, which I was convinced was awaiting me in the
forests of Valombrosa. The good padre was moved.
He took snuff with great fervor, and meditated deeply. At last he remembered "due lettini" in an ob-

scure part of the house, which he could perhaps give us, if we would be contented with them. We remarked with Montezuma that they were beds of roses, and joyfully went to housekeeping for the night, in the apartment usually allotted to travelers. Our sleeping-rooms were two alcoves curtained off from a large room where the brother Benigno prepared his arrangements for our meals, and where he was rattling away the next morning so early as fearfully to disturb our dreams. But before he had made ready our supper, we amused ourselves by strolling about the neighborhood of the convent to view the preparations for the next day. A terrible martyrdom of chickens and turkeys had taken place, so that we could almost walk knee-deep in the piles of feathers which surrounded the mortal remains of the former owners thereof. Great fires were kindled in various places, over which hung vast pots of soup, giving forth already not unsavory odors. A pile of heads lay in one place, one of combs in another, and beside the latter, not the brushes, but the gizzards, livers, etc., while spread out in due order, lay long rows of the dressed birds. Others in long rows also were suspended on spits at the fire, and slowly revolving, and gradually changing color, showed their intention of ministering to the feast next day. Many of the peasants stayed all night, and a great chamber in one of the barns was comfortably strewn with hay for their accommodation. The cooks I suppose cooked all night, as their fires were bright when we disappeared behind our curtains. The next morning, when Fra Benigno had ceased to adorn our dreams, and become a decided reality, we arose to prepare for his breakfast. And such a funny time as we had ! Half of our necessary articles of toilet had not been brought into the green-room, and we were forced to make an onslaught upon the napkins on account of the paucity of towels, and generally to make little darting excursions to the other side of the curtain, at the imminent danger of being surprised by the enemy. When we emerged, we found a comfortable breakfast awaiting us, and soon after we strolled into the church. This was attired in festal garments, whose red and gilt are never very becoming to churches. This one is rather a fine building, with some pretty good pictures and very good wood-carving. After dinner we went out into nature's great temple, and followed the paths through the woods until we emerged near the end of the domains of our kind hosts. The view is of the upper Val d'Arno, the river curving itself among the weird Apennines, rising tier upon tier against the horizon. In the valley, whose soft beauty is veiled in the distance, Florence dimly raises her towers to view, and at our feet opens a great gorge into whose mysteries the woods peeped curiously as well as ourselves. And as we looked, we felt ourselves lifted by the atmosphere we breathed and the grand scenes upon which we gazed to the heaven which bent over us, and the Heavenly Father, whose wondrous works we beheld. And then we strolled back to the convent to find ourselves kindly cared for and amused until the hour of retiring had arrived. Then the good Padre Decano arrayed himself in cloak and broad-brimmed hat, and conducted us to our new quarters through an old cloister and up a flight of narrow, steep stone stairs. He then desired us to ignore him when we should meet next day, bade us good-night, and we were safely locked in our queer dormitory. How we laughed as we thought of the sensation we might create at home—a party of Protestant ladies from America hidden away in the convent of Valombrosa, and locked up in an obscure corner thereof! However, we must correct the latter statement by saying that our servant had the key, and that we could also turn the bolt ourselves from the inside. Next morning, we opened our eyes upon a most curious scene. From our windows we looked down upon a number of splendid snowy Tuscan oxen, whose muzzles had been duly decorated with new and splendid worsted fringes to celebrate the day. Many of these had brought up our friends from the valley below in sledges. These are of the rudest possible construction, consisting of baskets fastened to poles summarily stripped from a friendly tree, and put to immediate use. The seats are made by piling hay to the due height at either end of the chariot, and confining it to its place by boards. Thousands of people were walking about, crowding into the church or feasting at the booths. The men were generally arrayed in velvet coats and short clothes, and their rosy faces and white teeth shone with delight. The girls are laughing, sun-burned creatures, without much beauty, but with good-nature rippling all over their faces, and overflowing in their bright eyes and red lips. Each one was adorned with any number of strings of pearls. The Tuscan peasant woman carries

her fortune around her throat. The servants even
expend all their spare money upon pearls, and expect
to add one or more to their store every month. Each
pearl is divided from its fellow by a knot, and thus
each one is distinctly seen, while to our eyes, of
course, the effect is entirely spoiled. The girls all
wore huge flats hanging at the back of their necks,
and trimmed with a variety of colors, the more the
merrier, apparently. At the booths eatables of various kinds were sold. Besides the more solid luxuries,
there were cakes, wines, candies, etc. One most extraordinary dainty was a half-cooked bit of dough,
looking at a distance like a gigantic bon-bon. It was
hollow, and into a hole in the middle was poured for
the buyer a few drops of sweet and strong *liqueur*.
The purchasers of this abomination were, of course,
generally boys. And they seemed at the height of
human felicity when with their mouths crammed with
one abomination, their hands were outstretched for a
second, and their eyes, which were always nearly
popping out of their heads with agony, were fixed
upon a third painful pleasure. Our rooms of the day
before were entirely given up to Doney, the great
confectioner of Florence. The large room was converted into a café, fitted up with chairs and tables, at
which latter, ices and various cool drinks were dis-
pensed. The attendants put their bottles to bed in
one of our alcoves, and themselves in another. As to
ourselves, we have been silent, mysterious, and almost
ghostly. Our coffee was brought to our rooms by
people who walked on tiptoe with bated breath. We
ate our dinner in the usual dining-room, but with our

own Festus as our attendant, and with every door and window closely barred. Festus performed his functions as if he were a parricide at least, assisting at the feast of a cannibal tribe. Whenever we left our rooms, we stole therefrom like conspirators and entered them like pirates. When we met the Padre Decano, or any of the brethren whom we knew, we exchanged the iciest of bows. Poor Padre Decano! there was always a quiver of his lips on these occasions which was very dangerous.

But with the fall of the shadows began the depopulation of Valombrosa. Long processions of priests and people began to wind down the hill. Mules and donkeys were loaded with spits and copper kettles. The Juno-eyed oxen were attached to their sledges. The gay laugh of lad and lassie floated fainter and fainter to our ears as they wound down to the valley, and by dark we were again alone, and windows and doors were unbarred. Upon the whole we have rather enjoyed the Assumption of the Virgin (whatever that is) and only hope that she does. The pictures of that event generally represent her as pushed about in a way which might be disagreeable, but then, perhaps the pictures do not give it just as it occured. And we concluded that other people had also enjoyed the festa, when we heard the good Padre's account of the doings of the convent kitchen. Among the provisions set before the convent guests, were three hundred pounds of beef and mutton, four hundred pounds of bread, twenty barrels of wine, and a hundred and sixty chickens. Two barrels and a half of water were used in the soup, and a good soup it is too, as I can testify. This was all given away. The holocausts we had witnessed being for those not received as guests.

We were having so charming a time at Valombrosa, that nobody knows how long we should have remained there had we not received the sad information that the rules required us to yield our places to other guests. This was a terrible blow. We had been unspeakably captivating, especially to the Padre Decano, with whom we were all six feet deep in love; those of us who had husbands only half a degree less than those who had not. We had hoped that our feelings were in some degree appreciated. Perhaps they were, for we were urged to return, but our rooms had been promised for the next two days, and our grief was great. Oh! to be a lay brother, or a Madonna, or a Padre Decano, or a sacred relic, or a pine-tree, or anything or anybody that could remain indefinitely at Valombrosa! Thus we mused the next day as we were making our preparations to descend to the lower world. Thus we mused many a long day afterward, when Valombrosa lay far away from our longing eyes.

The monks of Valombrosa are of the Benedictine order. They take the vows of obedience, but I should scarcely think they take those of poverty, as their fare is almost as good as one could ask for anywhere, and far better than one can find in any country inn in Italy. They are very hospitable, and no return is asked for the entertainment furnished. It is, however, customary to leave a sum of money which shall equal that paid for board at a hotel for the same length of time, and to remember the lay brother who waits at table and his satellites. When all this was done, and our last good-byes were said, we assumed the usual badge of mourning, and slowly plunged into the pine forest which surrounds our convent. And then we returned to the care of the Antonines, and in due time drove forth by the light of the pale moon on our way back to Florence, which we reached in the blush of early morning.

Another excursion yet was that to the Painted Tomb of Etruscan Veii. The story, as it here follows, is abridged, by omissions, from the form in which its author gave it to the press.

From the Monte Pincio, over which we are slowly riding one early summer morning, one has a charming view of modern Rome. There rises the great dome of St. Peter's. There stretches the huge pile of the Vatican, with its mile of extent, its long galleries, and its many apartments for the Head of the Church and the ruler of Rome. On the Janiculum beyond flows the triple fountain of St. Paul. The gateway, so prominent on the same hill, is the entrance to the Villa Doria. The church in the neighborhood is that erected over the spot where St. Peter is said to have suffered martyrdom. Just beneath us is the Piazza del Popolo, whence stream the three streets which pierce that portion of modern Rome where foreigners congregate; and hence churches and palaces and crowded streets sweep on toward the horizon.

Now, go backward in time. Let these lonely hills, where but an occasional convent or villa watches over the city, sparkle with magnificent palaces, long-drawn porticoes, and richly decorated theatres. Restore the Colosseum, whose huge bulk rises in the distance. People the forum with a moving crowd, of whom some shall enter its splendid temples; others be driven in costly chariots to the senate-house or to the Græcostasis, where ambassadors from foreign lands are to be received; or all, both rich and poor, throng to the Circus or the Amphitheatre. Throw down the buildings of the present city, and restore the valley to its primitive destination as a military parade-ground. Let the grand dome of the Pantheon still swell in its midst. In place of the modern church of Santa Maria sopra Minerva, let the worshipers of the goddess of Wisdom meet in a temple sacred to her fame. Place, also, for the mourners, who are slowly bearing the ashes of a beloved prince to the mausoleum of Augustus. And when we have gazed a moment on this scene, command the wave of time to roll back still further, and once more we look from this same height.

The Tiber flows on, but no imperial bridges cross its tide. The Palatine lifts no gorgeous palace to the sky. The Capitoline bears no temple to the Father of gods. Over no Via Sacra, no Via Triumphalis, rolls the conqueror's car. No prisoners groan in the dungeons of the Mamertine. No lion's roar is echoed through the vaults of the Amphitheatre. No living fountains pour their streams through the arches of the aqueducts. The obelisks which

were brought to adorn palace and circus of imperial
Rome, now guard the splendid temples on the banks
of the distant Nile. The arches of the Colosseum,
the walls with which the mistress of the world surrounded her seven hills, slumber in the quarries of
Cerbara and Monte Verde.

In those distant days there flourished here a city
over whose grave Rome has triumphed as she triumphed over the thousands of living cities which in
after days bowed beneath her sway. Its very name
has perished. Its very existence is denied. Its great
works have been attributed to a handful of barba-
rians and shepherds.

It is to visit the site of a city which was flourishing
and prosperous before the days of the foster-children
of the she-wolf, that we leave the gates of Rome,
and direct our steps toward Florence, on our way to
see the spot where once flourished the Etruscan city
of Veii. . . . .

A most picturesque dell is this in which we stand.
The great massive rock through which the tunnel has
been pierced rising above us, ilexes and ivy clinging
and waving in every direction, boulders scattered
about us as though giants had been at play; some
of these choking the stream, covered with moss, and
fit for footstools for the river-gods. It seems impossible to realize that we are standing on the site of a
populous city. And yet Veii lay stretched for a distance of seven miles in the happy valley she had
chosen for her home.

We can not toil through the heavy vegetation that
hangs over what were once crowded streets and lofty

5

walls, or urge our way through briers covering the
site of homes made comfortable by luxury and civilization when Rome was struggling into existence on
the Palatine, without remembering with deep interest
the history of the life and death of Veii. Before
visiting its most interesting memorials, let us recall
some of the bravery of the noble people who inhabited it.

Veii was the chief of the twelve Etruscan cities,
and well did she deserve her place at their head. She
early saw, with prophetic eye, the danger to her life
and liberty threatened by Rome, and early in the
career of the latter a series of struggles took place
between the two powers. She fought with Romulus,
with the first Tarquin, and in aid of Tarquin the
Proud when he was banished from Rome. Again
and again in the history of the republic, also, did
Veii rise to conquer or die. And again and again,
there is no doubt, was she successful. Amid all the
glamour which Roman historians throw over their
wars, this fact still shows forth. In the days of
Romulus, the Etruscans settled upon the Cœlian
Hill, which certainly conquered foes would never
have been allowed to do. And we read of long
treaties continually being made between Rome and
Veii; treaties for ten, twenty, forty, and even one
hundred years; while Veii was generally the first to
disturb the peace between the two powers. Some of
the most memorable and splendid passages of Roman
history occur in connection with her wars with Veii.
The Fabian gens for two years left their beloved city
and encamped six miles from her walls; erecting a

fortress, whence they emerged from time to time to harass their foes. At last they grew bolder, and strayed further from their camp, lured by the Veintines to their destruction. It fell upon them swift and sure. And the Romans were not strong enough to avenge a slaughter which plunged their whole city into mourning. The Veiians encamped on the Janiculum, crossed the Tiber, and stood before the gates. Another truce was made, we know not upon what terms, and so war followed truce, and truce attended after war again and again. And when, at last, Veii fell, it was in no ordinary battle. A mine was pierced, opening into her citadel, into the temple of her goddess. The Romans issued into the streets, opened the gates of the city to their hosts, and slaughtered their noble foes, or carried them captive to Rome. The statue of Juno looked on while the blood of her children flowed at her altar. "Wilt thou go to Rome, Juno?" said Camillus, and Juno, with the facile power of muscle and the desire for change which is apt to be characteristic of images of sacred and profane worship, bowed her head in assent. So she was conducted to Rome, and went to housekeeping in a bran-new marble-front house on the Aventine, where she was worshiped for a thousand years.

And now Veii, emptied of her inhabitants, was in the hands of her conquerors. It was a lovely city, beautifully built, with regular streets and splendid public edifices, with a citadel upon a commanding hill, with houses abounding in luxury and comfort all unknown to most of the population of Rome. It stretched away into a well-watered plain, occupying a space as large as that covered by Athens, and was in all respects a contrast to Rome. Rome climbed its seven hills; its streets were narrow, its buildings irregular, its houses destitute of comfort, its lands occupied by the rich, its poor forgotten and miserable. Many of the bone and sinew of Rome removed to Veii, but they were recalled. They were needed to labor and to fight, and strong measures were taken to prevent their leaving the city.

The next year the poor Veiian slave at labor for his new and cruel taskmasters heard the Gaul thunder at the gates of Rome, and the smoke of the proud city went up to heaven as she lay in ashes beneath the tread of the barbarian. Roman gold paid the price which redeemed the capitol and the buildings on the Palatine only.

But let us enter the last resting-place of a noble Etruscan, who, taken from the evil to come, was never forced, with brimming eyes and bursting heart, to behold the ruin of his country. A passage cut through the tufa rock, and guarded by two lions, leads to the sepulchral chamber. At the door of entrance two other lions are placed; all these grim sentinels are now headless and battered. I shall never forget my feelings when, having passed them, the door was opened, and I was admitted into this house of the dead. On either side of the room I entered is a stone bench, upon which, uncoffined, had been laid, on the one side, the body of a warrior in full armor, and on the other, as it is supposed, that of his wife. Part of the armor, a spear-head and helmet, lie upon the bench at the right hand, and also a candelabrum—all of bronze. There are about the room many jars containing ashes, and others for wine and oil. The next room is ceiled with carved beams, and contains a bronze brazier for burning perfumes, and several small square stone chests for human ashes. On the lid of each of these is sculptured the head of the occupant, so that he seems emerging from the urn which contains his remains. On the walls are painted particolored crowns.

Returning to the first room, and taking in my hand the helmet, I felt that I could read there, written in letters of bronze, a tale of pathetic interest. Long ago, before the days of Solomon, an Etruscan prince led his countrymen to the field. He was victorious. Pursuing his flying foes, urging on his troops, himself in the front rank, as the enemy turned at bay to sell their lives as dearly as they could, he was mortally wounded in a hand-to-hand combat. See, by this hole entered the spear, and by this one it passed out, having done its work well, and set free a noble soul as it pierced the active brain. His troops return to their home victorious, but singing no song of triumph. A melancholy dirge floats on the air, and is re-echoed in wilder, shriller accents from within the gates of the city. Again and again rises the strain of mourning as the soldiers bear him whom they loved and reverenced, and for whom hundreds would have willingly laid down their lives, to his honorable bed. They hewed out his tomb in the living rock, and placed about it the dread symbols of sovereignty and eternal guardianship. They depicted crowns of vic-

tory about the walls to symbolize his death as a conqueror.   They burned costly perfumes in his honor.
They poured libations of wine and oil.   And there,
" like a warrior taking his rest " on the battle-field,
they laid him.   Here his broken-hearted wife was
soon brought to share his repose.   Here his family
and friends were placed near him.   Here his depend-
ents and servants were laid beside him.   And when
all was done, when wife and friends and servants were
all gathered about him, when the tomb was finally
sealed up, and relinquished to the care of the mute
sentinels who lie still beside it, they carved no name,
they inscribed no record of his deeds.   These were
graven on the hearts of his countrymen.   They were
sung from age to age by the bards of Etruria.   Hundreds of years after his tomb was closed the poor
Veiian slave in the city of his foes sang at his toil in
plaintive accents the life and deeds and death of the
great Etruscan Lucumo.

But even here we do not leave the dead warrior.
The chambers are painted in quaint designs, but in
imperishable colors.   One of these only I shall describe.   It reminded me most strongly of a quaint
picture I had seen a few months before, painted by
old Luini, representing the scene of the Crucifixion.
The victim still on the cross, but dead.   The souls of
the penitent and of the impenitent thief in the guise
of new-born babes were just hovering over the cross.
The one was received of angels, the other seized and
borne away by a demon.

In the rude painting nearest the warrior's last resting-place we see a traveler unarmed and unclothed,

mounted on horseback. He is preceded by two attendants, one of whom bears a hammer. Seated behind him, with one paw resting on his shoulder, is an animal, who may perhaps represent a genius. The soul of the warrior is here represented setting forth upon its long journey. The attendants are the good and evil spirits, to one of whom he is to be delivered. The animal who rides behind him is the memory of his past deeds.

But the countenance of the traveler, his firm posture, his steadfast, onward gaze, betoken no fear. Naked, he is not ashamed ; alone and unarmed, he trusts and is safe. Surely, gleams of a better faith ; surely, hopes of a higher life are portrayed here. And around all the quaint, rude figures are portrayed garlands of lotus-flowers, the emblems of immortality. May it not be said of these who sleep here, and of those who laid them to their rest, that they obeyed the command : " That they should seek the Lord, if haply they might feel after Him and find Him ? "

VI.

1861–1866.

THE WALDENSES.

Rebuilding a Ruined Church—Visit to the Valleys of the Waldenses—The Stronghold of Angrogno—The Glorieuse Rentrée—A Sabbath in the Temple of the Balsille—The Lord's Supper—A Baptism.

ON her first arrival in Italy, as some pages already transcribed from her journal prove, Mrs. Gould's warm interest was drawn out toward the Waldensian Christians. And this interest grew from year to year as she became better acquainted with this interesting people in their own homes. For in the enforced journeys which she made each year, as the summer heats at Rome, and the annual access of the hay-fever combined to drive her to the higher parts of Switzerland and the Tyrol, she would often pass by Turin, and the opening in the mountains that leads up into the historic valleys and ravines in which the simplicity of the Gospel was so long harbored from persecution. She did not like to pass her friends without a visit; and it need not be said that she did not visit them without doing them some good, and leaving some grateful memory behind her. An incident soon occurred which gave to her interest in the Waldenses a practical turn. A lady living in one of our Western States, felt her sympathies strongly excited toward this ancient communion, and wished to do something in aid of it. She looked for some one who would make a wise disposition of her gift, and ended by putting a considerable sum of money into Mrs. Gould's hands, to be applied for the object, at her discretion. Through Mrs. Gould's agency the amount was increased by other contributions. In one of her visits to the Vaudois valleys, she had seen an ancient church that dated from before the days of persecution. It was ruined, roofless, and wasted by fire. Still, from generation to generation, the people had continued to meet there. Sometimes they would be driven away by persecution, but those whom the sword had spared would return to kneel where their fathers knelt. And now, from beyond the ocean, help came to them. The old church was roofed in and repaired at a considerable expense; so that what this impoverished people had lost by persecution at the hands of their fierce neighbors was restored by the charity of their fellow-Christians from a thousand leagues away.

Naturally, after being the agent of such a benefaction, Mrs. Gould was sure of a warm and grateful welcome among the mountaineers, whenever she was able to include the trip to La Tour and Pignerol, in her plans of summer

5*

travel. The following is taken from the description of a visit to the Waldensian valleys :

We were charmed with the situation of La Tour, as we beheld it the morning after our arrival. It is in a high valley, watered by two clear mountain streams, and surrounded by fertile hills and grand mountains. The valley is green with lovely meadows of rich grass, scattered all over with clover-heads. Patches of corn burn in the sunshine, and thrifty vines hang upon the hill-sides. The Catholic church is just at the entrance to the village, and just beyond the village on the opposite side is the Protestant church, a neat, pretty structure. Beside it is the parsonage, and in the immediate neighborhood are the college and the Professors' houses, each standing in a little garden. There is an Orphan Asylum for girls in La Tour, and a large number of schools. Indeed, throughout the Valais, the church and the school side by side in each village, remind one of the New England towns in their early settlement. In the Orphan Asylum, the children receive a good French and Italian education; are taught to sew, knit, and crochet, and perform all the labor of the establishment, so that they learn something of cooking, and can scrub, wash, and iron ; they also cultivate the little vegetable garden.

Education receives great care among the Vaudois. The children at a very early age are gathered into Infant Schools, where they learn to read and write, commence mental Arithmetic, and are taught something of the world into which they have so lately been introduced. Then come the primary, secondary, and high-schools. And there is a College for young men, and a Boarding-school for young ladies. The Theological Seminary is at Florence. The course of study pursued in the schools is very thorough in certain respects, but, like Italian education generally, is deficient in branches calculated to interest children. They are taught the grammar of the French and Italian languages with great care, write an excellent hand, and are well-exercised both in mental and practical Arithmetic. They have also a good knowledge of Geography. History and the Physical Sciences are too much neglected excepting in the higher schools. The best men among them are, however, aware of these defects, which are being gradually amended. The religious education is most carefully attended to. Not only are there Sunday-schools in all the parishes, but the Bible is diligently studied as a text-book in all the day-schools. Many of the schools in the upper valleys are closed during the summer. The services even of the children are required upon the farms, and the salaries of the masters are so small that they are obliged to eke out their means by farm-work.

From La Tour, excursions are made to the mountain valleys. About an hour thence is Angrogno, one of the valleys, which has witnessed some of the most terrible scenes in the history of the Valais. Here, at one time, every house was burned, save the two churches, which the flames refused to destroy. In the principal village is a simple white " temple " (as the Vaudois call their churches), where on one occasion a Catholic altar was erected, and a monk thundered forth denunciations of human and Divine wrath upon the humble flock in the wilderness obliged to attend the service. And not far distant, in the very heart of the mountain, is Pra da Tour, where they retreated to make their last stand. Here the women wept and watched and prayed one long day, while a handful of the men repulsed an army sent against them, and then the valley resounded with songs of praise. God had given to his people the victory. Again and again did the foe enter the defile; again and again was he repulsed. When we read the wonderful way in which rock and meadow, torrent and mountain fog, were made to fight for this people, we seem to feel a holy awe as we tread the hidden places of the earth which God prepared in the distant ages for a sanctuary for his truth. Here are rocky barriers which served as fortresses, where a little one could put ten thousand to flight. From this soft green terrace, a blaspheming leader of the enemy slipping upon the dry grass, was precipitated into the boiling torrent below. One day, the enemy had penetrated so far into the rocky defile that it seemed as if Pra du Tour, the refuge of the weak and helpless, the women and children, the aged and infirm, must be taken. Then a thick fog fell upon the combatants. The enemy could not trace the narrow path along the precipice. The Vaudois seized the opportunity, attacked them, and put them to flight. The fugitives often fell, to rise no more, into the deep pools of the river below. These and the sharp-pointed rocks were the weapons with which God discomfited them that day.

We had the privilege on the Sabbath which we spent in the Valais, of attending service in the neighborhood of the Balsille. Here the Vaudois first trod their native mountains on occasion of their "Glorieuse Rentrée." They had been almost destroyed, and the feeble remainder exiled. The Swiss had received and cared for them, and their own mountain homes knew them no more. With longings that could not be controlled, with sickness of heart that could not be healed, they looked back to their beloved land. There were the graves of their fathers; there the temples where they had worshiped God; there the cabins which had sheltered them in infancy; there the mountains they had so often climbed; there their homes. In vain did kind but stranger hands minister to their wants. That fearful home-sickness to which the mountaineer seems so subject took possession of them, and though innumerable dangers and privations assailed them, they climbed the mountains which separated them from their own. Through frost and snow, over fearful precipices, up bare and steep heights, they toiled and climbed for long days and nights. And at last over a solid wall of rock they looked down upon their desolate homes. And upon this mountain side of the Balsille they first rested on their native soil. Here, too, they spent their first winter after their return, living like the earlier disciples, in caves of the earth, and nourished almost by miracle.

On a sweet morning, when the valley was hushed in more than Sabbath stillness, we set forth to visit this sacred spot. Threading the defiles, crossing the stream, descending the mountain to mount again immediately on the opposite side of the torrent to a greater height, we toiled on our way to the village of the Balsille. This is situated on two shelves of rock separated from each other by the young and riotous waves of the Germanesca torrent. And thence we mounted an almost perpendicular grassy slope, the hiding-place and fortress of the saints in the dreadful days of their persecution. Above us were the rocky walls they had scaled to reach their homes again, and those still more steep and difficult by which they escaped when driven at last from their winter's stronghold. From the forest of pine trees below us the enemy had rushed to destroy them, and had been repulsed. Above the opposite heights, where the cattle were now peacefully feeding, they had been seen by the same enemy when escaped like the bird from the hand of the fowler. From a descendant of the Captain who led them in the darkness of night from the position which they could no longer hold, we received a bowl of bread and milk, our breakfast on that Sabbath morning.

From the Balsille, we sought the sanctuary to which the eleven villages of this parish are gathered. The congregation is composed entirely of peasants, and is most devout and attentive. The "Temple," like the other Vaudois churches, is white within and without. Upon the roof is depicted the Dove, and upon the wall, the Vaudois emblem, a lighted candle, and the words, "*Lux lucit in tenebrâ.*" The pulpit is of dark wood, and beneath it is the clerk's desk. The men sit upon one side of the church, and the women upon the other. The clerk reads the people into church. When all are assembled, the clergyman enters. As he came up the aisle, those of his congregation whom he passed rose in token of respect. The service had not commenced when two men and a woman entered, one of the men carrying a bundle tied with huge bows of red ribbon. A band of the same color was put about the woman's hat. They presented themselves, with a little salutation, just in front of the clerk's desk. I then perceived that the bundle was an infant, brought by its godfathers and godmother for baptism. The simple exhortation was given, the questions binding the sponsors asked and answered, and the child received the name of Henri Arnaud. The custom of having godfathers and godmothers is dying out. During the times of persecution, it was thought proper to provide children with guardians, beside their parents. So many fathers gave their lives for their religion, so many mothers were tortured and murdered, that the joy with which a child was received was mingled with tears and trembling in those doleful days. And it was a comfort that others had promised to care for it, should its parents be removed, and to watch over its religious education. But those times are over, and the more intelligent of the people do not understand why sponsors should take upon themselves vows which they will have no opportunity to fulfill.

After the baptism, the clergyman read the Commandments, and then a simple liturgy. Either written or unwritten prayers are used, according to the choice of the officiating clergyman. The singing is led by the clerk. The movement is slow, and the melody rather German than Italian. The voices are uncultivated, but not discordant. After the sermon, the Creed is read, the Levitical and Apostolic Benediction given, and with the injunction (never omitted), to remember the poor, the services are concluded.

The Lord's Supper is administered quarterly, on two successive Sabbaths. One of these services I attended. The bread and wine had been brought in and placed upon the table by the elders. The flagons were of pewter, and the goblets of glass. After an exhortation read from the pulpit, the clergyman descended, and putting a piece of money into the plate, partook himself of the bread and wine. The elders and clerk next came forward, and the men of the congregation two by two. Each, as he approached the little table, put into the plate a sou or double sou. The clergyman broke the bread, and with a certain wave of the hand presented it to the two persons standing before him. As they received it, they made a gesture of salutation with the hand. The wine was presented by the elder to the clergyman, and given and received as was the bread. As each communicant retired, he made a slight bend of the head. Two others immediately came forward, and the procession of men at an end, the women presented themselves in the same way. I think no stranger could have been present on this occasion without feeling himself carried back to the early days of the Christian Church. There, under the shadow of the great mountains which had been the bulwark of their fathers, the children met to celebrate the death of their Lord. On one occasion, their fathers had hoped to keep this sacred feast, but were called instead, many of them, to seal their love for their Saviour with their blood. Henri Arnaud, for whom the little babe was that day named, had prepared them for the communion, and when they were prevented from partaking of it, he led them forth to battle.

VII.

THE FLORENCE ORPHANAGE.

*An Exile caring for the Orphans of Exiles —
A Paternal Government — An American Wo-
man before a Roman Tribunal — A Christmas
Tree in an Alpine Village — The Florence
School and Orphanage—A Memorial Stone.*

WHILE, at Rome, the evil days continued, there came to Mrs. Gould at Florence, where she had frequent occasion to sojourn, a welcome opportunity of serving God by ministering to little children. She found there an asylum for Protestant orphans, that had been begun many years before in England, where one Salvatore Ferretti was then living, a refugee from religious persecution. When liberty of opinion came to Italy, he returned to Florence, bringing with him the orphan children of Italians who had died in exile. He struggled long and manfully to support both these and others who had come to him. His aim was to save the helpless orphan daughters of Italian Protestants from want and ignorance and sin, and put them in the

(114)

way of living honorably by their own labor, without the
sacrifice of their simple faith, and their clear conscience
before God. When, in 1866, this orphanage first came to
the notice of Mrs. Gould, it was in an unwholesome situation, and very comfortless, with some ten or twelve children, as well cared for as they could be with the means at
Mr. Ferretti's disposal. Efforts were immediately and
successfully made to furnish a more suitable house, and to
increase the usefulness of the institution. Mrs. Gould's
efforts were indefatigable in helping on the good work.
She interested many Americans at home and abroad in
this orphanage; and it largely depended upon her for its
support for several years. By the time her energies were
withdrawn from this work to another, it had been brought
to a position where it was secure from the dangers which
threatened its earlier days.

One winter, during these "evil days" of Rome, while
Mrs. Gould was earnestly engaged among her English and
American friends in that city, in collecting money for this
orphanage at Florence, an incident occurred which displayed something of her character, and something of the
character of that benign and "paternal government," the
overthrow of which, we are sometimes taught, was a monstrous and horrible sacrilege, and the restoration of which
is represented as a duty binding on all Christian nations,
that the wrath of God may so be averted from the world.

It became known to the Papal Government, through
some of those delicate expedients which were a part of
its ordinary machinery, that a vile and abominable thing

was committed in the Holy City; that a humane and Christian woman was actually collecting charitable gifts among her personal friends for the support of some orphan children in a neighboring town! There are some forms of vice and crime at which this apostolic Government, for a consideration, has sometimes been induced to connive. But not at enormities like this!

The house of Dr. Gould was from the beginning an object of suspicion to the Roman police. It was reported that American and English travelers would assemble there on Sunday evenings; and sounds like the singing of hymns had been heard proceeding from his parlors. There was reason to suspect that these strangers might surreptitiously be engaged in worshiping God. Dr. Gould was summoned before the police and questioned as to the proceedings. Had not the persons assembling at his house been engaged in acts of worship? He was not prepared to deny that their Sunday evening hymns were of this character. Would he give assurance that the occurrence should not be repeated? On the contrary, he thought it in the highest degree probable that his countrymen and countrywomen, gathering at his house on Sunday evening, would continue to join in Christian hymns according to their national custom. But were there not Italians among them? On this point Dr. Gould was enabled in some measure to relieve the anxiety of the paternal Government; it was not customary for Italians to be present at these social gatherings of strangers. And with a certain amount of browbeating, the culprit was given to under-

stand that his case would be held under consideration.
The authorities *did* consider it; and to such good purpose
that they concluded that to banish from the city the physician to the American legation, because his guests would
sing hymns of a Sunday night, might be attended with
more inconvenience than advantage. And the hymn-
singing went on from year to year, without serious moles-
tation.

But the present case was a different one, in two gravely
important respects: first, the crime was no longer that of
Christian worship, but that of acts of charity and mercy to
destitute and suffering orphan children; secondly, the of-
fender, summoned before the police court in her husband's
absence, at the instance of an eminent prelate, to answer
for this nefarious business, was a woman. It might have
been expected, and undoubtedly was, that a woman suddenly dragged into that position would be intimidated at
once. But the result was the furthest possible from that;
for she was "in nothing terrified by her adversaries, which
was to them an evident token of perdition, but to her of
salvation, and that of God." Present in court, to lend the
majesty of his purple to this dignified attempt to frighten
a foreigner and a lady with the threat of criminal proceedings, was Monsignor N——, one of the most noted society-
prelates of the Roman court, personally known to Mrs.
Gould, and at once recognized by her as the instigator of
this mischief. It may not have been according to the Roman Code of Procedure in such cases provided, but for
all that it was not the less effective, when the little Ameri-

can lady, with an immense dignity which those who knew her will at once imagine, turned sharply upon her eminent friend and charged him with the shameful insult that had been put upon her. At once Monsignor was all protestations of respect and disclaimer. "He purred over me like an old cat," said Mrs. Gould when she told the story, on reaching home. He was sure that no insult was intended, and trusted that no offense would be taken. "But you *have* insulted me," she answered; "you know perfectly well that if I have transgressed the law there is a proper way of dealing with a lady in my position, through the representative of my country. But go on, if you think best, and make me a criminal on such a charge as this! I promise you there is not a newspaper in America but shall tell the story of it." Obviously the relations between prosecution and defense were becoming painfully inverted. There was a little *sotto voce* consultation between the court and the eminent *amicus curiæ*, at the end of which they were fain to let their prisoner go without so much as a reprimand.

The following letter, dated at Rome so late as December 9, 1869, speaks both of the Waldensians in the valleys, and of the Florence Orphanage, and shows something of the progress which the latter had made in the few years which she had devoted to it. It is an appeal for help addressed to the Sunday-school children of the United States:

MY DEAR CHILDREN :—The happy Christmas time

is coming, and perhaps before this letter can reach you, you will have been gathered about your Christmas trees, enjoying the gifts which the season brings you. I know of other children who are looking forward also to the same day, because, thanks to you, they also are to have something to remind them that there is a little light shining in the darkness of their long cold winter. The Waldenses in the Alpine villages are long ago shut up among snows and ice. In the very early part of October their winter begins. I have heard from two of their clergymen lately, and I shall hear again after the Christmas season has passed. Ah! I wish we could do more for them, for childhood with so little comfort is very sad. I received such a beautiful letter from one of their clergymen after their little festa of last year, and then their teacher had written a little note of thanks, which they all signed. I will tell you a little about their Christmas.

They could not meet in the evening, for many of them live miles away from their school and church. There are no roads, and the foot-paths are covered with icy snow. Some of the little tiny ones were thought to be too little to come, but they begged so hard that they were brought on the father's or big brother's back, and they were all in the church at the appointed hour. There, the clergyman made a very short address and a prayer, and then the children, were conducted to the largest school-room of the parish. The clergyman is himself very poor. He never eats meat more than once a week, but he wanted to help make his little ones happy. So, he had got

in evergreen from the woods, and his wife had made
candles, which they cut up, and hung in their little
tree. A Christmas tree! The children had heard
of such a thing, but never seen it before. Some of
them screamed with delight; some of them stood
perfectly still, as if they could never move away from
the beautiful vision. Some of them had tears in
their eyes, the happiest they had ever shed. At last,
one or two broke out into an *Evviva*, and, in a moment, *Evvivas* loud and long sounded all over the
room. This exclamation is a little more musical
than our Hurrah, and means the same thing. When
the teachers could get them a little quiet, they began
one of the beautiful French hymns which I have so
often heard them sing, and the voices turned from
shout to song. And then began the distribution of
the presents.

"The tree was loaded with magnificent gifts,"
wrote the clergyman, "and each child received three
sets." I was frightened, for I thought he must have
run me in debt. But I read on. "First, each child
received a big tract and a little tract; second, each
child received an excellent bun and two mottoes;
third, each child received a gilded nut and an apple."
There, dear children, you see how little makes these
poor little creatures perfectly happy. Do you not think
we should be willing to give them this little taste of
pleasure once a year? I could not do it this Christmas, but I hope by next year to be able to send
enough money to light up one such little tree in
every Sunday-school in the Waldensian Alps. You
have helped me to make many happy this year;

many children like yourselves. God bless you for it !

What shall I tell you of our school and orphan-house? The school has now three hundred and fifty children. They are under the care of most excellent teachers, so devoted, that they take the little salary that can be afforded to them because they would rather be poor and be able to teach their children something of their Heavenly Father and Saviour than gain more money in other ways, as they might easily do. Indeed, a large sum of money is promised whenever the teachers will promise not to pray with the children, or read to them from the Bible. Thank God, these noble men and women say, "Thy money perish with thee!" In a letter just received from one of them, she says: "Catholics, Jews, Atheists, and Protestants all sing our hymns, and are present at our prayers."

This school was brought to our notice, as it seemed by accident, just as supplies which it had been re-ceiving were cut off. Ah! it was no accident which led us to its doors. It was the Heavenly Father of these little ones who guided our steps that day. And from that time, as one trouble after another has fallen upon us, until we find ourselves to-day almost in despair, we have been sure that God meant these children to be trained up for Him by our means. As one way has closed up, He will show us another. We can not, we will not turn these children into the street. We will not give them up to the priests. Tell us, Sunday-school children of America, that we need not! Tell us that you will help us to keep our promise.

6

And the orphan girls! What shall we tell you about them? My letter has grown so that I can not give you the details I would about them. In the letter which I have just received, the teacher tells me that the superintendent received, the day the letter was written (the 4th of December), eight pressing applications for places in the *Orfanotrofio* for eight girls. He had to refuse them all. We are in debt. Our beds are not properly furnished. Our little delicate children need warm, woolen stockings. (They shall not need those after Christmas, for I shall send them every one two pairs; so you need not think of their poor little cold toes). They need other warm clothing; and we are still liable to be turned out of our house for the rent. When I think of it all, I feel almost overwhelmed; but I remember who bade us commit the fatherless children to Him. He will, I believe, send help to the suffering little ones of Italy from the happy little ones of America. To you, children of loving mothers, to you, mothers of happy children, we commit them.

The work thus begun grew and prospered. In connection with it there grew up (as Mrs. Gould's letter indicates) a large and flourishing day-school. Of what sort this school was, in aim and methods, and especially in the unselfish, unpartisan, Christian spirit in which it was conducted, may best be learned from the example of the Roman schools in which, only a few months later, Mrs. Gould was able to apply the results of her Florentine experience.

The orphanage itself has grown into a permanent institution. No longer housed in an unwholesome tenement from which, on the failure of its precarious income, it was liable to be turned into the street, it occupies a fine building purchased and held in trust for its express use.

A lady who had known the whole work from its beginning, wrote thus in 1876: "To my mind the Florence Orphanage is at this moment the fairest monument of Mrs. Gould's noble, Christian philanthropy and indomitable energy that she has left behind her in Italy."

To the same dear friend is due a fitting memorial of this part of Mrs. Gould's work—a block of white marble set in the wall of the Orphanage, with this inscription:

IN MEMORY OF

MRS. EMILY BLISS GOULD,

ONE OF THE EARLIEST

AND MOST EFFICIENT PATRONESSES

OF THIS INSTITUTION.

VIII.

1859—1871.

CONTEMPORARY HISTORY.

IT needs a moment's retrospect to remind us of what a magnificent movement of history Mrs. Gould had been witness during her fifteen years' residence at Rome.

The year previous to her departure from America—the year 1859—was the year of the war of Austria against Sardinia, in which France under Napoleon III. joined the weaker party, and in a brilliant two months' campaign, made illustrious by the battles of Montebello, Magenta, and Solferino, drove the Austrians from Lombardy, and

(124)

annexed it to the Sardinian crown. Simultaneously with
the outbreak of this war, came the revolution in Tuscany
and the flight of the Grand Duke, resulting in the an-
nexation of this splendid and historic province, also, to
the dominions of Victor Emmanuel, and the inauguration
of the kingdom of Italy under a free Constitution .

In the spring of 1860, the insurrection in Sicily broke
out, and the news that electrified the party of travelers as
they landed from the steamer at Havre at the end of May,
was that Garibaldi had entered Palermo in triumph at the
head of his handful of red-shirts. A few weeks later the
epidemic of insurrection had spread to the city of Naples;
the king of the Two Sicilies ran away from his capital;
and on the 8th of September, Garibaldi entered the city,
and holding up his forefinger before the crowd, in symbol
of *Italia Una*, announced that the whole peninsula of
Italy was to be free and united. That year the forces of
the king of Italy entered the Papal territory, and the Two
Sicilies, the Marches, and Umbria were annexed to the
Italian crown.

When in April, 1861, Mrs. Gould, under Doctor Gould's
escort, made her first visit to Naples, she stopped on the
way at Gaeta, where the traces of tremendous fighting
were only two months old.

We entered the gate. The scene was tremendous.
The whole town was destroyed. Not a roof is left in
some parts of the town, and scarcely a whole wall
standing. Everything is torn to pieces. We saw the

fortification in which the young Rehoboam took refuge under the casemates where nothing could touch him. At the left of the gate are the masses of ruin caused by the explosion of the magazine, where the houses are almost reduced to dust. The citadel is built on a hill overlooking the town, whose foundation is a mighty rock rising sheer from the depths of the Mediterranean. The Piedmontese crept up from the hills around Gaeta and threw their bombs into the town, and Rehoboam was obliged to leave. We went up almost to the top of the hill. The view is splendid. The sea, frantic in the wild play of his waves, sent the foam in long white streaks all over the blue of his waters. The promontory of Circe, bold and blue and beautiful, stretched along beyond us to the north. The islands of Ponza and Palmarola and Zannone, with the larger ones of Ischia and Capri, lie along the horizon. A few boats in sight are tossing in the play of the waves. The Pontine Marshes stretch away in the distance. Gaeta itself, with its fortifications, its churches and its towers, lie beneath us, and the great rock on which we stand rises like a giant, lifting its head defyingly to the waves which scream and roar and leap at its feet. The mountains fill up the picture in the background. . . . . The sight of the many fortifications kept up for the purpose of enslaving the people, now fallen into the hands of the people themselves, filled us with great delight, and *Viva Verdi** was the cry of our hearts. We were full of the thought of Garibaldi and his no-

---

* Viva *V*-ittorio *E*-mmanuele *R*-e *D' I*-talia.

ble band. We saw his determined followers step by step approaching Gaeta, shutting up the tyrant within its walls, destroying one after another of its defenses, day by day besieging it closer, until the end was accomplished, the king fled, and Naples was free.

The capture of Gaeta took place .in February, 1860. There was outward peace for more than two years, until the unsanctioned expedition of Garibaldi, starting in the summer of 1862, on the island of Sicily, but aimed at Rome. He was met at Aspromonte in Catania, defeated, wounded, and taken prisoner by the troops of Victor Emmanuel.

What chapter, in what we so absurdly call "profane" history, more plainly manifests a divine work, than that which tells the story of the liberation and unification of Italy? It went forward so steadily, though sometimes so slowly and discouragingly to eager hearts, and all the while it was nobody's plan and nobody's doing. The Pope himself began it in 1846. Then "The Revolution" (they always speak of this on the Continent of Europe as a person) took it up. The House of Savoy was forced into the leadership of it in spite of itself. France gave it a mighty forward lift in '59, and then tried to stop it. Garibaldi would fain have pushed the work through at once, but Italy interfered to prevent him, and made compact with France to move down to Florence as capital, and hold the *status quo.* Then came the "Six Weeks' War" in '66, in which Italy acquired Venice by getting beaten, and France and the Prussians combined to consummate the acquisi-

tion. Once more, in '67, Garibaldi came within sight of
Rome, but he was beaten back by the Pope's mercenaries,
and the effect was only to fortify the Papal power more
strongly than ever in Rome. The final result was to come
"not by might nor by power." The Pope himself must
give the signal for his own overthrow. Catholic France,
which had first promoted Italian unity, and then opposed
it, was at length, by opposing, to accomplish it. War levied
in the interest of the Papacy was to result in its downfall;
and as the confederacy between France and Prussia had
liberated Venice, so the conflict between the same powers
was to be the emancipation of Rome. Among men, nothing but cross-purposes and changeful schemes. Providence seemed bent on upsetting the calculations of able
editors and "making diviners mad." And all the time the
divine plan, now so plainly manifest by the event, kept un-
folding from year to year, until it was consummated in the
unbroken unity and the well-ordered freedom of the new
nation.

After the tremendous events of 1866, Mrs. Gould was
continually looking forward to the time when there should
be freedom at Rome—liberty for her to do her own chosen
and delightful work in helping, comforting, and teaching
neglected and ignorant children. Her work at Florence,
in aiding the "Orfanotrofio" there, was wrought in hope
of larger and better opportunities of like work at her own
beloved home. It would have been a sorry record to say
of her that she did nothing but wait for better times. In
the day of small things and few things, she did heartily and

to the Lord what things her hand found to do, and looked forward not in vain to the fulfillment of the promise that is given to those that are faithful in few things.

It was with a view to her present and prospective work that—as events multiplied, and especially as the assembling of the portentous Council of the Vatican drew near— she undertook a vast amount of literary labor. Considered in connection with her frail health, with her time-consuming social duties, and with studies in art and history which were never intermitted, and most of which were recorded, for her own private benefit, in analyses of books and lectures, minutely careful descriptions of paintings, and detailed accounts of local archæology, the amount of literary work which she began now to contribute for the press is very remarkable. The series of six articles which she contributed to *Hours at Home*, under the title, " Rambles among the Italian Hills." were written as early as 1865. From these, considerable extracts have been made in an earlier chapter. But about 1869 she began a series of contributions for the *Overland Monthly*, and became the regular correspondent of the New York *Observer*, the Hartford *Churchman*, the *Advance* of Chicago, and the New York *Evening Post*. Her letters were not carefully preserved by her; but the imperfect files that remain, taken together with the copying-books in which much of her original manuscript is preserved in duplicate, show a prodigious facility in literary production, united with a prodigious industry. How good her literary work was, the readers of this book have some means of judging;

6*

but that which was done for the public was no whit better, either in substance or in neatness of finish, than the voluminous pages which she wrote for her own satisfaction and improvement.

She watched the Council almost through to its close, reporting its proceedings, so far as they transpired, to the various journals with which she was corresponding. A minute outside-history of this remarkable gathering could be made up from these letters; but it would not be more valuable than the journals of most newspaper correspondents, except as the writer's familiarity with various circles of Roman society gave her some advantages of observation. The History of General Councils, as hitherto written, gives us only uncertain glimpses of the history of the Lobby, which, nevertheless, has always been of prime consequence, in these assemblies, from the days of Nicæa to this present. A single paragraph from a letter of April 15, 1870, shows us some of the lobby-relations of the Council of the Vatican.

Among the most devout admirers of the Pope and the Council are a number of the old ladies—the matriarchs—of the oldest and wealthiest families residing in Rome. They are generally French or Italians, but may be Germans. They are all of the oldest of the old families, tracing their lineage directly to Benhadad or Tiglath-Pileser, and call the Bourbons *nouveaux riches*, although they believe in them as kings and well-meaning people. Their *salons* are the resort of Messeigneurs, the Fathers of the Council,

who lounge on their sofas nightly, are consoled from
their snuff-boxes, and answer them sigh for sigh, over
the good old times. I am sorry to say that while
refreshed with their *eau sucré* and country wine, and
assiduously waited on by their willing hands, the
Fathers of the Council laugh good-naturedly at them,
and the journals, both cismontane and ultramontane,
make impertinent remarks about them. These latter
declare that they have set up a private altar; that
when the real fathers of the true council are holding
their assemblies, these " monthly nurses " hold theirs ;
that they have their " postulates," their " general congregations," and their committees, and that they are
generally " the monkeys of Domineddio." The last
word, although it is compounded of two words only
applied to the Deity, is used greatly by the Italians,
without intentional irreverence. But the sarcasm of
the phrase as applied to these female busybodies is
tremendous.

I attended a little matriarchal and patriarchal session the other day; at least I was in company with
several of the good fathers and their lady adorers.
Of course nothing is so interesting to them all as the
Council ; and as far as it was proper in a mixed assembly, the conversation turned very much in that
direction. The fathers present were of both the
great parties, but all agreed that the dogma was sure
to be proclaimed, and the anti-infallibilists present
had all ceased to oppose it or to append amendments
to it. They all, I found, also agreed in the fact of its
great importance, and that politically. A theologian
of one of the great infallibilist lights, thought that it

would produce a great effect on Italian politics. His argument I give as nearly as possible in his own words: "The first practical consequence of the proclamation of the dogma ought to be the dismemberment of the kingdom of Italy, and the return of the alienated provinces to their old sovereigns."

This learned doctor, among his gifts and accomplishments, can not, in the light of later events, claim to number the gift of prophecy. The lady that listened to him had a keener foresight. She wrote, July 4, 1870:

The Pope's spiritual children have done their utmost to preserve for him his temporal as well as his spiritual power; but the Fourth of July has come to him as it came to England. The slavery of his people is sure to end. Day has already dawned for them. The public session will probably take place on the 17th. The people will cry, "It is the voice of a God and not of a man." The relics of St. Peter will be dislodged from the confessional and laid upon the high altar. All the bells of all the churches in Rome are to ring as that poor old man takes his place in the seat of his Master. A hundred and one guns will be fired from the Aventine and Janiculum hills, and from the Castle of St. Angelo. And an unseen hand will write on the walls of the Vatican, " Mene, Mene, Tekel, Upharsin."

By the time this letter had reached its destination, the editor of the *Observer* was able to add, in brackets, " All which has come to pass."

The intense heats of the Roman July, on which the Pope relied to bring his refractory bishops to terms, drove the most zealous of correspondents into the neighboring hills. Mrs. Gould withdrew to her familiar and favorite retreat of Perugia, and thence to the heights of the Engadine. No exile from Rome, among all her patriots, could have watched the tremendous march of events with more affectionate anxiety than did this adopted daughter of the Eternal City. At the first news that Rome was free, she started toward her home. "It was in vain," she writes, "that we tried to keep our steps from Italy another hour. The grand events which were occurring there were too important. Rome is too dear to us. We could not remain at a distance which forbade the daily receipt of telegrams. If possible, we should have gone to Rome at once. But no strangers were allowed to enter." She gathered all the details of the liberation of the city, and wrote them thus to the *Churchman :*

On the morning of the 20th [September, 1870,] the Italians surrounded the city from the Porta Pia to the Porta San Giovanni. A division took up its position at the Porta San Pancrazio. At five o'clock the first guns were fired at the Porta Pia. The barricades were taken, a breach made in the wall and in the gate itself, and a little after nine o'clock Rome had become the capital of Italy.

The scene was indescribable. The blood of Roman heroes and exiles flowed beneath the gate before it was opened. A young man by the name of Valenziani, long a homesick exile from the city of his birth, although ill and unfit for the fatigues of battle, insisted upon being one of the gallant besiegers of the gates of Rome. On the other side were his family, whom he had not seen for eleven years. Ten minutes after he fell the gates were open. His friends came to welcome him. He had " died without the sight." Four other Roman exiles, more happy than this young patriot, first passed through the Porta Pia. A few moments after, a Pontifical dragoon approached with a white flag. He was followed by the diplomatic corps, escorted by dragoons. The white flag soon streamed from the cupola of St. Peter's, the campanile of St. Maria Maggiore, and the Castle of St. Angelo. In an hour or two they were exchanged for the tricolor, which floated as if by magic all over the city.

I do not tell you of the reception of the troops in other portions of the Papal States. It was most exciting. The inhabitants of little villages and hamlets all ceased their labors, and came out to meet their liberators. Singing, dancing, weeping, embracing each other, and falling into the arms of the soldiers, who were bringing Italy and liberty to Rome. The poor hidden haters of the Vatican who had so long borne its yoke, fainting although so pitifully patient, seemed wild with joy. At every moment arrived Roman exiles, some who for long years had never seen the dome of St. Peter's, and were unspeakably happy as they saw it swinging in the horizon, and knew that they should soon stand under its shadow.

The whole of Italy—united at last—sends forth

the cry, " Come over and help us," to the Christian world. Redeemed Rome is free as a field to the laborers. The field is white for the harvest. Who will aid us in making these freedmen free in Christ Jesus?

Through the eventful days that followed, Mrs. Gould was part of the time at Rome and part at Florence —the two centers of public interest. The following letter, written from Rome early in 1871, under the title, " Everybody Excommunicated and Inundated," mentions some of the more notable events with which the "Annus Mirabilis," 1870, had concluded :

We are in a dreadful state in Rome just now. Everybody is *ipso facto* excommunicated. We have a prince and princess in a palace sacred as the holy house of Loretto, an ambassador of that mainstay and dependence of the Papacy, William of Germany, who pays a visit to the said bandits and outcasts. We have holy cannon sent from Belgium to kill the Pope's enemies, which thunder forth salvos when these princely usurpers enter the holy city. We have house-room given to the said guns in a villa claimed by a chamberlain of the Pope. We have a king who comes to Rome to help drowning people, and who goes into the holy house to rest a few hours. And, worse than all, we have a community which approves of all these iniquities, floats its banners, gets up torch-light processions, flings bouquets, indulges in prolonged vivas until its throat is sore, and refuses to weep with the prisoners of the Vatican. This is the condition of things in Rome at present, and holy wrath is the order of exercises. Cardinal Antonelli has issued his nine hundred and ninety-ninth note to the Papal representatives on the sub-ject of the king's having visited the city. I have read the document with much care, and in two lan-guages. I can see no possible object in writing it, except for the purpose of uttering an immense false-hood ; namely, that the king met with a cool recep-tion here. The fact is, simply, that the Romans went mad. They had a delirium of joy. His Majesty arrived about half-past three in the morning, and no creature was allowed to sleep from long before that time, until an hour after he had finally shut himself out of their sight for a little rest. They shouted, they screamed, they danced, they sang, they waved flags, they marched in procession, they laughed, they cried, and they did it all over again. They met him at the station, and accompanied him to the Quirinal ; lit up the streets through which he passed ; almost deafened him with a roar of vivas ; waited outside the Quirinal after his entrance until he twice came out to answer their salutations ; and after they had been persuaded to retire that his Majesty might re-pose a few hours after his journey, kept up their shouts and demonstrations of joy elsewhere, almost until daylight. During his drive through the city the next day, the king received the same ovation, and half of Rome accompanied him to the station when he left in the evening. If this was a cool re-ception, we only hope his Majesty may never have a hot one.

I have been prevented from writing as soon as I

should have done, by my absence from Rome on a
visit to Florence; and have not yet told you how
the dreadful inundation which reduced so many hundreds to poverty occurred. The spectacle was a fearful one. More than half the city was invaded by the
Tiber, which poured itself in torrents and rivers
through the city. From the Pincio the view was the
strangest imaginable. The houses, washed by the
strange, sullen waves of the river, arose like those of
Venice, excepting that the lower story was invisible.
The base of the obelisk in the Piazza del Popolo was
entirely covered; the heads of the lionesses were
alone visible, and they plunged hither and thither
with the motion of the current, as if not knowing
where to bear the huge towering edifice to which
they seemed yoked. St. Peter's and the Vatican
were reflected in the watery waste which stretched
beside them. The Campagna, which has so often
been compared to a sea, was one indeed; stranded
amid whose bosom were farm-houses and contadinos'
cabins. Boats and rafts sailed slowly through the
streets, carrying provisions or removing persons whose
houses were in danger from the devouring element.
All this was a sight most interesting and most wonderful. But the scenes presented in the neighborhood of the Vatican, in the Via Ripetta, about the
Pantheon, and especially in the Ghetto, were fearful.
The inhabitants were stupefied with the extent of
their misfortune. The children were crying with
fright and discomfort. The women were shrieking
for bread or loudly lamenting their ruin. The men
sat crouched, silently, wherever they found shelter,

careless both of the present and future, paralyzed by the dreadful misfortune which had come upon them. Their little all was swept away in a moment. Many of them were asleep when the first wave broke over the city, and had just time to escape with their lives ; first by ladders to the first story, and then by boats, as the waters invaded them there, to other parts of the city. (I should remind your readers that the lower floor is called here *piano terreno*, the ground floor ; and that the stories are only numbered from the one above it). Happily, the weather was very warm, so that few had gone to bed, and the men of the Trastevere, the Via Ripetta, etc., were sitting in their doors, or standing about the streets when the wave broke, so that they were able to aid in the rescue of their families. All that night the citizens labored, removing those in danger to places of safety. All the next day they labored again, carrying provisions to those imprisoned by the flood. The National Guard, especially, did yeoman service. Some of our own country people were among those who were imprisoned and fed from the boats under their windows. A regular service was arranged. A depot was established at the Monte Citorio, whence great fourgons carried provisions as far as horses could go, and then the baskets and hampers were placed in the boats and rafts which awaited them. The American physician had to make his visits by water, and from the boats was carried up the stairs on the shoulders of stout men, who made a comfortable penny by operations of this kind. In this way the artists in the Corso and elsewhere got into and out of their apartments. The water in certain parts of the city floated oil, wine, vegetables, meat, fish, animals, grain, and a heterogeneous mixture impossible to describe. In the Corso the wreck was frightful. Show-cases were dashed to atoms, and they and their contents ground together, sailed out of the stores into the street, and went to form the wonderful torrent which dashed relentlessly toward the Capitol. In a few hours silks, velvets, ribbons, flowers and satins, photographs, paper and pictures, were heaps of pulp and rubbish, afterward carried away in cart-loads, leaving broken shelves and discolored walls only where had been elegant stores full of magnificent goods.

And in the midst of all this ruin and alarm arrived Victor Emmanuel, to see for himself the sufferings of his people and provide for them. As he said when the authorities warmly welcomed him to his new capital, in answer to their thankful acknowledgments: "Ah! I came as soon as I could." No wonder that the city was awakened from its slumbers by the cries of delight with which he was greeted, and half Rome rushed into the streets to follow him to the Quirinal at half-past three o'clock in the morning. He was greatly overcome with the enthusiasm which greeted him on his arrival and accompanied his drive through the city the next day. At the Capitol he signed an order for 200,000 lire ($40,000), to be distributed to the sufferers. Then laying down his pen, he ordered his carriage to be sent around, and passing through the thousands who were waiting about the square, went down the stairs beside the Ara Cœli on foot, amid such applause as has seldom been heard in old Rome.

From the illumination which suddenly broke over the city at his arrival, to the serenade with which he was accompanied to the station, the whole visit of his Majesty was one long ovation. Ah! what a splendid checkmate it was to Pius IX., who shut himself up in his prison of eleven thousand rooms! What a contrast to the conduct of the prince cardinals, the descendants of the seventy disciples, not one of whom was to be seen aiding those whom they call their subjects in their hour of need!

And now we have with us the young heir and heiress to the throne, who have taken possession of the palace of the Quirinal, drive daily on the Pincio, receive constantly those who wish to be presented to them, visit at the houses of the Roman nobility, visit also the schools and benevolent institutions of Rome, and in every way behave in perfect contrast to a certain John Mastai. It is the fashion to be papaline; to sympathize with the "good old man" in question. This fashion prevails among some of the most elegant among our English and American visitors, although I do not find that it prevents their applying to be received by the Princess Margherita, or endeavoring to gain admittance into the salons of the liberal Roman princes; and to tell the truth, I have very little respect for the honesty of these Papal Protestants, and less for their good taste. The Roman families who close their houses, refuse to drive upon the Pincio, or assume mourning with the Papal court, are at least consistent in their behavior.

In her correspondence of this period, Mrs. Gould shows

a constant interest in the religious prospects of her home. Being absolutely without the petty zeal of those whose religious earnestness is identified with propagating a sect and making proselytes, she shared at first the generous illusions of those who looked for some movement of reformation to originate within the pale of the Roman Church; she watched with eager interest the cautious demonstrations of the group of "Old Catholics" in Germany, and the ardent, but solitary protests of Father Hyacinthe in France. Whatever there was of a genuine, religious "liberal Catholicism" in Rome or Florence, was naturally drawn to her. And if she was in advance of some of the rest of us in giving up the expectation of any practical outcome from this direction, it was not that she was less cordially hopeful, but that she had better opportunities of knowledge and a keener insight.

The missions that multiplied in Rome after the liberation, representing various Christian denominations, all found in her a cordial friend. Especially that touching "revenge of history" when the poor, humble Waldensian churches took their place among the evangelists of Rome, won her warmest sympathy.

But all the time her knowledge of the time and the people, and that inborn love for poor children that had marked her character from her own childhood up, was impelling her toward another enterprise as most hopeful of good for the Roman people.

IX.

1870—1871.

ONE YEAR'S WORK IN ROME.

Beginning the Italo-American Schools — A Six Months' Report — Dense Ignorance at Rome — Conflicts with Religious Intolerance—Abduction of a Girl—The First Roman Kindergarten—An International Christmas Tree—A Sunday-school —Patriotic Little Romans—The Planting of the Asylum.

a FEW weeks after the beginning of that work in Rome which was to be the crowning work of her life, Mrs. Gould wrote the story of how the beginning was made.

In the old days, when our hands were tied in Rome, we were in the habit of laying before our friends who came to us in their European wanderings, the needs of a school and an orphan house for girls, established in Florence. As we begged them to aid us in taking care of these noble institutions, I remember often saying to them, "I cast my bread upon the Arno, hoping after many days to find it upon the Tiber." When the events of the 20th of September

(142)

had occurred, we came down to Rome, from a visit
to the Waldensian valleys, to find, indeed, the bread
we had cast upon the Arno, awaiting us upon the
Tiber. Bibles were sold upon the very spot where, a
few years before, they were burned. The Gospel was
openly preached; no man forbidding. The books of
the lamented De Sanctis were bought with great
avidity, by his Roman fellow-citizens; the New Testament was freely read to those who could not read
for themselves; and, in short, Pope, as he could in no
other wise fulfill Bunyan's vision, had shut himself in
his cage, whence he glared on the pilgrims, but could
no more do them harm. All this was very delightful;
but to civilize and Christianize a community, you
must begin with the young. This is especially the
case in Rome, where woman occupies so low a place
in the social scale, and is so entirely under the dominion of the priests, and where the men are, so many
of them, infidel in their notions. We hoped that a
school would at once be started, which we could aid;
but no one took hold of such an enterprise, and when
I attempted it, I could not find in all Rome a proper
Italian female teacher. Nor did friends at home or
friends abroad put funds into my hands—as I had
hoped they would—to aid in hastening on the new
day which had dawned upon Rome.

At length, utterly discouraged, with fifty francs in
my pocket, and no teacher to aid me, I decided to go
forward alone, and open a school on the 20th of
March. The Vaudois clergyman kindly allowed me
the use of the rooms where his services are held
—a most convenient and comfortable suite of apart-

ments. Three children, whose parents attend the
Vaudois (Waldensian) church, were my first pupils.
In the course of the day, two others were brought to
me by an American lady; and in the course of the
week the same lady brought me four more. The
next week the school had grown very decidedly, and
at its close numbered twenty-two children; on the 1st
of May, thirty were present.

The school having been begun on the 20th of March,
its first six months terminated on the memorable anniver-
sary of the 20th of September. On that date Mrs. Gould
printed for circulation among her personal friends and
others whom she might hope to interest in her work, a full
account of what she was doing, and of the methods by
which she was doing it. These details are of double interest now, as showing both the work and the character of
its founder and promoter—her administrative talent, her
shrewd good sense; her tenderness of sentiment without
sentimentality; her Christlikeness of heart and purpose,
manifest alike in the work that she did, and the cant that
she avoided.

When children are presented for admission, we explain clearly to the parents that they are to receive
no pecuniary aid, that the children must be sent regularly, that we have no holidays excepting the Saturday, and that personal cleanliness is a *sine qua non*.
Where the mother's appearance is slatternly, or there
is an evident wish merely to get the child out of the
way, without any real desire for its improvement, we

refuse to receive it. If we were not strict in these regards, a perfect panorama of children would be continually passing in and out of our school-room, and our time would be almost altogether lost. In some instances, the same mother and child have presented themselves several times; on each occasion, with a slight improvement in their appearance. A little more soap and water had been used, a few stitches taken here and there, until finally a hopeful little subject was ready for admission.

The first business after seeing that the children were brought clean, was to engage their affections. Poor little things! they were so ready to be loved. But in order to show them that we really did care for them, it was necessary to avoid all shrinking from poor, diseased, deformed little bits of humanity, such as many of them were. No brushing away of little hands that sought your own; no untwining of little arms that wished to clasp your neck, or refusal of little lips that sought your hand or even your face. How often have I thought of the lesson our Saviour must have meant to teach us, when *he took the little ones in his arms* before he blessed them. Perhaps it was the caress that made the blessing precious to the infants who could not understand the words, but comprehended the tenderness by which they were accompanied.

For the first few days we were busied in finding out what the children knew, and trying to teach them to think. We soon discovered that they knew nothing. Not one of them could tell the days of the week, the months of the year, or the year in which

7

they were living. They had not the slightest idea of geography, history, or the elements of natural philosophy.   Some of them could spell words of one or even two syllables, but had never received a single idea from anything they had read.   One boy wrote beautifully, but could not read a word of writing. As to their religious instruction, I can not say that I ever examined them in the lives of the saints, but one day I told them the story of the birth of our Saviour; I went into all the details: telling them of the star in the East, and the journey of the wise men; of the songs of the angels, and the worship of the shepherds; of the wicked king Herod; the murder of the innocents, and the flight into Egypt.   They listened with great interest, and when I had finished, I said, "Tell me, my children, who was this little baby?" *Not one of them knew.*

Perhaps a few details with regard to the manner of conducting the school may be interesting. The door is opened some twenty minutes before the school commences, by a woman who keeps the rooms in order, attends to the children while eating, and teaches them to knit and sew. Each child has a comfortable little chair, and aprons are provided to cover torn frocks and jackets. At the hour for commencing the school, the directress or one of the Vaudois clergymen is always present, and the children are seated. The door is closed, and each child placing its little chair before it, kneels, and we repeat the Lord's prayer together. They then repeat certain texts of Scripture which we have taught them, and receive a lesson in the life of our Saviour. They have also begun to learn the Ten Commandments. With these exercises, are interspersed the learning and singing of Italian hymns, most of which are translated from our own. One feature of this first hour which interests them very much is the learning to sing some of our simplest English hymns. Their ear is very true, and they learn to pronounce our strange sounds with great readiness. Of course, great pains are taken to make them understand the meaning of each word. Our language is very necessary to the servants, work-people, and mechanics of Rome, and a course of thorough instruction in it will be commenced this winter. After an hour or an hour and a half spent in this way, the little ones spell and sing the syllables, Ba, Be, Bi, Bo, Bu, Da, De, etc. This exercise aids them very much in learning to read. Meanwhile the older children are preparing tables, removing chairs, placing books and copy-books, and reading, writing, and drawing go on for some three-quarters of an hour. Lessons in geography, natural philosophy, arithmetic, grammar, and history follow, with another reading and writing lesson. An intermission of an hour occurs at noon, during which they eat and amuse themselves. We had to teach them to play, for Italian children know no games. We make use of Froebel's play and others, for them, let them march, or send the little ones to a game of ball after they have been occupied at their lessons for an hour or two.

Italian children are very docile, so that we have been obliged to make use of but little punishment. They knew of nothing but blows, and often when I

attempted to draw a child to me to talk to it of some
little naughtiness of which it had been guilty, it
would shrink back, and try to cover its little face and
head. I was obliged to tell them that they were
never to be beaten at school. The brutality to which
they had been subjected had produced its legitimate
effect, and they were always ready to strike and kick
each other. We had to teach them that putting them
into a corner or into the next room was a punishment, and when they had learned this, the desired
effect was almost always produced at once. One little boy who would not learn this lesson had his
hands tied behind him with a handkerchief for five
minutes, which brought about great grief and entire
reformation. In every instance, punishment has produced a pleasant effect upon the child's temper, seem-
ing often to awaken intelligence and affection in a
surprising degree. We have a system of black and
red marks. A certain number of the latter entitles a
child to a ticket on Sunday. For four of these a
certificate is given, and every certificate entitles the
child to put a penny into a box for the Orphan
Asylum at Florence. There are some children who
never fail to receive their tickets at the Sunday-
school, or to put in their penny once a month for the
orphans. The Sunday-school is regularly attended
by about sixty children. The instruction given is the
same as that of the first morning hour of the day-
school. We have, however, for the Sunday-school a
few pictures illustrative of Bible History, presented
to us by an English lady, with which we interest our
little ones. For the winter, we shall be able, through

the kindness of our friends at home, to increase the number of these. We shall also form the older boys and girls into a sort of Bible class. Until now, they have been taught together, as they were all equally ignorant of Bible truth.

I can not but say of the Roman children that they are docile not only, but fond of learning, clever, affectionate, and appreciative of what is done for them. On one or two occasions, when something new has been introduced, they have burst out simultaneously into applause, clapping their little hands with all their might. The want of truth which prevails in Italy is one of our greatest troubles. But we are, we hope, succeeding in teaching our children something of the beauty of perfect truthfulness. I was very much delighted with an instance which showed how perfectly this lesson had been learned by one of our first scholars. The class in geography which was reciting with the teacher, all missed the capital of Spain. He called a little girl from another class to him, and put the question to her. She answered, as he supposed, correctly, and he repeated the answer, praising her, and ordered her a red mark. The little girl stood still a minute, and then faltered out, " But I did not say Madrid." Sometimes we are wonderfully struck with their appreciation of what they are learning. A little baby-thing who was only received to gratify a friend, as he seemed too young to learn anything, has a remarkable ear for music. The children were singing one morning to the tune, " I want to be an angel," Italian words, descriptive of the Good Shepherd with his lambs : " I am a little lamb, Jesus is my

Shepherd," * etc. This little fellow ran up to me, and putting his hands on my lap, said, " Lady, am I a little lamb?" " Indeed you are, my darling," I replied. He ran back to his seat, and long after the children had done singing, his clear little voice rang out, " I am a little lamb, Jesus is my Shepherd." Was there ever a more beautiful infant's profession of faith!

The school was commenced as an infant-school. It has now girls of seventeen and boys of fifteen among its pupils, and we have a class of twelve who are being fitted to pass the Government examination as teachers in the municipal schools. There are over eighty pupils in the school, and ere this letter reaches America, there will be a hundred. It is impossible to stop where we now are. This winter we shall open a Kindergarten, which will, I hope, number at least a hundred children.

Six months ago to-day the school was begun. To-day a large number of its members have finished their primary course, and several children ten and twelve

---

* " Io sono un agnellino ;
   Trovato dal pastor ;
 Un povero bambino,
   Salvato dal Signor.
 Il povero agnellino
   Non conosceva àncor
 Il vero buon cammino,
   Che mena al buon pastor."

" I am a little lamb, found by the Shepherd ;
   A poor child saved by the Lord.
 The poor little lamb did not know
 The right road leading to the Good Shepherd."

years of age are ready to compete with young men of seventeen, who have been all their life under instruction. I do not dare to tell in detail the progress that some of the pupils have made. Boys and girls who did not read a sentence when they came to us, are about to commence a course of mathematical studies, fully prepared to understand them. It must be remembered, however, that study is no task, but a delightful pleasure to them. Their countenances never fall until the hour for closing the school approaches, and the most inattentive child is sure to be aroused by the assurance that school is no place for idleness, and it may go home if it do not choose to be attentive.

The dense ignorance discovered by Mrs. Gould in the children that came under her instruction, was of the same sort with that which was reported by Commissioners of the Italian Government, as the result of inquiries made by them soon after the liberation of Rome. The extraordinary document presented by this Commission was widely circulated at the time by the Government as a sort of *pièce de justification* before the public opinion of the world. It brought to light ludicrous examples of ignorance, not merely among children of the lower classes, but among those who had enjoyed the privileges of some of the more advanced schools which the clerical government had provided for young ladies and gentlemen. When the alumni of the better schools of old Rome, being questioned upon the great names in Italian history, could answer (for example) that Christopher Columbus was another name for the Holy Ghost, it is less amazing that the little children from the street should be ignorant of the plainest and simplest facts in the life of Jesus Christ. If the Report were within reach, it might be largely quoted in further proof of the spiritual as well as intellectual darkness of the people who had lived in the very focus of the light of the Roman Catholic Church.

Some of the results of the census of the new Capital taken December 31, 1871, are given in the work of my venerable friend, pastor Gaberel, of Geneva, entitled "*Alma Mater:* Rome and Christian Civilization." I quote from an Italian translation, not having the original at hand. It appears that after an experience of that absolutely exclusive clerical and religious public instruction, which is the ideal Roman Catholic method for training up the youth of any people, an enormous proportion of the people of Rome were confessedly unable either to read or to write. Out of 235,484 inhabitants, all above the age of childhood were asked whether they could read and write, and there answered in the negative, to both parts of the question, 112,757 persons. There is reason to believe that if the inquiry had been accompanied by a practical examination, the number of the "*analfabeti*" would have been higher still.*

---

* Pastor Gaberel adds some interesting details of a visit made by him to certain of the public schools, as one of a Committee of the Scientific Congress that met at the Capitol in October, 1873. At one of these schools, a member of the Committee was

Such a condition of ignorance, in a people so admirably gifted as the Romans, must have been the result of something worse than negligence or indifference on the part of those who combined in the same persons absolute civil power and exclusive spiritual influence. It is one of the most inexplicable parts of the " mystery of iniquity " how even such a combination as this could succeed, as it did— in a nation whose language is absolutely phonographic in

---

struck by a certain marked physiognomy among the children, and on remarking upon it to the directress, was reminded that this school was in the neighborhood of the Ghetto. Whereupon the directress turned to the school and said, " Let the Jewish children step forward;" and some two-thirds of the scholars left their places. The chariman of the Committee, Cavalier Sacchi, deeply impressed by the scene, addressed them thus : " My dear girls, you are too young to understand the whole meaning of what I say ; but never forget to thank God for his goodness in permitting you to live and grow up in a free country, where law and education are equal for all. Never forget the unhappy condition that used to be imposed upon your fathers, and show your gratitude to God by profiting diligently by these benefits." Some of the older girls wept at these words, thinking, perhaps, of the days when their fathers, even down to 1870, were compelled to supplicate for leave to remain from year to year in the eternal city—a permission that must be paid for by a heavy tribute to be spent on the carnival frolics.

Observing a falling-off in the number of scholars above the age of twelve, the Committee asked the reason of it, and were told that as the age of confirmation approached, the priests redoubled their persuasions and threats, to compel the withdrawal of the children from the schools. Secretary Canini informed the Committee that one of the devices to accomplish this end, was to take the children into a dark underground chapel, and there display to them pictures of little children burning in hell-fire.

7*

the simplicity of its notation, so that the art of reading and writing is comprehended in the learning of twenty-four letters—in keeping an intelligent people, through generations and centuries, unable either to read or to write. There are few achievements that better prove the masterly ability, in certain directions, of the defunct Roman Government.

In a report of the school published in July, 1872, when it had entered on its second year, Mrs. Gould was able to add to her testimony of the prevailing ignorance of the children, the most gratifying testimony of their progress under instruction.

The children come to us utterly ignorant. This is true almost without exception. One of the scholars we have lately admitted, a fine, well-disposed lad, not only could not read a sentence correctly, or write a word legibly, but actually did not know his right hand from his left. As to history, geography, or the elements of natural philosophy, we find all our children on first coming to us as ignorant of these subjects as new-born babes. It may be well to repeat that with this ignorance of book-knowledge, exists that of every-day life. The children never have been taught the days of the week, the months of the year, the names of animals or plants: in short, their minds are perfectly blank.

By careful and repeated oral instruction, however, they soon acquire a great deal of general information. For the first year we used no books excepting those in which they were taught to read. Now the first and second classes study history and grammar at home, and I am preparing for their use a manual of English.* Our younger children have, we think, made astonishing progress. A class which we had formed for the pursuit of studies necessary to fit them for teachers in the municipal schools has been greatly diminished by our late removal from the Vicolo Soderini. We hope, however, in the autumn, from the nucleus still remaining with us, and from some of the elder and more intelligent of our new pupils, to have a large class of this kind organized. Our object will always be twofold; to preserve a high moral and religious tone in the school; and to prepare our pupils for their future career in life. To promote this latter object, technical instruction will be given as it shall become necessary.

Of course, the schools have met with the greatest possible opposition from the ultramontane party. While they were small they were despised; but when they put on larger proportions, every effort was made

---

* "The Children's Manual for Speaking and Writing the English Language. By Emily B. Gould, Directress of the Italo-American Schools, Florence, Claudian Press, 1874." "To Erminia Fua Fusinato, the sweet songstress, the ardent patriot, the devoted woman, this little effort to aid in the great work to which she gives her life is affectionately dedicated." It is an ingenious contrivance to overcome the endless difficulties of our English cacography by means of a phonetic notation attached to the letters. It had an admirable success, certainly, in the schools at Rome; and its author believed that if used by adult learners it would prove that, "in the study of a foreign tongue, as in greater things, one should 'humble himself and become as a little child.'"

to prevent children from attending them. To one priest, who was especially active in his opposition to the schools, I addressed a note, assuring him that the moral and religious character of the institution were such as must command the approval of every Christian clergyman, and requesting him to visit it; promising him full liberty to examine the books used, and be present at the instruction given. I never saw the gentleman, or received a reply to my note. During my absence from Rome last summer, two little boys were taken from the school, whose removal caused great distress to Signora Gotelli. The younger one, a little fellow about five years of age, was an especially interesting child, and as happy in his school as a little sunbeam. After an absence of three months, the little brothers were brought back. I made some objections to receiving them again, and insisted upon knowing why they had been removed. The mother then told me (and her story was fully confirmed), that she was taken very ill and was, as she supposed, about to die. She sent for the priest, who refused to give her absolution unless she took her children away from my school. " But," she added, "their father never wished them taken away, and you may be sure that I shall never listen to the priest again." I consented to receive the children, simply bidding her tell the priest that my school-room doors were always open, and that until he had seen the institution for himself, he had no right to speak against it.

The most violent attacks made upon the schools, however, do not proceed directly from the priests,

but from the " Society for the Promotion of Catholic
Interests." Our neighbors in the Vicolo Soderini,
who were members of it, were most venomous in
their spite, insulting us in the street, on the stairs and
terrace, calling out from the windows to the mothers
of the children, " Renegade," " Hypocrite," and
" Protestant," which latter was of course the most
opprobrious epithet in their estimation. " Oh ! fine
Catholics you are," they would say, " sending your
children to the school of that excommunicated one."
On one occasion, some of them mounted the roof,
which is in a most deplorable state, and commenced
something which I can only compare to an infernal
dance. The noise was really frightful. The mortar
fell about us in a shower, and it seemed as if the ceiling would come down bodily upon our heads. The
children, especially the elder ones, were terribly
alarmed. Their first impulse was to run out of the
room. It was necessary to prevent this at any cost.
The larger ones, girls and boys from twelve to sixteen years of age, would have knocked down the little ones; close beside the anteroom were the stairs,
steep, narrow, cruel, marble steps, down which they
would have precipitated each other in their flight.
The gentleman who was assisting me started for the
police, and for the moment I felt overwhelmed with
the reflection that I held the lives of ninety human
beings almost in my hands. A sudden inspiration,
for which I shall always be thankful, came to me.
Standing beside the first class, composed of the elder
children, and holding some of them by force in their
places, I started a hymn which we often sing at the

opening of the school. It describes the Saviour in
the storm. First, we have the calm summer day,
with the idle waves slumbering in the sunshine, and
the departure of the bark. Then comes the rising
of the tempest. "Even in a stormy night," says the
author, "he who has labored long sleeps sweetly, and
Jesus lay tranquil" in the midst of the hurricane.
"Did He perhaps forget His own?" Then there is
the cry for help to the Saviour, His stilling of the
tempest, and the loving reproof to the faithless disciples. The last verse is the following, the last two
lines being repeated :

> "Tal sovente nella vita
> La tempesta sorgerà :
> Ma il Signore pront' aita
> Per i suoi provvederà.
> Oh ! poniamo in Lui la speme :
> Viva fede nutra il cor :
> Sempre al misero che geme,
> Sta vicino il Salvator."

"So, often in life, storms will arise ; but the Lord
will give ready help to those who call upon Him.
Ah! let us put our trust in Him, let our hearts be
filled with faith. The Saviour is ever near to listen
to the groans of the miserable." The sweet sounds
of the young voices, as one after another they fell in
with mine, at first weak and trembling, but at last
gaining strength and volume, floated up, and partly
drowned the diabolical noise of our enemies, and as
we were singing the last two lines it almost ceased,
probably because its authors supposed they had been
unsuccessful in their attempt to frighten the poor

children. But I shall never think it was chance which led me to begin the singing of that hymn.

The next attack made upon the school by the members of this Society, came from persons in a different position in life. It occurred during the absence of the directress at Naples. Among the girls of our first class, was one whose parents had been ruined by the late inundation of the Tiber. She was very wild when she first came to us, but had gradually yielded to the kind but firm discipline we try to exercise, and had become exceedingly attached to her school and teachers. During my absence, certain noble ladies presented themselves to the mother of this child, a woman naturally feeble, and who has suffered much both in body and mind since her troubles of last year. These ladies told her that she was being punished by God for her sin in placing her children at the Italo-American schools, which were represented as sinks of iniquity (I should here mention that for months, most outrageous falsehoods had been circulated about the institution, of which we knew nothing until the events took place which I am about to narrate); but the new friends of the poor woman in question were ready to come to her relief. Her " padrone di casa," who was about to raise her rent, should be induced to be lenient, and above all, her daughter should be well provided for, if she would but follow their counsel. They would place her in an excellent seminary, where she would be brought up with young ladies, receive a thorough education, and on leaving the institution be presented with a dowry. The mother persuaded the father to allow her to accept the fine offers of these ladies, and the child, by their recommendation, was told herself, and directed to say at school, that she was to be taken to Florence. All went on as well as the zealous members of "The Society for the Promotion of Catholic Interests" could have desired. The child, who could not otherwise have been persuaded to leave her school, was consoled with the idea of a change, and of visiting an aunt to whom she is attached. The teachers at the school were thoroughly deceived, and so also was the poor mother. For when the carriage, in which the noble ladies came for their prize, left the humble door of her parents, they neither directed its steps to the railroad station as the child had expected, nor to an institution of learning as the mother had supposed, but to a house of correction under the charge of the nuns of St. Agatha. Here then, in company with far from repentant Magdalenes, this poor girl went through experiences, which, while they are quite too shocking to repeat, could never-have been invented by a young girl not yet thirteen years of age. The poor child was of course very unhappy, but as she was never allowed to see her mother alone, there seemed no hope of escape. At last she was advised, I may not say by whom, but of course by an inmate of the convent, to tell the story of her life there to her mother in the presence of the attending nun. She did so, and the poor distracted woman ran for her husband. It was in vain, however, that the parents insisted upon removing their child. To all their prayers and remonstrances, a cold refusal was the only reply. At last, the mother in her agony came for me. "Help me, help me," was her cry; "they have stolen my child."

The Vaudois teacher, Mr. Garnieri, who had charge of the school during my absence, was moved by the distress of the poor woman, and accompanied her to the convent. The nuns still persisted in their refusal, but as Mr. Garnieri was peremptory in his determination not to leave the house without her, and to call in the aid of the police if necessary, the required permission was obtained, and she was restored to her parents. For some time the appearance of the girl was like that of some frightened animal, but she has now recovered her spirits, and we trust that ultimately her terrible experience under the protection of the nuns of St. Agatha will leave no trace behind it.

I would by no means give my friends to understand that all Catholics acquainted with the schools are opposed to them. Many secretly approve of them, who do not even dare openly to visit them. I have lately had the pleasure of hearing that they are highly spoken of by a parish priest with whom I have no personal acquaintance. Others visit the schools regularly, and take the greatest possible interest in their welfare.

The general principle was laid down in the commencement of the enterprise, that the religious instruction should mainly consist in teaching our children the life and precepts of Jesus Christ. From this principle, we have as yet seen no reason to deviate. So many new children are being constantly received that the sweet "old, old story" is always falling upon ears which never before listened to it. The school is opened with the repetition of the Lord's Prayer by teachers and scholars, singing, the repetition of certain verses from the Bible, and the lesson of which I have just spoken. *Our aim is to Christianize and civilize, not to propagandize:* to fill the mind with thoughts of a Heavenly Father and a loving Saviour, and we trust that our efforts are not altogether in vain.

On the 15th of November I opened the first Roman Kindergarten. I can not here go into a description of this admirable system, but will only refer to its effects, which we find most excellent. Beside the actual instruction the children receive, which includes the elements of Arithmetic, Physiology, Natural Philosophy, History, Astronomy, Botany, Geometry, etc., their hearts and minds receive the best possible training. The book of nature is spread open before them, and by a regularly organized system they become acquainted with the world into which they have so lately been introduced. They learn also to love work. Their little hands are every day busied in producing results which are to them most interesting. While they are learning some of the deepest secrets of creation, moreover, the study of the works of their Heavenly Father, and the respect they are taught to pay to the rights of others in the little objects with which they perform their simple tasks, bring before their young minds the two great commandments of the law. In short, while this most excellent system of instruction is adapted to the children of all nations, while it is, perhaps, the discovery *par excellence* of our age, it seems to me an absolute necessity in Italian education, an antidote to, and a preventive of, the defects of the new-born nation.

Our Christmas tree was, of course, a great event to our children, many of whom had never seen anything of the kind. By the kindness of friends, and particularly by the self-denying labors of a little group who devoted from two to four evenings every week to the task of preparation, it was made a perfect success. Its decorations were the work of representatives of five different nations. A German friend presented us with the tree itself, hung a golden star above it, and placed a little "infant Jesus" on its topmost branch, according to the German custom, bearing the title, "Suffer little children to come unto me." Some young Danish girls hung golden and rich-colored tinsel in showers over its branches, which bore, with a variety of other ornamentation, a lace bag worked in worsted and filled with bonbons for each child, a ball in a bright-colored net for every boy, and a nicely-dressed doll for every girl. On an adjoining table were piles of white bread, plain cake, and oranges. On another were rolls of clothing, dresses for the girls and pantaloons for the boys, with a variety of little articles in worsted, presented by friends. The room and tree were brilliantly lighted. At the appointed time, the children entered the room at opposite doors—one column bearing the American and the other the Italian flag, and were placed in a circle about the tree. A few moments were given them in which to admire it, and then at an appointed signal they burst into a Christmas song. They next repeated the story of the birth of our Saviour, as given in St. Matthew and St. Luke. Various recitations, interspersed with hymns and patriotic songs, followed, and brought what may be called the literary part of the performance to an end. The distribution of the gifts followed. The little ones of the Crêche were now introduced. This charitable institution was founded soon after the entrance of the Italians into Rome, principally by the exertions of Mrs. J. E. Freeman, and is supported by our country people, under the charge of the clergyman of the Episcopal Church. It is a most necessary and Christian charity. The little guests were just old enough to be delighted with the brightness and coloring about them, and themselves made a beautiful scene in the picture. One affecting little incident occurred in connection with these children. A mother who had recently lost her child had sent a portion of its wardrobe to the Crêche. As the little ones were brought in, she lifted one of them in her arms to show it the tree, and found that it was dressed in a little coat which she had but lately wrapped about her own babe.

The clothing given out on occasion of our Christmas tree is still worn by many children who would otherwise be literally in rags; but I think the fete did much in many other ways, producing an excellent impression on the community, and encouraging the children and parents by showing them the interest taken in the schools. It stirred up the ire of the ultramontanes in our neighborhood to a terrible degree, and was the remote cause, we think, of the brutal attempt to frighten the children, and of the abduction of Matilde Tornelli.

Early in April we left our large hall in the Vicolo Soderini, which so many of our friends visited last winter. We were busied for months in looking for a proper place. The same malign influence, to which I have before referred, was at work to prevent our obtaining an apartment. During my absence in Naples, two Catholic young women interested in the school exerted themselves to find one. They met with various experiences, of which I will mention but one. A Roman lady to whom they addressed themselves, and whose apartment they thought might be suitable, received them with great suavity, and was quite willing to let them her rooms. They soon discovered, however, that she supposed they wished to use them for immoral purposes. They hastened, of course, to undeceive her, but when they had fully explained that they wished them for our schools, all her suavity vanished in a moment, and she refused further parley, with a "Get thee behind me, Satan," series of gestures, which were ludicrous in the dismay they portrayed.

At the time of our removal from the Vicolo Soderini, our school numbered over a hundred and thirty children. The distance to the new place is so great that but few could follow us to it, and the pain with which I parted from those among whom I had passed so many of the happiest hours of my life I can never describe. I left, however, between sixty or seventy of them under the care of Mr. Garnieri, so that we

may say that in the course of fifteen months two
institutions have already been founded in different
parts of the city, each of which will doubtless, ere
long, be as large as was the one at the time of our
removal.   Our new rooms are in the Palazzo del
Governo Vecchio, in the street of the same name, not
far from the Piazza Navona and the Palazzo Braschi.
They are airy and pleasant, but too small.   I had
expected to secure the apartment below us, and had
indeed already signed the contract for it, but the hope
of at last resting for some years in an appropriate
haven has gone, like so many of its predecessors.
This last disappointment was the more severe, because after signing the contract for rooms sufficiently
large for the schools if they should include two hundred or two hundred and fifty children, I concluded
to devote those I now occupy as an asylum for
orphaned and destitute children, and at once admitted two poor little girls, whose home was a particularly sad one, and who were suffering for want of
the actual necessities of life.   One of them is deformed.   I should like to bring her up so that, if her
life is spared, she may become a teacher where she is
now a pupil, and by ministering to others learn the
secret of true happiness.   I am at present so earnestly
solicited by my friends to take charge of two other
little girls left worse than motherless, that I can not
refuse to do so, and am looking for two or three
rooms in the near neighborhood of the school, where
I can place them under the charge of my matron, who
has two little children of her own.   I can not but
hope that this first asylum in Rome under the charge

of foreigners, begun after the experience and careful study of sixteen months, and begun *on so very small a scale*, will lead to happy results, as it will not only give the children a comfortable home, but remove them from unhappy influences with which most of them are surrounded.

Our Sunday-school is a very important branch of our work; we have been able to enroll nearly all our pupils among its attendants. Until my late illness, I always attended it myself, and a little circle of the mothers accompanied their children every Sunday, and listened with the greatest interest to the lessons given. It is held after the hours of service. It will be put in excellent hands during the summer, and in the autumn I shall hope to renew the care of it myself. I may add here, that the very first spontaneous exercise of the children's minds occurred in the Sabbath-school. It is the easiest thing in the world to fill a Roman child's mind with words, but one of the hardest to put ideas into it. It was very long before we could get from them the oral instruction we had imparted, without repeating it at the moment of examining them. Our habit has been for the last six months to keep the school all together for the opening exercises, and then to separate the elder children from the younger; the latter remaining with me. On the occasion to which I refer, I said: "I have been thinking about Jesus Christ, and how very much He loves little children. Can you tell me how He showed us when He lived here on earth that He loved children so dearly?" "Because He died on the cross for them," said one. "Because He raised up the little girl that was dead," said another. "Because He made well that little boy that had the dreadful convulsions," said a third. These answers came without any help from me, and by guiding their minds a little, I got them to tell me of the blessing and the promise pronounced as the Saviour took the little ones in His arms. The replies would have been nothing in an American or English Sabbath-school, but here in Rome they were a precious token of good. They showed interest and reflection such as we had long sought for in vain. I am very sure that these children will never forget these lessons; that the seed has been sown, although other eyes than ours behold the harvest.

Another thing which gives me pleasure is the knowledge our children are acquiring that they have a country; that they are Italians, and not Romans only. On the king's birthday, I ordered a flag, which I have had made for the school, carried there. But on entering our drawing-room, two of whose windows command the Piazza di Spagna, I found that the flag which should have been displayed from our house, had also been taken to the Vicolo Soderini. I sent for it directly, but on my way to the school, I met the servant returning with the report that the children would not let it go. It was still early; the exercises of the day had not commenced, but the children were assembled, and had taken their places. I explained to the teachers that I must have one of the flags, and we proceeded to take it down. But at once there commenced such a burst of "No, no," and such a hubbub of little voices, that all my personal authority was required in order to call them to order. When they were hushed, I told them that they were very bad Italians, that they were rebels. I favored them with a sermon upon the conduct of a true patriot, and added: "And then you are so selfish. Do you think I do not love Victor Emmanuel also? But for him, I could not have opened the school, and we should never have known and loved each other. Do you wish everybody who passes my house to think, as they will, that I do not love Italy and the king?" "Oh, no, no, Signora! *la prenda pure;* take it!" they exclaimed, and some of them came forward to help to take it down. One boy asked and obtained permission to get a second flag from his own house, and in a few moments the school was opened as usual. But while we were in the midst of our instruction, there was again a great uproar. This time there were vivas and clapping of hands from my excited little patriots. Their companion had returned with the flag, was carrying it aloft in triumph, and in a moment was leading off the chorus of Viva Vittorio Emanuele! Viva l'Italia! We finally thought it best to suspend the usual lessons, and give ourselves up for the morning to patriotic songs and declamations.

The "Asylum," the beginning of which was so small and "without observation," was destined to grow into the most useful and enduring of Mrs. Gould's charitable undertakings at Rome. Her work in the organization of day-schools began, in the course of a few months, to de-

8

feat itself in a way which she was foremost to recognize and rejoice at. Her own methods and principles, under the administration of her eminent friends, Signors Correnti and Bonghi and Signora Fua Fusinato, were adopted in the public schools of Rome; and none were more ready than these honored leaders in the cause of Italian education to acknowledge the debt of obligation to their American fellow-worker. On her own part there was nothing of the spirit of selfish benevolence, that she should reckon nothing done unless she did it herself. So that she was content, as the general cause of Roman popular education went nobly forward, to decrease while others increased. But that more tender and motherly work which began of itself (as one might say) in this beginning of the "Home," grew and prospered, and could not die, even though bereaved of the wise and energetic mind and the loving heart that nursed its feeble infancy.

X.

1871—1873.

THE BEGINNING OF THE HOME.

Friends and Enemies—A Breaking down of Health —Helpers in Time of Need—A Christmas-Tree, and Mary Howitt's Address—A Sunday-school Festival, and a Lady's Lay-Sermon—Prayer and Providence—The Children's Home begun in a Maronite Convent—Teaching Trades—The Liberality of Friends—The Love of the Scholars.

THE opposition encountered by Mrs. Gould's work was no more than might have been expected. She had no occasion for "resisting unto blood, striving against sin." But there was no end of petty annoyance. To be hooted in the streets as a *scomunicata*, was frequent enough; and insulting and calumnious talk against her abounded in the ultramontane press. But such things were generally let pass without notice. On one occasion only, after an exceptionally scurrilous newspaper attack, she had recourse to the excellent press-law of Italy. The Italian press is the freest in Europe; but when it takes too many liberties with an individual, he has this redress, that the offending sheet may be required

to give to his counter-statement equal space and circulation with the original libel. Not in her own defense, but
in defense of her cherished schools, she went, in one instance, to a magistrate and exacted this mild penalty from
one of the leading " Papaline " journals.

All care was taken in the conduct of the schools to pro-
voke no reasonable objection in any quarter. The absence
of all proselytism, and of all attack upon religious prejudices, was, indeed, a matter not of precaution, but of
principle. On the other hand, a good understanding was
always maintained with the Government by loyal com-
pliance with the perfectly reasonable requirements of
Government inspection—for failure in which some well-
meaning people got themselves into trouble with the police. Some of the most distinguished Roman citizens
delighted to manifest their interest in the schools, by personal visits and by subscriptions to the treasury. Among
these may be mentioned that venerable patriot, the blind
Duke of Sermoneta, and the poet and scholar, Signora
Fua Fusinato.

The prodigious labors of Mrs. Gould, the organizing
and personal instruction of the schools, the wide social
duties toward her friends in Rome, both Italian and foreign—duties now more than ever imperative, since the
maintenance of the schools depended mainly on the sustained interest of her personal friends—the voluminous
correspondence in which she was engaged with several
different American journals at once, and which was made
doubly to contribute to her work for the children—these,

of course, broke down her health. A letter to a friend, dated in December, 1871, gives a very exact account of her regular course of life at this time. It is an illustration of what the letter says, to observe that the letter itself consists of *thirteen* closely written pages.

I have been obliged to neglect sending you my promised letter, having been literally *drowned* in work since my return to Rome. I found that my school had greatly increased in numbers, but was suffering for want of my personal care in many other ways. So I have gone into it each day and remained during the entire school session, with the exception of a run home to breakfast. This I shall have to do for some weeks longer, when I hope to have properly trained both children and teachers, so that I shall have some little time to myself. My correspondence is all carried on after eleven o'clock at night. Indeed, this is my life at present. Breakfast at nine. A few words on housekeeping matters, and then at once to the school. My kind friend, the young Vaudois clergyman, has been so occupied that he could not give the religious instruction, so all this has fallen upon me. I took alternately after the opening of the school the different classes, but I was seized with sudden and violent bronchitis, and my husband became so alarmed that I only take the English, the opening exercises, and the first class, with the general oversight and discipline. It is nearly five when I leave the school, and I step straight into bed, where I remain until nearly eight. In the evening, friends always come in, as that is the only time when I am at home, and after they leave, comes the correspondence of the day, which is simply tremendous; husband, house, and friends, all go to the wall.

The tender and skillful care of Dr. Gould delayed the break-down, but it had to come. She *would not* be sick while the great work of her life might be imperilled by it. But when she saw the way clear to the fulfilling of her heart's desire in the founding of the Home for Roman Children, and when, in January, 1873, Miss Mary Ellis, of the Mount Holyoke Seminary, arrived in Rome, to aid in the direction of the schools, there was nothing imperatively to hinder her being sick; and so she lay down, in utter nervous prostration, and passed through a severe and perilous illness. In this emergency, there came forward to the help of the schools a band of young American and English ladies, who devoted the priceless hours of a tourist at Rome, to teaching these little children. The sight of these young ladies at the work drew from the pen of Signora Fua Fusinato, in the *Italie* newspaper, an eloquent expression of thanks:

The strangers who visit us now have done and are doing so much good among us, that they force us almost to forget and forgive the wrong that other foreigners have inflicted upon us. It would seem as if Providence desired in this instance also, as in so many others, to confide to woman the healing mission of the angel of charity, love, and peace. They come to us, these lovely women, to enjoy our smiling skies, to breathe the perfume of our flowers, to revel in the treasures of art we present to them, and while their bodies are healed and their minds refreshed, they are filled with the desire of repaying the benefits they have received by labors of intelligent benevolence and true piety. Many of them, not content with aiding this charitable institution with their means, give their time also, and busy themselves in teaching their language, in which decided progress has been made. Indeed, while we Italians were affected by hearing these eighty-five children sing (thanks to a foreigner) our patriotic songs, the English and Americans present were no less moved by hearing them sing the simple songs and hymns which recalled to them their youth, their distant fatherland, and their absent friends.

Another friend, whose sympathy and practical help never failed Mrs. Gould, was Mrs. Mary Howitt—name beloved in both hemispheres. At the Christmas-tree festival, which was held (a little late) in January, 1873, in the Young Men's Christian Association rooms, an account of the work from its beginning, prepared by Mrs. Howitt, was read; and the festival was not only a delight to the children, but a commendation of the work to a crowded company, whose friendly interest was of vital use. "I think," says Mrs. Gould, "I never saw, outside of a sardine-box, such packing as there was in the *salon* of the Christian Association that day."

Mrs. Howitt, in a characteristic paper, briefly re-

lated the story of the schools, and announced the purposes
of their founder for the opening year.

Under these favorable circumstances, Mrs. Gould
will now, with the cordial good wishes of all her
friends, venture on the equally bold. step of meeting
the present need, by opening a new school in another
part of the city, trusting all, with the same spirit of
faith in which the work was begun, to the Fatherly
care of him who loves little children to come to
him, and reproves such as would keep them away.
Mrs. Gould's present experience amongst the lower
population of Rome, in two different parts of the
city, has made her acquainted with a fact which it
may be interesting to some to learn.   The children
who attended the first school in the Vicolo Soderini,
were apparently of a higher type of intellect and
moral intuition, belonging as it were to a more cultivated race than these that are gathered from the immediate vicinity of the Governo Vecchio.   Nevertheless—and this is a very encouraging circumstance—
these almost utterly ignorant children are most eager
for, and intensely interested in, such simple religious
instruction, the very rudiments, so to speak, of the
Divine love and knowledge, as is given in the school.

And here, perhaps, it may be well to remark that
as regards religious instruction, no attempt is made
to interfere with, to undervalue, or to overturn the
established religion of the nation.   That which is
here instilled is simply based upon the great fact of
a loving Heavenly Father and a Saviour his Son,
who became man, became a little child, was poor like

themselves, suffered cold and hunger, and often had not where to lay his head; who spent his life in doing good, and finally died a cruel death for them, and left us his parting words, to them as to all, that they should love one another. This touching, sublime story, whose simple, pathetic truth is ever new to them, finds an answer in every young heart, however dull and unawakened the intellect may be. The story of the life and death of our Saviour never falls upon careless or unwilling ears.

Scarcely a day passes without the occurrence of some beautiful instance of the power which this Divine example exercises in the school. One day two furious combatants angrily appealed to Mrs. Gould, detailing their wrongs and bitterly accusing each other. Taking one in each hand, the affectionate directress said mildly, but with a somewhat sorrowful countenance, " But what did we repeat to-day? Was it not that we should love one another? If we love one another we should not tell tales of each other nor wish to hurt each other." This was enough; the angry color passed from the childish faces, and friendly play went on once more. Again: two still younger children were seen in the act of fighting. Taking their hands, Mrs. Gould said, " Let us love one another!" and stooped and kissed first one and then the other, and without saying more, drew them together. Peace was made; the quarrel and the anger were over. Truly the Saviour had spoken in those young passionate hearts, " Peace, be still." . . . .

Long residence in Rome and a thorough knowledge of the lower class has taught the excellent directress

8*

of these schools that the less pecuniary aid extended to them the better, and that, excepting under peculiar circumstances, neither food nor clothing, nor anything which might act as a *bribe*, either to the child or the parent, should be given. This being the principle on which the school has been established, it becomes valued for its own worth, a worth soon found to be beyond that of mere material help. The parents, as well as the children, gain hereby an independence of character which raises them out of pauperism, the shame of the poor Romans in the eyes of all strangers.

Nevertheless, whilst this is the rule, cases occur which necessarily demand an exception. Thus, six children out of the whole school, have, after long attendance, been found in such painful circumstances, that it has appeared not only desirable, but absolutely necessary to provide food for them at noon. The latest case, which occurred only last week, may be mentioned.

A little girl of about ten, who had attended school for about six months, the child of a very poor, worse than widowed, mother, having fainted whilst at her afternoon lessons, was carried into the matron's apartment, when it appeared she had fainted from absolute want. "What time had you your breakfast, my child?" asked the matron, knowing that she had brought nothing with her for her dinner. "Mamma mia had no breakfast for me to-day," answered the poor child. No food literally had passed her lips all that day, yet she had never complained, but gone steadily through her lessons till exhausted nature

gave way. On this, her name was immediately put
on the list of those who dine at the school, and she
makes the sixth. This fainting in the room of the
matron led also to another discovery regarding the
insufficiency of her clothing. The dress she wore
was a very old and washed-out summer barège, which
now being dirty, she was told to come cleaner to
school. In a day or two the poor thin skirt had been
washed, but not the body. "How was this, why had
not both been washed together?" Again the reply
was a revelation of their poverty. She had literally
no other clothing on under the little waist!

In connection with the schools must be mentioned,
as an important adjunct to them, though as yet in its
infancy, the Home for destitute children, in which at
present are four little girls, not orphans, but whose
domestic circumstances are worse than orphanage.
One of these children, first admitted and mentioned
in last year's report, a little cripple, then laden with
irons, from which she is now happily released, is so
much improved in general health as scarcely to appear deformed. She is still one of the best and
brightest of the children, and will, it is hoped, become
in time a valuable assistant teacher. Three other little girls wait to be admitted as soon as sufficient
funds will justify Mrs. Gould in enlarging her responsi-
bilities, and a suitable locality be found. In the
meantime a little boy is sheltered in her house,
brought thither from his home on the Campagna,
where his life was endangered by fever. He too is a
very tractable and singularly bright child.

The Sunday-school, mentioned in the last report,

is also an interesting feature of these important educational undertakings. About three weeks ago, on making out a list of the children, it was found that more were present at the Sunday-school than had been in attendance on any one day during the week, showing how popular was the instruction given on that day. The exercises are exactly those which occupy the first half hour of the daily school. The Rev. Mr. Burtchaell, well known to all the English and American friends of the cause, has a class of the elder children, which he instructs according to the mode usual with the elder or junior classes in the Sunday-schools at home. The whole school unites for the opening exercises, after which Mr. Burtchaell removes his children ; the others grouping into little classes of four or six, round their respective monitor or monitress, recite verses from the New Testament. About every ten minutes a bell is rung, the monitors rise, and are taught a little in advance of the others, after which, turning again to their own classes, they teach that which they have just learned. This alternation of first learning and then communicating that which has been learned, is found to be productive of excellent results. Occasionally the entire school rise and one of their favorite hymns is sung.

Sometimes, however, this routine is not wholly followed, and the younger ones are kept together grouped round their beloved directress, listening with enchanted attention to the story perhaps of a lost sheep for whom the Good Shepherd is in search, or to some other sweet incident of the Saviour's life and love, the comprehension of the subject being evident on every eager upturned young face (many of them really beautiful), and still more by the replies which follow the questioning of the teacher, often full of tender, childlike and not unfrequently original thought.

Besides this Sunday-school for the children, morning Sunday-classes have been formed for adults and such elder children as are prevented by their avocations from attending the daily school. Owing to her late ill health, the directress has been reluctantly compelled to give up her part in this branch of the school to one of the teachers. She hopes, however, to be able to resume her place in the course of the winter. In this school, which numbers about twenty-five, reading and writing only are taught, but as it meets a want of so many who have not had, and might not otherwise find, the means of acquiring these elementary branches, the number will, no doubt, greatly increase. . . . .

We have thus endeavored to give a brief account of the labors of our estimable friends—labors which, as we have before said, are as seed sown not alone for the harvest of time, but for the immortal harvest of eternity.

As for ourselves, the lookers-on, let us bear in mind that if we have pleasure in this world-famous old city, the soil and stones of which are full of ancient memories; the city of empire, the city sanctified by the blood of Christian martyrs; if we rejoice in the picturesque and the beautiful with which it surrounds us; if our daily pleasures are enhanced by the amenity of its climate, its glorious sunsets, its flowers and its fruits; let us spare of the wealth which God has given us, be it more or be it less, to help in lifting up its young sons and daughters, its little children, with their rich, but unawakened intellects, their infant hearts open to every tender, elevating religious sentiment, and so indeed help to regenerate Rome— Rome, which whether for evil or for good has so many ages held rule over the souls of men.

The Sunday-schools described by Mrs. Howitt, which from the beginning had attached themselves to Mrs. Gould's enterprises, grew more and more interesting. In July, a little festival was given to such of the grown-up scholars as had been regular and constant in attendance. It was held at the rooms that had been secured for the use of the Home in a spacious building, once a Maronite convent. The account of this in Mrs. Gould's annual report gives a good idea of the religious impressions made by her work:

As I entered our large school-room, after they had assembled that evening, I thought I had seldom seen a more interesting group of young people. They were principally girls from seventeen to twenty-five years of age, with a sprinkling of young men, and some younger girls, kept at home, during the week, to tend the inevitable "pupa." We had made our festa in some degree a picnic, by desiring everybody to bring his or her knife, fork, plates, etc. These having been placed on the tables, our guests were

requested to pass into the next room, and seat themselves wherever they found their property.

The supper-room of the evening is a particularly
pretty one, the roof being supported by columns.
Between these our tables were spread. The doors
stood open into the garden, which was partially
illuminated by a young moon. A fabulous amount
of maccaroni had been prepared, and was served.
But the standard of good manners, which prevails in
the class of society to which our guests belong, did
not permit them to begin to eat until particularly requested to do so, when with a volley of "Thanks,"
they fell upon their national dish with great vigor.
Our boys, under the direction of Mr. Garnieri, meanwhile gave a serenade of patriotic and other airs.
They were invisible minstrels, and after their concert
was over, went contentedly off to bed. The maccaroni was followed by a dish of beef, and I am sure
the meal eaten by these hungry people was one more
enjoyable to us who were lookers-on, than the best
dinner we could have eaten ourselves. The customary finale of a Roman supper is a salad, but, as we
were anxious to give a lesson of caution, in these
days when the cholera has invaded Italy, we substituted a *zuppa inglese*, a favorite sweet dish. This
was received with great favor, and we accompanied
it with a little lecture on diet, whence a digression
treating of cleanliness of their persons and their
homes was easy. It was evident that the moment
was a favorable one to make an impression upon our
pupils, and we took advantage of it. I presented
Signora Fua Fusinato to them, told them how much

she had done for the unity of our beloved Italy, and
for its improvement in literature and education, and
reminded them that they too could some of them
perhaps aid their country, as she had done; at least
all might imitate her as a woman, and as a woman
we best loved her, and she best filled her lot in life.
I wish I could remember all that she said to them;
how feelingly she spoke of the days, so lately past,
when no poor man or woman could hope to rise,
no matter how great his merit, no matter how diligently he labored or studied. She reminded them
of their duties and privileges as citizens under a free
Government, and exhorted them to profit by the
advantages they were enjoying. Monteverde, the
greatest perhaps of living Italian sculptors, she told
them, began life in a position like their own. (Indeed
this remarkable young man was apprenticed as a boy
to a chair-maker, and worked with him for some
years). I suppose this sort of address had never
been made to any one of these young people before;
that the idea that they might rise in life, might make
a position for themselves, had never occurred to
them. We took care not to weary them, and as soon
as all had finished supper, invited them to return to
the other room, where a series of megalethescopic
views, principally of Italian scenes, were shown and
explained to them. Then, as it grew late, and some
of the elder of the party remembered for a moment,
in the midst of their delight, that we must be wearied,
they suddenly withdrew to another part of the room,
and sang for us a very sweet patriotic song. When it
was over, the time for the last words had come. We

tried to make them such as they would remember. There were but two things that we had to beg them to think of during our separation from each other: One was, that God was our Heavenly Father, who loved us with a love so great that we could never understand it, and was always ready to hear our prayers. They answered this with a spontaneous burst of " We will pray for you, Signora, we will never forget to pray always for you." This promise we accepted, with the assurance that God would surely hear their prayers, as he had those of our children. The other injunction we gave them is particularly necessary, in the midst of the community in which they live. The young women were entreated to remember and respect their womanhood, and the young men to respect their female friends. In this way only could they be good members of families, good Italians, and good Christians. I wish every preacher could have so attentive an audience as we had that night. I wish every sermon were received with such gladness as were our few words on that occasion. It seemed as if they could not make up their minds to take their eyes off from us, and again and again one and another returned for one more good-bye, and one more assurance that they would never forget to pray for us, and never be absent from the Sunday-school. Signora Gotelli writes me that the result of this gathering has been excellent; that the young people speak of it with great emotion, and she considers them in a most impressible state of mind.

I think I should explain our meaning in telling

our guests that evening, that God would hear their prayers, as he had those of the children. Last summer I was ill, and became at one time very much discouraged with regard to future improvement. I was writing to the schools, and, partly to let my teachers understand how ill I felt, and partly because we endeavor every day to teach our children to lay their desires before Him who cares for them, I said : "I want you all to pray our Heavenly Father for me, and perhaps he will make me well again." The time necessary for a letter to reach Rome had just about elapsed, when I began to feel better, and the improvement was so marked that it was impossible not to connect it with our children's prayers, while the next post brought me a budget of little letters, of which their artless assurances that they all were praying for me every day was the burden. These letters were answered by one in which they were told that they were always to remember that God was the answerer of prayer ; that if they ever met with people silly or wicked enough to say that God was too far off, and too great a Being to hear the prayers of children, they were to answer : "I know better ; for he heard mine, when I asked him to make the Signora well again." This winter, ill-health obliged me to be absent a long time from my duties. One day, before the opening of the school, the children present asked some one from the house how I was. The reply was not favorable ; upon which one of the little girls said : "But we are not praying for our Signora ; we must pray for her ;" and down the little things dropped on their knees, showing how well they had under-

stood the lesson of the preceding season. But, indeed, it can never be too often repeated that the first
dawn of interest and intelligence in their minds is
always on religious subjects. We were telling them
some time since of the resurrection of the ruler's
daughter, and the remark was made that Jesus did
this miracle, not only for the sake of that one little
girl and her mother and father, but to show all little
children how much he loved them. One of the little
girls said something in a low voice, which she was at
first too timid to repeat. But on being urged to do
so, she said: "And he wanted to show them that he
was Jesus." Was not this an intelligent remark for a
little girl between seven and eight years old ?

And yet the difficulties of giving to these Roman
children anything like a thorough education are exceedingly great. They learn words with astonishing
rapidity, but their hatred for ideas is almost insurmountable. We have been obliged to make a boy of
fifteen read over a sentence of two lines and a half six
times before he was able to tell what it was about,
and this after first ascertaining that he understood
every word of it. One of our children was repeating
one day in his history lesson the story of Brutus. He
is one of those boys who will learn by heart in spite
of you ; and so, with his hands twisted behind his
back, and his eyes almost starting from their sockets
in his eagerness, he got the affectionate father, the
lictors, and the poor boys down into the Forum together, and Brutus with his foot upon the door-sill of
the temple of Mars, when he was suddenly interrupted
with the question—" Who was Mars ? " " Mars," said

the young sage, in a dreadful state of impatience to get back again to the words of the book once more, "Mars! Why, Mars was the sister of Lazarus!" It must be said in very partial extenuation of the young man's ignorance, that the two words Mars and Martha differ from each other but very slightly in Italian. I mention this absurd mistake to show what our difficulties are. This boy would have passed a most splendid examination in history, and yet he . was utterly ignorant of it and everything else. We never have any foundation upon which to build, and our efforts to keep our children from learning by rote have to be constant, both because of their own disposition to learn long strings of words, and that of their teachers to encourage them in it. Those who are learning the Froebel system will never give us the same trouble, as their intelligence is thoroughly developed before books are put into their hands.

The conviction was growing daily in Mrs. Gould's mind that all these means of influence were inferior in importance to the institution of a *Home* into which children could be received, not only for *instruction* in certain useful matters, but for *education* under the best influences, in seclusion from the damaging influences to which they were ordinarily exposed. Already, for strong reasons in each particular case, she had assumed the entire support of six girls, on account of circumstances of especial need, distress, or exposure, or of especial promise. But she found that such an opportunity was even more needed for boys than for girls. "The Roman boys are infinitely less guarded and shielded from evil than the Roman girls. The latter are much less in-dulged, and are kept at home sewing, knitting, or aiding in household work, while their brothers are exposed to all the evil influences of the street. It is almost impossible to counteract in six hours the evil influences exerted dur-ing the rest of the day."

In pursuance of this plan she had secured, at a reason-able rent, the first and second floors of a house which was once a monastery of the Maronite monks.

Connected with the apartment is a garden, which, although small, contains an immense deal of beauty. There are such lemon trees as are scarcely ever seen save in the famous groves of Sorrento, a fountain trickling over maiden's hair and other aquatic plants into a basin, the home of a large family of fish; a famous grape-vine; roses which look into the upper windows; magnolia and pepper trees; Japan fruit; violets hemming in the flower-beds with a wall of sweetness, and withal walks, up and down which our boys course like wild things in their play-hours. There are four good school-rooms on the ground floor, a dining-room and kitchen, and rooms which will be devoted to a printing-press this winter, as we hope. The boys' dormitory up-stairs is a charming room: lofty, with large windows opening upon the balcony, and its wealth of climbing flowers. Next this, is the room of the director of the boarding-school depart-ment. We were able to persuade Mr. Garnieri to ac-cept the position of head of our little family, for which he is eminently qualified. A matron and the three little girls occupy a room on the other side of the house, and a suite of rooms has been let to a friend, so that our rent will be somewhat lessened.

The plan was to receive the most promising candidates to this Home, at first on probation ; and then, when they had proved themselves diligent, faithful and teachable, to receive them under a legal apprenticeship until the age of seventeen or eighteen years, by which time they would be prepared with good principles and a good trade, to go home and help their parents, who in most cases would be of the neediest classes. Amid the thousand organized charities of Rome, with their great funds accumulated through centuries, not one, it seems, had ever undertaken to teach a poor boy a trade, although many of them had been devoted to the assiduous cultivation of ignorance, indolence, and beggary as Christian virtues.

In one of her letters to the New York *Evening Post*, a few months later, in commenting on some of the speeches of Garibaldi at Rome, Mrs. Gould had an opportunity of emphasizing the importance of this work of true charity. Garibaldi had visited the Orphan Asylum at the Termini, where the boys welcomed him with "Garibaldi's Hymn."

The General made a little speech to them, in which he reminded them that Italy needed good workmen, and that in preparing themselves to become such, they would aid in promoting the glory of their country as well as their own welfare. Garibaldi is decidedly conservative in some of his ideas. At the workmen's dinner given soon after his arrival in Rome, he exhorted his audience to bring up their sons each one to the trade of his father. We should scarcely expect such advice in America, where every one is constantly admonished to seek to rise himself and to raise his family. But a different state of things prevails here. If a young man is educated beyond his station he has but few doors opened to him. He naturally looks to an employment under the Government, and after having found one (if he be, indeed, a fortunate candidate among the many who apply) he is no longer his own master. To-day he may be an engineer, a secretary, a lawyer, even in Rome; to-morrow he may be ordered to some little town in the Apennines. He is a fair mark for the criticism of every journal, of every disappointed member of his profession. It is therefore the wisest course for persons who wish to aid the young men of Italy to give them first a trade. Then, if their education, their talent, and their good fortune enable them to rise above their birthright, all the better; but in any case they will have the means of livelihood.

The first beginnings of the new work were difficult. In her report written in July, 1873, Mrs. Gould was compelled to say:

We regret that we have no trade for our boys at present. We visited Paris last year, haunted the offices for the employment of the Alsacians and Lorrainese, made applications at the various schools of arts, besieged the clergymen, but all in vain. We could get no mechanic to come down to Rome to teach his trade in our schools, without paying simply fabulous prices. Here, the difficulty of getting an honest and thoroughly competent mechanic is insurmountable. There is one thing only that we can at present do toward putting our boys in the way of earning their living, beside teaching them drawing and modelling. It is to teach them printing. For this purpose, we must beg our friends to send us a printing-press. We have rooms on the ground floor in the Via Marroniti, which were formerly let to a carpenter, and which we destined, from the first moment we saw them, for printing-rooms. There are many reasons which make it desirable to introduce this trade into our institution. It is certainly very necessary that when they leave us, they should be fitted for making their own way in life. If we have a printing-press for them, the boys can always be under our personal supervision while at work. The trade is a perfectly healthy one. By fitting, as we should know how to do, the workshop into the school, their general intelligence will be increased. Good printers will hereafter be more and more in demand in Italy, from the constantly and greatly increasing number of newspapers and books issued in the country, and thus the future of our children will be secured. The schools will, after a very short time, become partly self-supporting. Our friends will be sure to give us work, in the way of printing handbills, circulars, and cards. This very report will, we hope, ere long, issue from our own printing-press. Finally, our boys and girls (for we shall teach printing to all our children, as soon as they are old enough) will have pleasant associations with their work, will learn to really love it, and thus we shall have done our little part in solving the labor question, which is such a serious one in our day, and threatens to be more so in the future.

With impaired health, with many an embarrassment and hindrance in her work, the butt of public insult in the street, as she "went about doing good," Mrs. Gould was a happy woman. The history of her charitable treasury was a story of human sympathy directed by Providential care. She says of it:

The many sweet thoughts and tender affections and earnest prayers which have accompanied the gifts cast into it, have enhanced their value a thousandfold. Now one has approached it, with a song of thanksgiving in her mouth, because God had looked upon her affliction, and in exchange for an angel in heaven, placed a new-born babe in her arms. Now a mother, in memory of one whom she was rearing for God's service on earth, but of whom the Master had need in heaven, has sent us a gift in memory of this son. Again and again, friends in the far-off land, for the sake of the love they bore to those whose names are too sacred to be pronounced here, have sped their offerings in aid of our labors. And those, too, who knew us only or principally by means of these labors, have been unceasing in their collections for our benefit. How often has help come to us, when, in spite of ourselves, we were greatly discouraged ! This was

9

especially the case last winter, when in consequence of
circumstances which it is not necessary to relate, our
treasury had been unreplenished, while the necessity
of assuming other and greater obligations was pressing upon us.

Among those who came to her aid at this crisis, she
names the Rev. Horace James, Henry Day, Esq., and the
Rev. Mr. Waite, whose timely words opened streams of
supply toward the empty treasury; and mentions one
gift of a generous lady which deserves to be "told as a
memorial of her." One day, in the absence of Mrs. Gould,
Mrs. Gouverneur Morris Wilkins visited the schools, and
left behind her, to Mrs. Gould's address, an envelope containing five thousand francs, and then slipped away from
Rome without giving so much as an opportunity for ac-
knowledgment.

But the best reward of all this arduous labor was found
in the individual improvement and personal gratitude of
the objects of it. Every reader of this volume must have
remarked how personal was the interest of Mrs. Gould in
her work—to what extent her love toward the flock which
she had gathered around her was like the love of the Good
Shepherd who "knoweth his sheep and calleth them all
by name." Consequently, the personal gratitude of the
pupils grew to be beautifully tender. One instance out of
many is that of a girl in whom, in very lowly circumstances, were discovered qualities that gave good promise
of usefulness in the work of teaching. After a little pre-

paration she was sent to the Government training-school for teachers at Torre-Pellice, at the expense of a few of Mrs. Gould's friends who made special gifts for her support. Her diligence and success and her gratitude to her benefactress were a bountiful reward. Ten months after her admission to the school, Mrs. Gould (who had visited her in the meanwhile, to make sure that she was doing well) describes her progress thus :

The instruction is given in French, of which she did not know a word when she entered. I never dreamed of the possibility of her keeping up with her class, and being promoted into a more advanced one at the end of the year. Her examinations are just over, and to my surprise and her great delight, they were successful, and she enters a more advanced class this autumn. Her letter to me announcing the fact is written in French, and is overflowing with her delight. " What happiness, what pleasure," she says ; " I felt so sad at the idea that I must remain two years in the same class, not only for myself, but for you ! . . . . I thank the good God who helped me so much." This child is one who can be governed entirely through her affections, which are wonderfully strong. During my illness of last winter, she was neglected with all other correspondents. She wrote again and again, and at last she poured out her poor little heart thus : " My dear and good Lady, I can not think why I have no more letters from you. Are they lost on the way ? Are you angry with me ? Are you ill ? Dear Lady, I am so unhappy. I am afraid

you are ill, for nobody tells me anything about you. As soon as I come home from school, I ask if there are any letters from you, but I must always hear that horrible word *No*. Dear Lady, I do beg you to answer me, or else I do not know what I shall do. When I get up in the morning I pray, and I say, 'O Lord, let me get a letter to-day,' but none ever comes. I long for a letter as if it were an angel, but the more I long for one, the more I do not get it. Then I ask God to keep you well, and to make me a better girl and give me patience. . . . . I do not believe you have given me up. I think you will love me until the day that God calls me away. Will you not? Oh ! I never forget you, and I love you so much."
. . . .

XI.

LAST LABORS.

Mrs. Gould's Delight in the Home — Growth and Prosperity—An Italian Friend—Rest and Labor in the Apennines — Boscolungo—Lessons in Charity—Marietta and Beppino—Letters from the Children—And Mrs. Gould's Answer — A Report Broken Off.

AS the enterprise grew and prospered, it is easy to see that Mrs. Gould found a peculiar delight in the *Home.* The destitute children whom she gathered in from the streets or from desolate dwellings, wound themselves about her heart. Her interest in the Schools, and her laborious zeal for them never flagged; but the Home was yet dearer to her. It added vastly to her already excessive burden, but the burden was borne with delight, even when it was crushing her. One by one the number of six children with whom the establishment began in June, 1873, increased, within a year, to nineteen. It was never a question now how to find suitable candidates for the various schools, but how, out of a multitude of applicants, to choose the worthiest. Mrs. Howitt tells

(197)

how, as the winter of 1873 approached, and it became necessary to close the windows, Doctor Gould, always watchful over the sanitary condition of the schools, insisted on reducing the number of pupils. Mrs. Gould at once began "weeding out" the less hopeful plants from her garden. "The school," says Mrs. Howitt, "has thus been reduced to about a hundred. But although a third have been dismissed from the school since Mrs. Gould's return, no less than a hundred and fifty have been refused admission since the removal of the schools, for want of accommodation in the present rooms."

We have already had occasion to mention more than once the name of Signora Fua Fusinato. She was one of those exceptional women whose names have adorned in successive ages the history of Italian learning and literature, and the only one who in recent times has received the honor of a Professor's chair in a University. But it marks the character of the present age of Italian progress, that this lady, instead of being occupied solely with the writing of poems or the delivery of university prelections, should be devoted to raising the prevailing low standard of female education, and to encouraging efforts for elevating the children of the lowest of the people. It was at her earnest recommendation that a highly qualified teacher of the Italian language, Professor Rebecchini, was secured, who should enable the pupils to avoid the vulgarisms of their local dialects, and to use their national tongue, the exquisite language which is the common possession of all Italy, with correctness and elegance.

It was with consciously-failing strength, and yet with just exultation over the work that had risen now to " the full tide of successful experiment," that Mrs. Gould re-treated into the Apennines from the summer heats of 1874. What sort of place it was, she recovered strength, after a long period of prostration, to describe in a newspaper-letter, dated " Boscolungo, September 25th."

The Pistoian Apennines, among whose recesses we have been hiding ourselves for a few weeks, are but little known to the ordinary traveler. He traverses them, it is true, on his way from Bologna to Florence, and has some glimpses of very wonderful scenery, but the greater part of his journey in this neighbor-hood is made inside the giant peaks. Scarcely does he emerge breathless from one tunnel before he plunges headlong into another. It is not until one leaves the railroads, and drives in among the folds of the mountains, that the beauty and sublimity of the Apennines are spread before the eye. To reach Boscolungo we were obliged to make a journey of some thirty miles from the nearest railroad station, that of Pracchia, passing through almost every variety of scenery: overhanging slopes, smiling with vine-yards and orchards; traversing gorges, down which huge boulders had been tumbled by fierce torrents; mounting heights covered as far as the eye could reach with chestnut trees, rising still higher among forests of beech trees and finally creeping slowly up into the region of pine, spruce, and larch. The road is a very fine one; the bridges are wonders of engineering, adorned with fountains and architectural ornaments, and each of the thousand twists and turns which the great highway makes in its upward course reveals some new beauty of scene. We approached its summit just at evening, and the sound of the little chapel bell close beside our hotel was the only noise which broke the silence. The sharp cry of the cicala is heard in the sunshine, but at night the stillness is unbroken.

Our hotel is a large, rambling building, divided off into apartments for the use of the Duke of Tuscany and his suite during the hunting season. The lower part of it was occupied by his customs officers. A little higher up in the road are planted two remarkably ugly dwarf pyramids, bearing white balls on their heads, and the arms of the duke on their faces. These are at the very summit of the road, and mark the Tuscan boundaries. Thence the road curves and sweeps down toward Modena, from which we are distant fifty-nine miles. Opposite us there is a building let out as tenements to the wood-cutters. A chapel, two or three other tenement-houses, and the post-house, now also let out for apartments, compose the hamlet of Boscolungo, or Abetone, as its inhabitants and neighbors call it, from the great forest of pine (*pinus abies*). The Ximenes road, which terminates at the pyramids, is met by that called the Via Giardinia, from its engineer, Giardini, who laid it out in the reign of Francis III., Duke of Modena, in 1777. It is not kept in quite as good order as that on the Tuscan side, but we found five miles of it a very delightful ride. A mountain which we have constantly in view, whose peak is shaped something like a human face, is called Furmalbo, and at its foot, washed by two mountain torrents, is the village which bears its name. There is nothing like a carriage to be hired in our hamlet, and the walk to the village and back again, climbing the mountains, was a little too much for our unaccustomed feet.

But the forester was our very good friend, and he is allowed a horse; his superior officer has a caratella, and on a festival day horse, caratella and forester were at our command. So, one beautiful September morning the forester, radiant in blue-cloth uniform, the horse well fed and groomed, and the caratella, new-roped and with its wheels well greased, drew up at our door. The caratella is simply four bits of wood netted together with rope, upon which is perched a seat, the ropes forming a footstool and the body of the vehicle. The horse is tied, harnessed and roped in some inexplicable manner, and the passengers must be well provided with faith and patience, also with parasols for the sunshine and vast umbrellas for the rain, both of which the clerk of the weather is sure to produce in unknown and unexpected quantities during all autumn excursions in the Apennines.

We traveled to Furmalbo through burning sunshine; we returned in the midst of a second deluge, but we enjoyed our trip exceedingly. Furmalbo, so little known to the modern tourist, was well known to the Romans. Several of the houses are built out of their wonderful architectural remains. The church, which is a basilica, contains several pillars from old

9*

temples.　Three of them are of the richest composite style, and others of plain Doric.　It was built in the year 1000, but has been restored, and horrible Renaissance capitals placed above the ancient ones to support the nave, which is higher than the aisles.　The ceiling is of carved wood.

On a height a little above the village is one of the ninety-nine castles of the Countess Matilda, who made of Furmalbo one of her favorite residences. The arms of the town are the three towers with which the castle was guarded.　The ruins of one of them remain; another has long ago been covered by a fruitful garden and shady pergola.　Upon the foundations of the third its present owner has erected a modern tower, which is his *maison de plaisance*.　The host, hearing that *forestieri* were in town inquiring if the ruins were to be seen, sent us word that we would be made welcome, and was on the spot to receive us. But through what a heap of human misery we were forced to mount to reach the height from which Matilda looked forth upon her domains!　Foul, ill-smelling, steep, crooked streets, inhabited by so wretched a population that they scarcely seemed human.　We were told that some of the frightful objects we saw were afflicted with leprosy, and, indeed, they were like no human beings that we had ever seen.　Even on these heights, under these smiling skies, breathing this pure air, man has succeeded in tainting all that God has made.　The want of drainage, the allowing of foul water to pour its poison into the living springs, the crowding of large families into one ill-ventilated room, has sufficed to make part of this beautiful mountain-side a vast pest-house, a laz-aretto of filth, disease and misery.

We forgot all that we had seen, as the gates opened to admit us into the grounds of the old castle. There one neither sees nor hears nor smells aught that is offensive. Its owner has divided the new tower into three stories. The lower one is his studio, where he works in clay in a very respectable way for an amateur sculptor. The second is his study, where one of the party greatly enjoyed a perfect library of herbariums. The upper floor is a museum, where there are some very interesting remains of Roman and mediæval armor, and one or two most valuable and exquisite bits of bronze. One of these is the support of an incense-burner, or miniature furnace, wonderfully wrought, and more perfect than anything to be found in the Naples Museum. One of the Roman helmets is very interesting. Its first owner had evidently been killed by a pike, and the hole in the helmet had been carefully repaired. Human life had long ago passed out of the opening in the bit of bronze, but the hel-met remained for generations to tell of the fierce war-fare of the former rulers of the soil.

In a wonderful walk we sometimes take, we are out of sight of every mountain visible from our hotel. The path is through the thick beech wood, and sud-denly emerging on a sort of shelf of slate, the remains of an old quarry, we find range upon range of mount-ains closing in about us ; some bristling with pines, some utterly bare, some bearing cultivated fields upon their breasts. The nearer mountains fold over each other, and all lean toward a narrow valley where the busy waters of a torrent are making sweet music, but are invisible to our eyes. Upon our right the mountains draw back a little, and a smile or two of cultivated fields break over their sad-looking faces. But the pines are our nearer neighbors. Plunging in among them, we seem to plunge into an almost pathless wilderness, as yet scarcely trodden by the foot of man. But a slow tramp is heard among the spines of last year's cones, and a procession passes us. Men issue forth, bearing these enormous monarchs of the forest stripped of their branches, and shaped to take their places on the deck of some, as yet, unconstructed vessel. The men wear a sort of double bag upon their heads and shoulders, which keeps them from being bruised, and on this they lift the great burden. The forest is very extensive. One can get lost with all ease by going in almost any direction.

Nothing in Mrs. Gould's work was more characteristic of her than her way of resting from it. Among the woodcutters and charcoal-burners, who constituted the entire population of little Boscolungo, far away from railroads and telegraphs and schools, exhausted with excessive work and care, and prostrated with the beginnings of a fatal sickness, it struck her that here was "an opportunity of teaching our children [in the schools at Rome] a lesson of self-denial for the good of others, as well as of linking together their interests and some of those of their little country people." The children of Boscolungo, she observed, spent the whole of the long summer days in idleness. It is hardly necessary to add that she sought refreshment and comfort at once by opening a school for the poor little mountaineers. Each member of the party of tourists lent a hand. With Dr. and Mrs. Gould were the Rev. Somerset Burtchaell, a most devoted and large-hearted clergyman of the English Church, and his family, and the Rev. Pierce Conolly, of Florence. The story of this school was briefly told in Mrs. Gould's last and unfinished Report of the Italo-American Schools.

We opened a little school for them which was regularly attended by about thirty girls and boys from four to fifteen years of age, none of whom could read or write, and most of whom did not know a single letter. It was rather hard work. There was not a shop within several miles, and of course no books could be obtained. But our friends painted a series of letters, syllables and words upon card-board. We rifled old newspapers of their headings, and pasted them upon postal cards, and our little people made in the few lessons we were able to give them, most extraordinary progress. We saw, too, in them the change we saw in early days among our Roman pupils. Their hands and faces grew more delicately white, their step more graceful, their shrill voices softer and sweeter. Sometimes we took them into the woods, which rang again with the echoes of their happy voices, as they sang the same hymns which so delight our own children.

We remained in the neighborhood so late that the fingers of Autumn were busy weaving among the

beech-woods a robe which was, like Joseph's, a coat
of many colors. The sheep were brought down from
the higher peaks, and our children were set to watch
them, or trudged sturdily along under heaps of chips
and twigs. We used to hear the voices of the little
shepherds above our heads, or of the wood-gatherers
in the forests, singing "*io sono un agnellino;*" and
the chorus which broke forth when they met us again
after a day or two's separation, was so full that we
feel sure they will never forget that they are indeed
lambs of the Good Shepherd, although they had
known but now of his infinite love and tenderness.
Meanwhile, we wrote to our children of the Home,
that we needed books for our little scholars in the
Apennines, asking them if they could not think of
some means by which they could be procured. Immediately there followed a little package of letters.
Those who had a few soldi of pocket money, wished
to give them at once ; those who had not, begged to
deprive themselves of some little luxury in order to
save their share in the gift ; not one was willing to be
left out. Mr. Burtchaell, whose wife and sister taught
constantly in our little mountain school, procured in
Florence for each child, a copy of the First Reader,
used in the municipal schools, which he distributed
when he left the hamlet. These books were the gift
of our children. To the father of one of the families,
who, not being from the neighborhood, had learned
to read, a hymn-book was given, and he promised to
get the children together on festas, and endeavor
at least to prevent them from forgetting what they
had learned. We feel sure that even these efforts,

few and feeble as they were, will be heard from, in
that blessed day, when the King shall "make up his
jewels."

Before dismissing our little mountaineers, I can not
help mentioning an interesting circumstance that
occurred one Sunday, when we had gathered them
about us in one of the kitchens of the great, straggling building where we were lodging. A few miles
from the hamlet where they live, is the home of a
most extraordinary woman, Beatrice d'Onaglia. She
is perfectly illiterate, over seventy years of age, unable to read or write, but with a remarkable gift as
an *improvisatrice*. She was visiting us, and had come
in to see the school. The children were listening
most attentively to the story of the Babe of Bethlehem. Beatrice listened also, but suddenly her voice
rang out clear and strong, like the sound of some
powerful wind-instrument. Slowly and distinctly,
she began to repeat the same story in verse. Her
eyes were fixed, with a gaze so distant and so earnest,
that she seemed looking back through the ages upon
the star in the East, the manger and the new-born
Child. One could have imagined that the fable of
the Sibyls had for the first time become a living
truth, and that from the lips of one to whom the
gift of second-sight was permitted, dropped words of
inspired wisdom. It was a scene never to be forgotten. A thrill ran through the little assembly, and
we realized how surely God reveals his wondrous
deeds, not to the wise and great ones of the earth,
but to the humble and unlearned. If I should not
be straying too far from my present subject, I could

tell my friends much that is interesting of the inhabitants of these high places of the earth, of the ill-
doers who have no comforter, of the poor who have
none to minister to them. Our friends were able to
relieve some of their physical wants, to speak to
some of them words of consolation and sympathy.
But we had the prevailing feeling while we were
among these poor people, that their pitiful cry
was ever ascending to heaven, "No man careth for
our souls."

This example is only one of many that might illustrate
that beautiful thing in Mrs. Gould's conduct of the schools
—her training of the children to the love of doing good.
The reward of a week's good behavior, when the schools
were first begun, was the privilege of putting a *soldo* into
the box for the Florence orphans. By-and-by she welcomed as an able assistant in her work, the coming into
the house, of one more helpless and weak than any of the
children themselves; and counted that this had much to
do with "the religious and moral growth of the institution." And the distress of a party of desolate little waifs,
left on the hands of the city officers, was made to minister
to the Christian graces of her pupils.

Rather more than a year ago, God gave to a married pair who have been connected with our institution from its earliest days, a dear little babe. She
was, of course, adopted by us all, and every one of
our children aspires to be its little nurse. It is charming to see how our roughest and rudest boys become

in a moment as tender and careful as our gentlest girls, when trusted for a little while with the care of our little Lena. She reigns like a queen in our small community, and we have never yet found our children unwilling to acknowledge her sway. She teaches them lessons of unselfishness and tenderness, which perhaps they could learn in no other way.

One thing which we especially try to impress upon our young people, is the duty and privilege of self-denial, and our success in this respect has been, we think, very remarkable. Last winter two ill-looking men were seen getting out of a third-class car at the Roman station, with a number of little *ciocciari* (peasants of the mountain frontiers of the Neapolitan provinces) under their charge. Suspicions were aroused that something wrong was taking place, and they were arrested. It was found on investigation that the children were from Sora, and had been sold by their wretched parents to these men, who were about to take them to Civita-Vecchia, and thence embark with them for Great Britain. They were to have swelled the number of organ-boys, chimney-sweeps, etc., which abound in London. The men were put in prison, and the children taken in charge by the city authorities.

The newspaper *Fanfulla* opened a subscription for their benefit, and at the same time conferred a great benefit upon the children of Italy, by inviting them to come to the aid of those of their own age who were deprived of sweet homes and loving parents. For months we had been wondering how to teach our children that it is more blessed to give than to

receive, and we were delighted with this opportunity
of impressing upon them this most necessary lesson.
We told them the story of these poor children, and
added that we so much desired to have them par-
takers in the privilege of helping them. "But," we
said, "you have no money to give them, and we must
help you to get some.   If you will work for them in
your play-hours, we will give you five centimes (one
cent) an hour, and if you will go without sugar in
your coffee, you shall have five centimes for every
time that you choose to take it unsweetened." Every
one of them wished to help. A little book was given
to each child, in which he or she wrote down the
hours spent in work, and the days the sugar was not
touched. We could not allow them to work excepting on their half-holiday, for they are busy little
people at all times, but their zeal was something tremendous. It was affecting to witness a scene presented the first Saturday after this proposition was
made to them. Every child was full of business
under the surveillance of our young teacher-pupil.
In a corner was the smallest little girl, seated in a little chair, the tears running down her cheeks. On
inquiry, it was found that the task given her was to
learn a piece of poetry, and one of the elder girls was
desired to teach it to her, as she had not yet learned
to read. She was crying from sheer fatigue. The
teacher at once told her to run away and play. But
the little thing refused: "No, no," she said, "I want ·
my soldo to give to those poor children." And the
same spirit ran through the whole community. They
none of them failed to raise the sum apportioned to

them, although every care was taken to make their self-denial entirely voluntary. When the sum decided upon had been raised, two of the best boys were sent to the *Fanfulla* office with it. But just as they were being dispatched, a note was put into my hands from their young mentor. All the summer they had been saving up the centimes, given them sometimes by their parents. They intended asking permission to spend them in getting up for themselves a little festa in the country. But they had all decided that they preferred to deprive themselves of this pleasure, for the sake of increasing their contribution for the benefit of the unfortunate little children of Sora. So the little parcel of coppers went with the rest. I may add, that great as was the temptation, we have never given them the picnic which they had hoped to have.

When the October frosts warned them away from Boscolungo, the little party of foreigners went down the mountain-side, taking with them the blessings of the poor people. After all farewells were said, and they were well on their way down the steep road, a clear little piping voice, like a bird's note, was heard from far up the height, and they stopped to look and listen. Presently (the words of John Bunyan happen to tell the story exactly), " they espied a boy feeding his sheep. The boy was in very mean clothes, but of a fresh and well-favored countenance ; and as he sat by himself, he sang. Hark, said they, to what the shepherd boy saith. So they harkened, and he said : "

Io sono un agnellino
Trovato dal pastor.

The little shepherd in his sheepskin breeches and with his crook leaning against his shoulder, as he sat perched on a rock, outlined against the blue sky, and sang to his " silly sheep," was all unconscious how sweet and significant was the picture he was leaving on the memory of his benefactors.

There was business connected with her cherished plan of a kindergarten at Rome, which required Mrs. Gould to go round about by way of Venice, before returning to Rome. It was at Venice that she heard of a peculiarly touching case of distress among children, which she describes herself in a letter to children, which was widely circulated, in lithographed copies, among the American Sunday-schools.

This autumn, when we were in Venice, the Waldensian clergyman told us about Marietta and Beppino. Where they lived, the sea came in every day, and they never ate anything but polenta. This polenta is made of coarse corn-flour. It is not good at all, but they could not get enough even of that. One of the children died, and while we were in Venice, the poor mother died too, just of want. We began our " Home," some eighteen months ago, but when we made up our accounts, we found that we had spent three thousand dollars more than we had received. And yet, what could we do? We could not let Marietta and Beppino starve and die, like their mother and the baby. We had to take them, and we did. The wife of the Waldensian clergyman gave them two warm baths to make them clean, and threw away their old, dirty rags. Then she made them some clean night-clothes, and put them in a nice bed to sleep. The next day she dressed them in new clothes. Marietta laughed and cried when they were tried on her. A kind young lady who had been studying in Venice how to teach our children took them, and brought them to the Italo-American Home in Rome. Dear children, you know what a home means. It means father and mother, little brothers and sisters, happy play, learning lessons, sitting down to dinner almost before you are hungry, sleeping in clean, soft beds at night. It means mother's love, father's kind words, and the blessing of the Father in heaven. We give what we can in our Home; the love without which children can not be good and happy, beds that are clean, if not soft. They have their soup every day, and rice, or maccaroni, or beans. Three times a week, they have a piece of meat. We should like to give them pudding on Sunday, but we can not afford it. And it is no great matter. Most of them have grown fat and rosy, because they have enough to eat. They learn lessons every day, and the older ones are taught to print. Every day, too, they are taught from the Bible, and they have their play-hours, when they make a great deal of noise, but we do not mind that, because it does them good. And so we try to do our part; to be the fathers and mothers of these children. And now I want to know if you will not do your part toward being their brothers and sisters? Sometimes we are afraid that we may have to send them away, because we can not get money enough to buy them food, and pay for a house for them to live in. By and by we who have founded this Home shall die, and sometimes we are very sad, because we do not know what will become of these poor children then. But if the Sunday scholars at home would promise to send us what they can every year, we should not feel so. What do you say? Will this Sunday-school help us? May we be sure that the children we have now will be fed, and clothed, and educated until they can take care of themselves? May we take care of others who have poor, ignorant, wicked parents, or who have no father and mother, and bring them up to be Christian men and women? We tell them that they must work and study hard now, so that they can be teachers themselves by and by. Most of them are willing to work in their play-hours, or to go without sugar in their coffee, so as to help children who are poorer than themselves. This makes us hope that by-and-by, when they have learned to be printers, or teachers, when they have grown to be men and women, when they are earning their own living, they will be glad to help to take care of our Home, when they have left it. But we must wait some years before that time will come. And so, I beg you, dear children, to help us to keep up and enlarge our Italo-American Home.

These two children, Marietta and Beppino Bartoli, were so peculiarly dear to Mrs. Gould that we add from her unfinished report of 1875 some additional details about them:

The parents were members of the Waldensian

Church. The man worked as a mason, receiving a franc and a half or two francs a day, and on this scanty sum (often not earned, because of the scarcity of building work going on in Venice) a family of eight lived, or, rather, starved. In order to keep life in their poor bodies, the mother was in the habit of taking the youngest child in her arms, and through the sleet and biting cold of the winter, standing on one of the bridges to beg for a few centimes. The child died of the exposure and of want. The home of the family was in one of those cellars which can exist only in Venice, into which the sea enters daily. . . . . Not long after the birth of another baby, the poor mother fell ill of a disease contracted through the unwholesomeness of the atmosphere and the scanty nourishment. She was buried by charity, and then the living were to be thought of. We were urged to come to their help, and the children were brought to us. Seldom was a sadder picture of infant misery presented. Thin, pale, aged little faces ; little feet dragging wearily to support weak little bodies ; dull eyes from which all the glorious light of childhood seemed to have faded ; oh ! it was pitiful. We should like to have shown our friends the two little ones whom we finally decided to take, as we saw them first, and then again as we saw them the night before they left Venice, after they had been fed and bathed and clothed in clean night-dresses, sleeping the sweet sleep of infancy, in a bed lent us by the wife of the Waldensian clergyman. They were brought to Rome by the teacher-pupil, of whom mention has been made in our former Reports, and I doubt if two happier, lovelier children are gathered to-night about any fireside.

Before transcribing Mrs. Gould's letter to the Home, in which she tells her children of her acquisition of this new treasure, it is well to give two of the little notes that had come to her, and to which she refers in her reply. The first is in an elaborate and beautiful handwriting :

MY DEAR DIRECTRESS, MRS. GOULD :

I am very sorry that you are ill ; but we must always say to the Lord : " Not mine, but thy will be done."

And I hope that soon you will be able to come with us to stay ten days, as you promised ; and that you soon will come to give us our lessons, and to live as a family once more—father, mother, sons, and daughters.

My dear mother, I keep all my trust in God. With a kiss I clos my little note. I am your

Affectionated son,

——— ———.

ROME, 12 *June*, 1874.

(Exuse me the mistakes).

The following is in the cramped and irregular hand of a very little child :

ROME, 15*th Sept.*, 1874.

DEAR MADAME :—The other day when we came back from school, Mme. Gotelli gave me a very pretty letter from Miss Mary and a card. The paper was very pretty, with a big fly on the envelope. I shall write to her very soon. I have put by for the poor boys of your mountains six sous. Tell us wich books we must buy, and we will ask Mr. Garnieri to send them to you. Scarcely can we pass to our new school, because there is the engine and so much earth all along the street, and to-day is all wet ; it is raining very much. The street Babuino is all in a muddly. Yesterday it is worse. Mrs. Gotelli does not correct our letters, only she tells us the words we do not know.

Good-bye, Miss,
and I am your devoted

—— ——.

Miss, pardon our Luigi.

VENICE, *October* 21, 1874.

MY DEAR CHILDREN :—I thank you for all your good letters, some of which have been really excellent. I can not answer them as I would like, for I have a great deal of writing to do just now. But you shall have, at least, one letter. I want you to know that Signorina —— is ready to take her diploma as *kindergartnerin ;* she will have to study still further to receive her other diplomas, and I do not see how she can do this at Rome, so that I have proposed to her to stay here a few months more. But she is homesick away from us and wants to come back to Rome. She could do it, if you would be faithful and not make her so much trouble as you did last year. The larger children ought by this time to have conscientious principles and to help us with the little ones. Write to the Signorina whether you wish her to come back and will be good to her.

And now I have something important to tell you. Less than a week ago a woman died here leaving several children. The father earns a franc and a half or two francs a day when he can find work ; and you can judge how wretched they are now that their mother is gone. I have thought of taking two of the

10

children—a girl of about ten, and a little boy nearly
six years old, but looking much younger. But this
is the way the matter stands. You know that I do
not take such little children as this. They do not
know how to wash nor dress themselves. You larger
children will seem to them so grown up and so educated that if you set them a bad example they will
be sure to follow it. In that case, I should be doing
him harm and not good. Ought I to take him? It
depends on you. Are you ready to deny yourself
on his account? Each one of you, will you love him,
and try always to set him a good example? Will the
older ones take turns in washing and dressing him,
and taking care of him, comforting him sometimes,
poor little orphan, and letting him have a share of
your little books? You will be ready, perhaps, to
promise everything for these poor children. But
wait a little. Go and ask God for Christ's sake to
help you. Tell him you are poor sinners, proud
of the little good you do, prone to think you can
do everything, when you can do nothing without
him.

Once, when Jesus Christ was here on earth, there
came to see him a young man, handsome, intelligent,
well educated, amiable. Every one loved him. Jesus
loved him; but he said to him, "One thing thou
lackest." So it is with you. We love you for your
smiling faces, your quick minds, your affectionate-
ness; we love you because you are *ours*. But if
Jesus Christ were to come to our house to-day, I am
afraid he would say to each of you, "One thing thou
lackest." This one thing is to love him; to do

right, not because you love to be praised or rewarded for it, but because you love him. My dearly-loved children, go to him to-day. Each one of you tell him you want to be his true children. Ask him for help to do your duty by each other, and especially by these little children, if I bring them. To-morrow go to Signor Garnieri and Signora Gotelli and tell them whether I am to send the little children.

I must let you know that I have been suffering from fever for two days, and am still in bed, so that I must say good-bye for the present. I had not told you of my leaving Boscolungo and the children there. We distributed among them the books you sent, and they were very thankful. The forester promises to get them together to read and sing every holiday.

Give salutations to every one, from

Your affectionate

EMILY B. GOULD.

Quoting from the foregoing letter in her unfinished Report for the year 1874–5, the writer adds:

It is thus that we strive to bring our children face to face with their Heavenly Father in every act of their lives. On one occasion, when our " *fille du regiment*," as we playfully call the baby, was drooping, we wished that her mother should take her for a day or two to the country. She felt that she could not leave the children. But we got them together, and asked them to promise that they would be good during her absence. We made it a serious affair with them, and they all promised but one. He was sent away for the moment, and afterward taken apart, and asked why he refused to promise. " Because," said he, " if I promised and afterward forgot and did something wrong, I should tell a lie." The little fellow was asked if he was not willing to promise to try and be good. That promise he was willing to make; I need scarcely add that he kept it.

For one who loves children, the happiness of the members of our Home is one of its most delightful features. When we are absent from them, we can scarcely recall any but smiling countenances. They seem always to find some fresh pleasure; a visit, a walk, some wonderful exploit of the "*fille du regiment*," a difficulty vanquished, a word of commendation, a new scholar, a new lesson, even a new rule; each and every one of these is a reason for the buoyancy of childhood to manifest itself.

On one occasion our youngest child was found not to be well, and was sent to our own house, to see the physician. I shall never forget the tenderness with which the " little mamma" lifted the child in her arms and carried her away. When she reached the house, she found the doctor absent, and was obliged to return to the institution, leaving the child to await his return. Soon after, the directress went home, and was met at the door by the little one, who, with the tears streaming down her face, ran to her with outstretched arms, and the petition, " Send me home, Signora; oh! will you not send me home?" It was an affecting thought that every tender caress, every loving word, every happy hour—in short, all that she had known of the joy and blessings of childhood, were encircled within the walls which stranger hands had provided for her refuge. . . . .

At this point, the writer's hand was interrupted by the onset of her last sickness.

XII.

A LETTER FROM A SICK-BED.

American Citizens Abroad in War-time — Forbearance from Hard Words — Letter to a Colored Citizen — The Church of Rome and Slavery — Prospect of Liberty in Romanism — The Regeneration of a Race.

T HE patriotic American whose duty kept him abroad during the dreadful years from 1861 to 1865, had some hardships to bear and conflicts to maintain that were spared to those in the field. The anguish of waiting from one mail to another, in those days before the Cable, for news which, in moments of crisis, was to decide the fate of the Republic; the duty of repelling the ignorant insolence to which one was liable, especially from a certain class of ill-bred English people, anywhere on the Continent; the duty of keeping oneself constantly and accurately prepared with information for the benefit of those who were willing to understand the matter;—these were burdens that rested heavily on the heart of Mrs. Gould, throughout the years of the war. Withal, she was not unmindful of another, like them, but more congenial to a mind like hers—the duty of encouraging and helping those nearer the field or on the field by words of cheer from a distance, and the benefit of such a comprehensive, bird's-eye view of the conflict as can best be got through such a long perspective. Every citizen had to act as an accredited representative of the United States to the citizens of other countries. This spontaneous, unofficial diplomacy was of priceless value to the nation. It is doubtful whether the services of ambassadors at courts were more gravely important to the national cause, than the services of Henry Ward Beecher and Andrew White, and the less conspicuous services of many others, as ambassadors to the people. It could hardly serve any good purpose, at this day, to reproduce incidents illustrating the zeal and resolution as well as tact with which Mrs. Gould served her native country and the cause of liberty in this way. But it is pleasant to see that there was not so much of tact and discretion in her social diplomacies, but that she knew the right moment to let fly in a fury of righteous indignation, and sin not. Some of those extraordinary vacations of hers, in which she sought repose in doing what to other people commonly seems like work, were devoted to diligent study of national questions. The ninth volume of her Journal records the summer of 1862 (volume I. begins in June, 1860) spent on the Voirons, near Geneva. Forty pages of this are occupied with a careful abstract of Professor Cairns' work on the Civil War, which she had been studying, and in part committing to memory.

But the most complete expression of her patriotic feeling, and of her sympathy with those sentiments of humanity and justice and love of the kingdom of God on earth, which in religious minds were wrapped up with a true patriotism, was written, as we may almost literally say, by her dying hand, ten years after the war had closed. It is worthy of being transcribed here in full, both as the utterance of the best type of American feeling, and as the latest important production of its author's pen. Withal there is an additional reason why it should be given here unabridged.

Many who read this story of the life of a Protestant Christian lady at the capital of the Roman Catholic Church, will be surprised, and some will be disappointed, to find hardly a word of denunciation or of ridicule, where there was so much (in the earlier times) of outrage upon personal rights, so much that was offensive to the moral sense, and so much, at the same time, that was irresistibly provoking to so quick a sense of the ludicrous as Mrs. Gould's. There were many good and Christian reasons for this forbearance—reasons which it might be wished that others would ponder before speaking unadvisedly on such matters, either with their lips or with their pens. But among these reasons was *not* the lack of clear knowledge or strong conviction. And when, by-and-by, the occasion for speaking arose, there was no uncertain sound in her utterance.

The occasion presented itself in the month of April, 1875, in the midst of the most pressing cares for her great family of needy children, and when the prostration of fatal sickness was already beginning to overcome her. An American paper reached her, into which was copied from a Roman Catholic journal a letter written by one of the most prominent and influential colored citizens of the United States, in which, piqued by what seemed to him a neglect of his people on the part of Protestant Christians, he half recommended them to join the Roman Catholic communion. Such a recommendation, even though only half serious (and as the writer freely declared afterward, it was less than half serious, being meant rather as an indirect argument to those to whom it was not addressed), might nevertheless be the occasion of most serious mischief among uninstructed minds; and Mrs. Gould, feeling herself to be called to the duty by many Providential indications, replied from her sick-bed, through the press, in the following letter to her colored friend :

107 VIA BABUINO, ROME, ITALY, }
April 21, 1875. }

MY DEAR FRIEND :—A copy of your letter to the *Pilot*, as reprinted in the *Congregationalist*, has just reached me in Rome. Anything from your pen would be of interest to me, for my earliest recollections are connected with your family. Although I lost my mother at a very early age, I can perfectly remember her expressions of respect for your parents ; and my father, the late Dr. James C. Bliss, was for

10*

more than thirty years their beloved physician. As an only child, I was brought into relations of uncommon sympathy with him, and I know well how greatly he loved and respected your mother. I remember his grief when she exchanged her earthly home for the better land. Your father was our life-long friend, and his memory will always be held in honor by us. I remember one beautiful incident in his life. The family of his parents' old master, if not his own (for here my memory is not quite clear), became reduced to poverty. Your father was applied to by them for relief. He loaded a sloop with provisions and other necessaries for them; and so fed and supported those who had lived upon the unpaid toil of his family. I remember much that is interesting in your history, and not one thing that does not do you honor: from the extinguishing of the great New York fire by your father, to the school-boy letters written from France by your younger brother. And so, you will let me say a word to you in all friendship with regard to your letter to the *Pilot*.

I recognize fully the frightful effects of the institution of slavery. I know what it has brought upon the white race—the frightful immorality, the deadening of the moral sense, the perjury, the treachery, the rebellion, and at last the fratricidal war; the firesides it has left forever desolate, the battle-fields it stained with rich young blood, the Rachels weeping for their children, who will never be comforted until God shall wipe away all tears. I know that it transformed human beings into incarnate demons. I remember Libby Prison, and its infernal horrors. I have heard women, elegant, refined women, calling themselves Christian women, wish that they had the power to sink the whole North into the ocean. These are some of the effects of slavery upon our race. And I contend that they are worse than the sufferings it entailed upon yours. It killed your bodies; it destroyed our immortal souls! And can we wonder, you and I, that this deadly poison still continues to work in our veins! Alas! we too long clasped the serpent to our bosoms. We may not yet cease to feel its sting.

But to answer your letter more particularly. I shall say little of the political side of the question. If more is needed to be said upon this head than has been already said by the *Congregationalist*, it must be left to abler pens than mine. I would simply remind you, that every persecution of the black man at the North, every mob which has disgraced its cities, was headed by Roman Catholics. They sacked your houses, insulted your women, and did your men to death. They broke into the Colored Orphan Asylum, they kept you in hiding for your lives, until the city was put under martial law for your protection, and I have yet to learn that one of these wretches was placed under the discipline of his Church for his deeds of cruelty. But I wish to speak more particularly of the religious side of the question. You speak of our Protestant faith as "*cant*." Dear friend, was the religion of your parents and mine "cant?" When my father stood beside your mother in the land of Beulah, and gave her into the hands of the ministering angels, was their sweet converse,

were their prayers *"cant?"*   While I write these
words, my heart is stirred within me, as I know yours
will be when you read them.   Ah, beloved ones, fear
not.   Your God shall be our God; your Saviour our
Saviour; your Protestant Church ours.   God forbid
that your children should prostrate themselves at the
feet of the man who worships himself, and calls upon
the world to worship him as God; who has but now
stigmatized those of his own faith who deny him the
attributes of Omnipotence as "damned heretics;"
who, had he the power, would light again the fires of
the Inquisition and put to death the children of God's
saints.   My lot has been cast for nearly fifteen years
under the shadow of the Vatican, and I know how
deep and baneful is that shadow; that if slavery has
destroyed its thousands, Vaticanism has ruined, soul
and body, its tens of thousands.   I know that so cor-
rupt are the highest in clerical dignity in this city,
that decent women will not live as servants in the
houses where they visit, because they fear their outrageous insults.   I know that an ecclesiastic who has
stood for years on the steps of the papal throne,
neither knows nor cares how many children he has.
That their name is legion, he and everybody else here
knows.   I know that an American young girl who
was copying in the Vatican, had her rights disputed
by an Italian woman, who based her pretensions on
the simple fact that she was a cardinal's plaything.   I
know that a Roman artist of distinction was con-
demned to long years of poverty because his wife
would not break her marriage vow for one of these
same red-petticoated corrupters of society.   I know—

what do I not know—of the horrors of this Church, here in its center, in the abode of its head.

And do you dream of liberty in the embrace of this Church? Then I will tell you what that liberty is. When the Pope was king, I was myself dragged before the police to answer for the crime of having collected money to save orphan girls from starvation, or worse. Our house was again and again visited by the police, and your friend, Dr. Gould, summoned before it, because we had sometimes gathered together our own country-people in our own hired house to worship God after the religion of our fathers. I saw in Florence, a few years ago, a woman who had been imprisoned for three years here in the Inquisition, and then banished, because she had had the Bible in her house. Just after the Pope's return from Gaeta, Bibles were taken out of the house of our consul and publicly burned. (This consul is living in Rome now, and I have the story from his own lips). Yes, this Bible, which your mother and mine revered, whose precepts they followed, was burned, year after year, in Rome on the Piazza di San Carlo. Here, in the old days, the Pope's subjects were forced to show their communion-tickets once a year, or be imprisoned; and men and women took the communion over and over again, and sold their tickets to those who would not commune and yet were afraid of the priests; thus, as a Catholic lady said to me, they traded in what they believed to be the real flesh and blood of their Lord and Saviour. You say that "the Catholic Church is strong enough with the members of its communion to sweep from existence anything within its fold which seeks to mar the unity of its own brotherhood." But I tell you that it is so weak here in its stronghold that most of the young men of Italy, and at least three-quarters of the young men of Rome, are infidels to-day; and, as one of them said to me not two hours ago, " We are so because we have seen the corruption of the Roman Catholic Church." It held its followers here once by force ; it can do so no longer.

Is this the liberty you would impose upon your country and your race ? Remember, I am my father's child, and I can not tell you anything which I do not believe and know to be the solemn truth. I have never before exposed what I know of the errors and corruption of this Church, principally for the sake of the noble band of men and women who, refusing to acknowledge the late blasphemous dogmas forced upon the consciences of the Roman Catholic Church, are striving for reform within its communion. There are no men and women on earth whom I more truly respect than those "damned heretics," as Pius IX. styles them. Theirs shall be the martyrs' palm, as theirs is the martyrs' cross. But even for their sakes I can not keep silence when I see the frightful danger to which your race is exposed. For you, and this noble band alike, there is no choice. You must be the slaves of the Vatican, or its accursed. I adjure you by the names of those we hold dearest and best, do not enchain yourself; do not fetter your children with the gyves which dangle from the Vatican throne. You were born a freeman ; you may not put your feet into the stocks, your hands into the manacles which the Church of Rome. holds out to you. Here, it is true, you may kneel beside a prince at St. Peter's; you may kiss the toe of the hideous bronze image in its nave just before or after he shall have pressed his lips to its feet; your son may walk beside the child of a descendant of an Etruscan lucumo; and yet, both prince and black man—your child and the heir of Prince Massimo—will be alike the bondsmen of Antichrist himself, if you give in your allegiance to Pius IX. and the Jesuit directors of his so-called conscience.

And now do you ask me what you are to do? I am the younger, and I am a woman; but you will let me answer you as I think my father would have done. In the first place, you are to suffer for Christ's sake, as he suffered for yours. Do not forget that Abraham Lincoln and John Brown were white men, and that they suffered unto death for the black man. No race ever rose from degradation without being made perfect through suffering. Then hold fast your Protestant faith, with the liberty it gives you of a free Bible; of life eternal, independent of the fiat of a sinful man; of heaven without a purgatory; of a Saviour who wills no intercessor between you and him. If you have lost this faith, go and seek it again at your Saviour's feet, from your mother's God.

But this is not all. Consecrate your life to the regeneration of your race. In order to do this, you must look at things as they are. Your race is not at present the equal of ours. How many peers have you among men of your own color. Strange indeed it would be if the black man, after long generations of oppression and ignorance, could be the equal of the white man, with all his advantages. Admit this fact, and go to work to raise up a generation which shall be equal to yourself and your children in intelligence and culture. Do what we are doing here among the neglected children of the former subjects of the Pope; not one of whom among the many hundreds I examined during the first two years of my work (and many of them were from twelve to fifteen years of age) knew their right hand from their left; while not one of a large class to whom I had told in detail the story of the Babe of Bethlehem, knew of whom I had been speaking. (This is a specimen of the education which the Romish Church gives its children—where it dares). Take, then, the youth of your race, the little ones, free now, thank God, and educate them so that they can stand side by side with their white brethren. Do all that you can to benefit the land in which God has given to you and your children a birthright. Put yourself shoulder to shoulder with those white men who will not see our land the kingdom of the Vatican, or the hunting-ground of a so-called Southern aristocracy. If they deny you equal social rights with themselves, very well. Bear it; you are not to hope to accomplish everything you could wish. Something may, nay must, be left for another generation to do. But there is a great work to be done in our day. Let us do it, never forgetting the God of our fathers. So shall he fight for us and give us the victory.

Your affectionate friend,

EMILY B. GOULD.

XIII.

SHE RESTS FROM HER LABORS.

Perugia—Rome—Perugia again—Sickness and Death—Grief of the Children—Little Beppino follows his "Dear Lady."

THE scene of the saddest chapter of our story is in that beautiful town of the Umbrian hills, Perugia, a favorite resort of Mrs. Gould during all the period of her residence at Rome. With its history, ancient and modern, its monuments of antiquity, its objects of art, its natural beauties, its quiet little industries, its social and domestic life both among the high and among the lowly, it occupies a larger space in the volumes of her journal than any other place except Rome and Florence. When, in May, that restless right hand of hers was compelled at last to rest in the midst of her unfinished work, and the warning of physicians equired her to flee to the mountains for her life, it was naturally enough that she found her way at once to the congenial home of a gentle Italian family with whom she had been

(233)

wont to spend part of the early summer *in villeggiatura.*
The hope of her recovery lay in her long and uninterrupted rest, and relief from care.   But the question that
she put so tenderly to the Sunday-school children of
America, "Who will take care of my poor children?"
kept pressing upon her mind, and after a fortnight's refreshment among cherished friends and scenes at Perugia,
she hurried back to Rome, arriving on the 29th of May.
Three days afterward, June 1st, she was seized with the
mortal illness from which she was never more to rally.

A letter of one of the friends who tenderly watched her
through the three months of this sickness, gives us the full
history of it.

It commenced with such fearful pain that it was
feared her delicate frame could not bear up against it.
The days wore on and brought her no relief.   A distinguished Italian physician, now a member of the
Italian Parliament, who had been Garibaldi's chief
medical officer in all his campaigns in Italy, took a
profound interest in the invalid who had sacrificed
herself for the good of Italian children, and visited
her almost daily as long as he remained at Rome.
When the regular medical adviser of his family had
left the city, Dr. Gould called in Dr. Bacelli, a man
whose reputation now extends throughout Europe,
to take charge of the case.   His attendance lasted
up to the period when at his express desire the
patient was removed to Perugia.

Although it was so late in the summer—a time
when the exodus of foreign visitors and residents from

the Eternal City is usually complete—by a providential exception, as Mrs. Gould herself remarked again and again, there were this year some of her personal friends who had remained in Rome in defiance of the heat. Some half dozen in all watched, with her nurses, night and day, alternating their services and doing all in their power to alleviate the pangs and support the strength of the dear sufferer. Each of these will bear loving testimony to the sweetness and patience with which the great agony was borne —how, while it wrung from her lips uncontrollable cries of appeal to God for mercy and relief, it never led her into forgetfulness of the sympathetic suffering of those who were with her. How often she prayed that she might lose the power of making those cries aloud, and begged her husband to press his hand upon her mouth and prevent her voice from being heard! She was constantly expressing her fears lest the health of those at her bedside might suffer, imploring them to take rest and food, and wine; to pardon her the pain she must cause them. "God grant that if I am to die, I may not last long enough to wear you all out;" "Nothing can ever repay your kindness to me;" "Pray, that I may not make you all suffer so!"—such were the expressions that all who were with her will remember. More than once when she was beseeching her Heavenly Father that he would send Death to relieve her, her husband asked her if she could realize what life would be to him without her, and if in that case she could ask to be taken from him? whether she would consent, were he in her state of suffering, that he should pray to be taken away and leave her desolate? "Yes," she said, "were you suffering the agony I am in I would wish you to go, to have you released from it."

Mrs. Gould was removed from Rome in a condition of such acute agony that we scarcely thought she could reach Perugia alive. The journey is described by Dr. Gould to have been a fearful one. At Perugia she was received into the house of some dear old friends, an Italian family, with whom she had been in the habit of passing weeks at a time, *en pension*, in past years. She had every care and comfort here that the heart could desire. Some of her intimate friends were passing the summer months in this, the coolest spot among the Umbrian hills. The air of Perugia had always proved most beneficial to her. We could not but believe in Dr. Bacelli's encouraging words, when he left her bedside in Rome. "Take courage, Doctor," he said, "your wife's illness is one that will be long and painful, but is not dangerous. Remember my words." Who would not have been buoyed up by such a sentence from a medical man of such eminence?

We could not venture to interrupt this sacred and solemn story for a less reason than to introduce here some of the English letters of her children, addressed to her during this summer, that were a solace of the dying woman in the midst of her agonies. We give them in the order of their dates. They are written, some on scraps of paper that might have been torn from the leaf of a copy-book, and some on dainty little colored and decorated sheets such as children like.

ROME, *June* 12, 1875.

MY DEAR DIRECTRESS : — I'm very sorry because you are ill, I will be very glad if you come yet with we. Il Signor Garnieri pray for you, also we first of the dinner we will do one little pray. Good by take sixteen kiss of your boy. No more Naughty but Good.

———— ————.

MY DEAR MOTHER MRS. GOULD :—I am very glad that you are a little better, and I am certain that God heard our supplications in Mr. Garnieri's church, and Mr. Ribetti said the prayer about 11 o'clock.

The Lord's my light and saving health, who shall make me dismay'd ? My life's strength is the Lord, of whom then shall I be afraid ? (Psalms xxvii. v. 1°.) The Lord's my Shepherd, I'll not want, he makes me down to lie in pastures green ; he leadeth me the quite waters by. (Psalms xxiii. v. 1.) My dear mother, never forget these two verses ; and I hope you will be better every day, and receive my respect and thankfulness's sentiments from your

Affnated Son,

ROME, 21 *June*, 1875.

———— ————.

July 24th, 1875.

DEAR MADAM :—I am very sorry that you are ill so long. I should like to be able to help you but I am only a little girl and can do nothing else but to be good and pray for you—and this I never forget dear Madam.

I kiss your hands.

———— ————.

IN MORNING, 12 *August*, 1875.

MY DEAR MRS. GOULD :—I am very sorry that you are ill and fear I have made you so by being naughty. Now I will try to be good and not make you sorry any more.

I pray that Jesus may make me good so that when you come back you will see a change in me such as will make you glad.

I have asked him to make you well but fear he has not heard, because I was naughty. I wish you good health and happy days. I am

Your scholar

———— ————.

DEAR MOTHER—MRS. GOULD :—I cannot choose words for to explain to you my gladness when I heard from Miss Marietta that you was a little better. Oh! may you continue so, until you will be able to come with us once more before we die.

Dear Mother, I hope that God who is the Doctor of doctors, and the King of kings will make you better, and enable you to come to give us English lessons. I believe that it is His will you should come again with us.

Receive the respects of your
Affectionate Son

ROME, 24 *August*, 1875.   ———— ————.

ROME, 25 *August*, 1875.

MY DEAR BENEFACTOR :—I am very glad that you are better, and I hope that you will soon come to Rome, with us, and speak us in English about many things. Every day we remember you, and I think that our God have heard our supplications. Good by my dear dear mother and I am

Your son,

———— ————.

We resume the narrative of the dying woman's friend.

The change of air from Rome to Perugia made no improvement. Her sufferings were to endure just so long as her already well-nigh exhausted frame could hold out. During the last ten days, the crises of pain became less acute, and there were longer and longer intervals of comparative rest. This, which naturally gave us gleams of hope, was really the sign of the approaching end. Her mind was perfectly clear; she dictated letters, chiefly having reference to her schools; she begged to have letters from all "her children;" she was as full of bright, eager interest about her friends as ever, when almost suddenly came the great change.

For the last twenty-four hours of her existence she sank into a lethargy and breathed her last, to all appearance painlessly, in the arms of her husband, with dear friends around her, on the night of the 31st August, just three months from the date of her first seizure. Some of us can remember her saying during the first days of her illness, when some allusion was made as to her being soon better: "You will see," she said, "that this will be a three months' illness." Often she spoke of the impossibility of her ever really recovering from the shock of such an illness, and she said towards the end, to her husband, " Dear, it would be so much better, if you could only think so, for me to die than to linger on a burden on your hands, a poor nervous invalid perhaps for years to come." Who can doubt that knew them, what was his loving reply to such words as these?

That true friend and work-fellow, the Rev. Somerset Burtchaell, hastened to Perugia from Spoleto, when he heard that the death of his friend was impending, and arrived in time to minister in the funeral services that were held in the room in which she died. Some twenty friends and fellow-countrymen of the departed Christian were in Perugia, all of whom were present, "and few could keep back their tears in looking for the last time on that slight form and on that dear face with its sad, sweet smile in the awful composure of eternal rest."

When the letter arrived at the Home which told that all hope of Mrs. Gould's recovery must be given up, and asking the prayers of all connected with the Home in behalf of the dear sufferer, the children melted into tears, and with a spontaneous impulse knelt down to offer up their prayers. The lady in charge of the children describes the scene :

It was about three o'clock in the afternoon, and the children of the day-schools were present, and knelt with the others. Professor Rebecchini, who was about to give his daily lesson to the upper classes, knelt also, and the new teacher of the day-schools, Signora Angelini, prayed aloud that God might yet in his great mercy spare their benefactress. The young Scotch printer made an earnest prayer aloud in English, beseeching that the Lord would relieve her great suffering in the way he thought fit. The children then made each one his own mental prayer.

Shortly after this, on the same afternoon, a young teacher heard the sad news of her death. Coming back to the Home, she was met on the staircase by the two eldest girls, Lucia and Clelia, and overwhelmed them with the tidings of their great loss. The news spread at once through the Home. The two girls went each into her own room, and wept inconsolably through the evening. The two youngest children, Mariangiola and the little Venetian, Beppino, were told by the teacher, who, putting her arms around them, said: "Do you know, my poor little ones, that you have lost the Signora, your dear mother?" and the little Beppino said, "Yes, but then she has gone to heaven," and clung sobbing to the teacher. Poor little fellow, after apparently entirely recovering the previous effects of misery and starvation, his present state of health is such as to render it more than probable that he will soon follow his dear benefactress to heaven.

For three or four days her name was constantly on the lips of all. The girls were, on the whole, the most affected by their loss. They could not eat at meals, especially the elder ones. One of the boys had a dream, which he related with great fervor to the teacher, of how he saw the dear Signora all in white, lying upon what seemed like a long white chair, in a white coffin filled with flowers of the sweetest perfume, and "looking so beautiful, so beautiful." The eldest and best among the boys, when he was told that the "Signora" was no more, could only repeat with a sob: "E morta!" and burst into uncontrollable tears. The mention of her name to any of them brings instant tears to their eyes; they are all more generally subdued, and with rare exceptions, are at all times better behaved than before.

Poor little Beppino! He had not the heart to stay, when the *cara Signora* who had rescued him from misery and starvation had gone. A spinal tumor, necessitating a formidable surgical operation, had declared itself, and through the kind offices of a friend, a bed was secured for him in the children's hospital of Rome. The fruit of the

11

tender care that had been bestowed on him was thankfully recognized in the patience and childlike trust with which he lay month after month on his hospital bed, waiting to die. All to himself, in his feeble voice, he would lie crooning the hymns he had been taught by the *cara Signora.* Sometimes he would utter happy words about the Home —"our own house, the home of those who have been so kind to me always." Then he would speak reverently of the Saviour who loves little children and died for sinners, generally winding up with—"When I die, Jesus will take me to live with him in heaven, and then I shall see our dear Signora again." As he lay a-dying, he was urged with kindly-intended importunity, to say a strange prayer, of form and import unlike any he had heard. He answered: "I pray to Jesus. He loves me and I love him. I will go to Jesus and to my dear mother, Mrs. Gould." So they kindly left him saying to himself, "I love him, I love him!" And when they came back they found a look of deep repose on his worn little face. He had died in his sleep.

XIV.

HER MEMORY IS BLESSED.

" By Strangers Honored " — Expressions of the Italian Press—"A Wreath of Stray Leaves "— Words of Mr. Adolphus Trollope and of Mrs. Mary Howitt — Honor to her Memory from those of her Own Country—Memorial Service in New York — Address of Dr. William Adams—The Grave at Woodlawn.

T HE death, "in the midst of life," of one so endowed with gifts of nature and of Divine grace, so loving and so beloved, drew forth expressions of respect, admiration, and grief from far beyond the circle of her personal friends and beneficiaries.

The Roman newspapers, including those that had rarely any word to say in behalf of anything Christian, and excepting only the organs of the hierarchy, spoke of the departed friend of little children in such terms of love and gratitude as it is a pleasure to transcribe. The following example is from an editorial in the *Gazzetta d' Italia :*

We think it no exaggeration to say that the death of Mrs. Gould, the founder and directress of the

Italo-American schools, was felt with pain by all that knew her. Having no children of her own, she occupied herself the more earnestly, in Rome, with her schools. In a short time she established two—one in the Via dei Marroniti, the other in the Via del Governo Vecchio. There were frequently in attendance on them from 120 to 150 day-scholars of both sexes, besides forty others who lived in an asylum which she had established. Withal she had provided a kindergarten for the training of very little children, according to the system of Frœbel. . . . . Latterly she had brought to Rome a printer, with all the materials of his business, and the older scholars were instructed in this trade. All this, be it understood, including the asylum, was gratuitous. The cost of it has been great. In 1873 it amounted to 51,000 lire. This sum came from Mrs. Gould's private means, supplemented by contributions which no American coming to Rome refused, and by various expedients suggested by her own mind, which was ever active to promote the success of the schools.

The Catholic journals accused Mrs. Gould of making her schools a Protestant Propaganda. But the charge was groundless. At her school examinations and at her evening receptions, which were frequented by the best society, we have seen Catholic ladies of the highest orthodoxy. . . . .

During the last winter Mrs. Gould was accustomed to receive at her elegant apartments on the Piazza di Spagna a numerous company; but there were no idlers among them. Both ladies and gentlemen were expected to do some little work, the proceeds of which should go to the support of the schools.

Mrs. Gould, whose physical strength was not proportionate to an energy and force of will characteristically American, has died a martyr to her zeal.

" *Fanfulla* " spoke of her departure in terms the tone of which may be judged from these few sentences:

Our readers will remember that more than once we have had occasion to speak of Mrs. Gould, directress of the Italo-American schools, that have been so much frequented and have accomplished so much for the education of our people. We have now the sorrow of announcing the death of this distinguished lady, which took place in Perugia yesterday morning. She has fallen a victim to her own zeal. Of delicate constitution, but gifted with amazing energy, she had attempted more than her strength would consent to. . . . .

We seem to see her still, full of grace and of care for others, in the midst of her children at the examination and giving of rewards, coming forward with a courteous word of thanks to us for our constant encouragement of her work. Poor, dear woman! by what a multitude will her death be mourned!

A briefer notice in *Il Diritto* evinced a feeling no less tender and sincere:

The name of this American lady has for years been dear and blessed at Rome. She was the founder of the Italo-American schools, a good angel who gave bread and instruction to thousands of the children of the poor—an astonishing example of generosity, constancy, love, and self-denial. What courage in that modest heart! What greatness of soul in that woman who consecrated her fortune and sacrificed her health to become the mother, the teacher, the protector of a whole phalanx of little children. We seem still to see her in the humble dress of a maid-servant seated in the midst of her little ones, covering them with kisses and delighting herself in the smile of grateful recognition on those innocent lips. We know not whether any noble heart will be found to take up the work which Mrs. Gould bequeaths, and continue these schools of hers which have been an apostolate of civilization and humanity. Assuredly her name will not be forgotten; and in proportion to the blessing which flowed from her life to others, will be the bitterness of the lasting grief felt for her departure in all gentle hearts.

The Roman newspaper in the French language, *L'Italie,* spoke in a like strain; and the Italian journal in far-away San Francisco, *La Voce del Popolo,* received the news from its Roman correspondent in this form:

Rome has lost one of her noblest benefactors. Mrs. Gould, founder and directress of the Italo-American schools, is no more. Her death is a heavy misfortune to the poor children of Rome. . . . .
Good and generous Mrs. Gould! Having no children of her own, she became a loving mother to the children of others. She was the goddess of charity

personated. Her heart was an inexhaustible fountain of affection. She left not behind her one, two, or three orphans, but over two hundred. If these poor little ones could understand their loss they would water with tears the grave of their benefactress. How much better humanity would advance in the paths of virtue, honesty, knowledge, if women who now spend their time in the vain luxury of courts would imitate Mrs. Gould.

O generous daughter of a free land, thou wert an angel of consolation to the poor, living far above the vanities of this world! Well hast thou understood and fulfilled the holy mission of woman! Thy name shall be cherished by Romans with deepest veneration.

These utterances of the Italian press were no exaggerated expression of the feeling of all humane and patriotic Italians that knew her good deeds, so far as this feeling was not restrained or perverted by religious bigotry. Her eminent friend, Signora Fua Fusinato, Inspector of the Roman Schools, had purposed that the bust of Emily Gould should be placed among those of public benefactors in one of the buildings devoted to national education; and was already seeking materials for a eulogy to be uttered at the unveiling of it, when her own lamented death defeated or at least postponed the plan. The beautiful and beloved Princess Margaret, now Queen of Italy, had showed a marked interest in her and in her work. Successive Ministers of Public Instruction had repeatedly expressed their approval of her labors, and taken counsel of her regarding the management of the common schools— had aided her, withal, by substantial personal gifts to the treasury; and they testified how much they had learned from Mrs. Gould and her American methods of organization and teaching. It would not even be difficult to give the names of Roman ecclesiastics who had taken an earnest and intelligent interest in her work, and on whose minds the sight of her example of unselfish, loving beneficence, too strong for the fierce narrowness of their system, had wrought a conviction, like that of the centurion at the cross, that "surely this was a righteous woman."

Among the various expedients devised in aid of the schools had been a volume of miscellaneous pieces, the free contribution of distinguished authors, to be issued from the school press. It is interesting, as an illustration of what sort of minds the genial ardor of Mrs. Gould's beneficence drew into the current of its purposes, to note some of the names of her helpers in this volume. The list includes the names of George P. Marsh, William W. Story, Matthew Arnold, Lord Houghton, T. A. Trollope, William and Mary Howitt, Mr. and Mrs. Cowden Clarke, and others of like reputation. This "Wreath of Stray Leaves" (as they entitled it) was laid as a chaplet on her grave. Mr. Trollope thus dedicated the volume to her memory:

This is not the place for any attempt to give an account of the good work undertaken and done by

Mrs. Gould, or of the truly rare spirit of entire self-devotion with which it was carried out. All those (and they were many) who witnessed her life in Rome, can testify that the above expression is as simply unexaggerated a statement as if it were the enunciation of a mathematical fact. She gave her life to the work! So little did she ever look back from the plow to which she had set her hand, that even amid the paroxysms of pain which it was her lot to suffer during many long weeks, her mind was constantly reverting to the arrangements to be made for the bringing out of this volume.

And now it is brought out—posthumously! And we, all of us, the contributors to its pages, though we may still hope that the publication may, by the help of the public, be of some avail toward giving the aid so urgently needed to the funds for the support of the school, shall never have the pleasure we had promised ourselves in seeing her pleasure for whose sake each did his best.

Our plans were laid, our suggestions were made so merrily, so laughingly! All sorts of jesting titles for our projected volume were proposed; and one, conceived in merry mood, by her who will never jest more, was by acclamation voted the best. We have none of us the heart to put any such words on our title-page now. We did each his part as a testimonial of affection and admiration for one who lived only for others. Let it stand now as a memorial and tribute to her memory.

In writing a Preface to the volume, her unfailing friend
11*

and the friend of all good works, Mary Howitt, added these affectionate words :

She is gone, like the true and noble of all times, from works to rewards. But is the work which she began, to perish? Surely not. . . . . Let the motherless and homeless children whom she gathered into a home of labor and love, become your children now that she is gone ; so that they, if not others also, may become a living, noble, lasting monument, enduring through them to countless generations, to the memory of her who did all that she could, and perished in the doing of it.

In letters to the New York *Observer* and *Evening Post*, Mrs. Howitt spoke again of her American friend :

She, alas ! who gladdened and enlightened so many minds in America, and who devoted herself to the instruction and enlightenment of the Roman child, is no more. . . . . But she had accomplished much. She had proved how receptive of a pure and Christian teaching was the youthful mind of old Papal Rome, and had laid the foundations of an industrial school and home for orphan or friendless children. She, an American, with the large, free views and warm philanthropy of her country, made America from the first a participator in all her work. Italy—long-fettered, down-trodden Italy—found, as she lifted herself from the dust, young free America by her side, to support her and lead her onward into life and liberty—that glorious liberty which comes from the pure teaching of the Gospel of Christ. Mrs. Gould did not arrogate to herself the honor of this good work, though she was one of the very first who entered the field. She regarded herself but as the handmaid of America, and whatever she undertook and accomplished belonged to her country. Her schools and her Industrial Home were Italo-American, and her country gratefully and graciously acknowledged the offering of her philanthropy and patriotism. Her best and most efficient friends were Americans. With a liberal hand they supplied the necessary funds, and cheered her onward by their cordial approval. . . . .

Wonderful was the sweet, tender influence which she had over children. Love was innate to her, and also that wisdom, so sublime in its simplicity, which is the special gift of God to the true mother, and which, to my mind, must have been so pre-eminent in the mind of the Holy Mary, the mother of our Lord—that of leading the child, by the uprightness of a pure, loving spirit, to the very being of the Divine Father. Often have I sat in her schools and found myself looking on with admiring delight to see revealed in her the true power of the divinely-taught mother—the loveliest of teachers—to hear her telling of the Saviour, of his love to the little children, of the Good Shepherd and his lambs—her face beaming with an ineffable tenderness and devotion which is beyond all beauty except that of the angels. . . . . The Home of orphan industry, the institution to which her womanly heart gave its tenderest and most untiring energies, is now motherless. Is there no warm-hearted, child-loving, childless woman in America ready and willing to step into her place? Is there no woman there filled with the wisdom and energy of a strong Christian love, who has not yet found her true place in life, yet prays God daily to open it before her? How beautiful, how self-forgetting, how full of the heroism of the purest love is the character of many a woman drawn to the life by Mrs. Whitney and many another female American writer. My heart has burned within me, as did the hearts of the disciples in company with the risen Lord on the way to Emmaus, as I have read of these loving, devoted women — women who have been wounded in the battle of life, or whose large capacity for active service in goodness and love has found ordinary life too narrow, and who, living out of themselves, have lived in others. I am persuaded that in America there are many such. It is not all fiction which is written in books. There are, I believe, hundreds of women in free, unconventional America, who are capable of doing what our dear dead friend has done. Here, then, is scope enough for the exercise of the noblest gifts of their womanhood. Here are children to be loved and trained; here is an opening for the expenditure of wealth which will cause no regret, no deathbed pang, but which will yield an untold interest in that great day when the Master Householder reckons with his stewards.

MARY HOWITT.

In like terms others of her English friends and helpers uttered the common feeling of love, admiration, and bereavement. But for the danger of extending this chapter too far, we should love to quote the words of the Rev. Mr. Burtchaell, of Madame Jessie White Mario, and of that dear Catholic friend and fellow-laborer, Mrs. Geraldine Macpherson, who followed her so soon to her heavenly reward and rest.

Mrs. Gould's own countrymen, who had expressed their confidence and love in their constant support of her work, were no less ready with their words of eulogy when the time had come that they might be uttered without offense to herself. A published letter from Mr. Pierce, the biographer of Sumner, declares: "Her place is among the noble women of our time. Amid scenes of refined enjoyment she consecrated herself to the service of mankind." And then, having recounted the exquisite delight of visiting the Alban Hills in company with Mrs. Gould and some of the choicest of her friends, he adds: "Scenery and historic associations like these are indeed attractive to the imagination, but better far is communion with one who toiled for a people rising into freedom, and who by her unselfish devotion has lifted higher the ideals of her sex." One of the most full, clear, and just appreciations of her character and work was from the pen of one who had peculiar opportunities for knowing them both, and who wrote as follows to an American journal:

She was never a strong woman, although her tenacity of purpose and her nervous energy accomplished what many a more robust person would have shrunk from. But she expended her very self in her chosen work. When a teacher failed, she went to teach;

when a child was ill, she nursed it, and, if need were, shared her own chamber with it; she braved all weathers; fought against her own weakness and ailments, and infused a vitality into all parts of an enterprise which often seemed too great and too diversified for a single person to direct and urge on.   And all this time she had not neglected her social and private duties.   Every Sunday evening there was the same assembly of strangers and residents in her room.   One needed no formal introduction; it was enough to say: "I am an American; I have heard of you, and I want you to let me share your Sunday evening sing," and her welcome was as warm and her smile as sunny as one could wish.   And many a time as I have sat behind the piano-forte I have seen eighty or a hundred Americans singing the tunes and hymns which they had learned at school, or had been wont to sing in their own family circles in their distant homes. . . . . Those who knew her thoroughly, who had tested her friendship, and found how true she was to her principles and her affections, will recognize more and more that, exceptional as were the vivacity and brilliancy of her lighter moments; no less rare were her graver qualities and her determination never to relax in her work while strength and life were left her.

In a long review of Mrs. Gould's career, Miss Elizabeth H. Denio, an active helper in the last months of her work, speaks of one incident of it to which neither Mrs. Gould nor her husband makes any allusion, but which more than one of their intimate friends record after her death.

When the "Home" was opened there was a large sum of money in the treasury, and Mrs. Gould felt authorized to enlarge the work. Later came the panic in America and hard times; contributions fell off, while expenses increased. Both Dr. and Mrs. Gould began to retrench at home, and to draw from their own income to keep up the work. One servant was dismissed, the carriage was given up, and Mrs. Gould, accustomed from childhood to have every wish gratified, began to deny herself luxuries, and even necessary comforts.

Under the title, "A Brave Woman's Memorial," Dr. Theo·dore Cuyler has given some reminiscences of his own in an article in the New York *Evangelist.*

One morning, after a pleasant hour on the Pincian, I went with my traveling companion, the Rev. Newman Hall, to call upon the late Mrs. Emily Gould. Her husband, Dr. Gould, was then residing in the heart of that portion of Rome most occupied by Americans. We climbed the stairway of a house which had more of the modern air than can often be found in the city of the Cæsars, and were shown to Mrs. Gould's apartment. She was too feeble to sit up that day; but the thin pale countenance was all aglow with intellect and enthusiasm. She received us with great cordiality, and began to talk at once about that love-labor for poor Italian children, which was burning in her brain, and consuming her very life.

Mrs. Gould told us the story of her brave struggles

to educate the bright-eyed children of Rome. With that romantic story—and how she had established her day-school, and handed it over to the Waldensian pastors, and how she was then starting an "Industrial Home" for the Christian training of orphans and other destitute children—with all this beautiful story the Christian people of America are somewhat familiar. My friend, Newman Hall, was intensely interested in her narrative of the work. "This is one of the most remarkable women I have ever met," he said to me as we left the door-way. "You Americans may be proud of such a representative here in Papal Rome."

Two years more of untiring toil wore out that frail and delicate frame, which we saw that morning propped up by the pillows. During the midsummer of 1875, Mrs. Gould fell asleep in Jesus: and great lamentation was made for her among the little brown-faced Italians of the "Home," and the Waldensian day-schools. She had been so long the moving spirit of this Italo-American effort to bring new ideas into old Rome, that it was feared lest the movement might be buried in her tomb. But God is the most faithful of trustees, and he never forsakes the enterprises of love which are committed to his care.

Our American Christians, amid their thousand calls at home, are not willing to have that promising plant die out under the very eaves of the Vatican. We have not many distinctively American enterprises in ancient Europe; this one in the most venerable of European capitals stands by itself. Its failure now would be a national reproach, as well as an extinguishment of one of the lamps of Evangelical influence lately lighted in the city where Paul once taught Jesus to Cæsar's household.

We have been set upon this train of reminiscence to-day by reading the last statement made in behalf of this "Gould Memorial."

American womanhood sometimes wins admiration abroad by physical charms, often by elegance of costume and adornments. But plain Harriet Newell, teaching Christ to the Hindoos, and frail, refined Emily Gould, gathering in poor orphans from the streets of Papal Rome, and the band of female missionaries who have gone out from "Mount Holyoke," are the best representatives of womanly beauty. No diamond necklace exhibited at the Centennial flashes with such lustre as this one which the Master wove for his faithful handmaids out of these words: "She hath done what she could."

More than a year after the death of Mrs. Gould at Perugia, there was gathered a great assembly of her friends and of the friends of her father and mother, for a Memorial Service, in the Fourth Avenue Presbyterian Church, in New York, of which Chancellor Howard Crosby is pastor. The church was without decoration except that a wreath of white flowers lay on the communion-table.

Besides such services of prayer and thanksgiving as are becoming at the commemoration of a saint sleeping in the Lord, there were addresses by Dr. Crosby, by Dr. Hutton, by Dr. Charles S. Robinson, and by Dr. William Adams. It is natural that many words should have been uttered of the father and mother of the deceased—the "beloved physician," and the "honorable woman," whose "toils and cares were given" to holy works in the earlier days of New York—by the venerable pastors who remembered them as work-fellows. But their thoughts reached rather toward the future than toward the past. The tone of thankfulness and hope was well expressed in these sentences from the address of Dr. Adams:

We have here a new lesson concerning true greatness. What the common notion of greatness is has been expressed in the words of our Lord, and this in contrast with that greatness which is to be attained by His disciples: "The princes of the Gentiles exercise dominion over them, and they that are great exercise authority upon them. But it shall not be so among you; but whosoever will be great among you, let him be your minister; and whosoever will be chief among you, let him be your servant."

There is no place on earth that is distinguished by so many monuments and memorials of what the world has called great, as the city of Rome. Arches, columns, statues, obelisks, pillars, mausoleums, surviving the ravages of time, perpetuate, on every hand, the names of the mighty dead. We commemorate this day another kind of greatness, which will live here on earth when bronze and marble shall have crumbled to dust, and shine afterward "above the brightness of the firmament, and as the stars forever and ever."

When the Italian army under Victor Emmanuel— how many associations do such names suggest?—entered through the Porta Pia, that "Eternal City" so

identified with art and history, there went in also the
gentle and modest form of a Christian woman, intent
on doing good in the name of Jesus Christ. With
no political ambition, with no thought of self-aggran-
dizement, her single purpose was, in the spirit of her
Master, to feed his lambs. The work which she had
begun so prosperously on the Arno, she now begins
on the Tiber. When freedom was given, and "a great
door and an effectual was opened," many hearts, on
both sides of the sea, rejoiced because of the good
things that were done "in Rome also." The work
which she projected was fundamental. She gathered
about her little children and instructed them in the
name of Jesus of Nazareth. Others in due time
might heave the arches and carve the friezes and dec-
orate the capitals. Hers was it, with unapplauded
toil, to lay the foundations of a great improvement.
It was an undertaking which called for self-sacrifice
and toil, and patient endurance. These were not with-
held. Herein did she exhibit that form of *greatness*
extolled by our divine Lord—ministering to others
at an expense to ourselves. Better and greater is
it that Christ should say of one such disciple, "She
hath done what she could; wheresoever the Gospel
shall be preached in the whole world, there shall also
this that this woman hath done be told for a memorial of her"—than any inscription ever engraved
on imperial pillar or tablet. When the tombs of
Hadrian and Cecilia Metella, the Column of Trajan
and the Arch of Titus, and all other monuments of
worldly greatness at Rome, shall have perished from
the sight of men, the good that was done to the

minds of groups of children, molding their character and shaping their destiny, will brighten more and more, for it concerns souls for which Christ died and which are in their nature immortal. We wonder not that sobs were heard in the schools and orphanages at Florence and Rome, that day when it was announced that their Founder and Benefactress was dead. But the greatness of her work will be revealed hereafter, when glorified spirits shall recognize her earthly labors as the chosen means of mercy to themselves, and are permitted, in the presence of their divine Redeemer, to hail her with secondary gratitude and the mention of a human love.

> " They mourn the dead who live as they require."

Thus happily has a poet expressed the sentiment that the best token and proof of our regard for the dead is a disposition to meet their wishes, to take the work from their hands and carry it on to completion. From the success of what has been done already, we borrow motives which incite to greater endeavors for time to come. Why may not that which was begun in feebleness be continued and extended in strength? We long for the time to come when the whole of Italy, from Sicily to the Alps—that beautiful land of the vine and the olive; that land of history and of the arts—shall see all her children, so bright and expert in native qualities, gathered about the living Christ, to be taught and blessed by him in whose days the righteous shall flourish, and abundance of peace so long as the moon endureth. The kings of the earth will die, but IMMANUEL, our incarnate Redeemer, shall reign throughout all generations. Concerning incipient measures, looking to the extension of this kingdom, we may say both of their beginning and their result, in the language of the Psalm: " There shall be a *handful* of corn in the earth upon the top of the mountains: the *fruit* thereof shall shake like Lebanon, and they of the city shall flourish like grass of the earth. His name shall endure forever: His name shall be continued as long as the sun, and all nations shall call Him blessed."

Thus, with good men making lamentation for her departure, and thanking God at every remembrance of her, the body of Emily Bliss Gould was laid to rest in Woodlawn Cemetery.

During the last visit of Doctor Gould to America, before her death, Mrs. Gould, already pressed by many premonitions of her approaching departure, had sent to him a commission, surrounded with many words of affection too sacred to be transcribed, in which she " gave commandment concerning her bones."

I do not feel about it as I once did, when I clung almost with agony to the thought of bringing our father to rest where I should be. As I go on in life, I feel as if the body. precious as it is, were only the garment which we love because they wore it once, while they in richer array have forgotten it, and are often much nearer to us than their graves are, even when these are but little removed from our roof-tree. But you could give me nothing I should prize so greatly as a plot in which to lay the bodies of my parents, and a simple stone to bear their names and a few words of the promises they so loved. If I were to choose, I would have a plain shaft of the form least likely to be affected by the weather. On the one side I would put:

Sacred to the Memory of

JAMES C. BLISS,

"the beloved physician,"

WHO DIED JULY 31st, 1855.

"Strong in faith, giving glory to God."

"And the end, everlasting life."

You know he would not have liked us to put such words of praise as he deserved.

On the opposite side I would put:

Sacred to the Memory of

MARIA A. MUMFORD,

wife of James C. Bliss,

WHO DIED MARCH 1st, 1831.

"O woman, great is thy faith."

On one of the remaining sides:

EMILY, JAMES, AUGUSTUS, MARY,

infant children of

JAMES C. AND MARIA A. BLISS.

"He shall gather the lambs with his arm and carry them in his bosom."

Opposite this:

"Eye hath not seen, nor ear heard, neither have entered into the heart of man, the things which God hath prepared for them that love Him."

"Their works do follow them."

In the spot thus consecrated by her filial piety, she lies at rest, and with the names that were so dear to her is inscribed her own name, with the words:

SHE HATH DONE WHAT SHE COULD.

XV.

1876—1879.

HER WORK GOES ON.

THE death of Mrs. Gould, occurring in the midst of the season when all the customary supporters of her schools were scattered from Rome, left her enterprise almost helpless. After many months' delay, and not a little hesitation and anxiety, a Committee was organized which took the bereaved and orphaned institutions under its charge. In this long interval, the efficiency of the institutions had become impaired, the funds were exhausted, and a debt of nearly 4,000 francs had accumulated. The Committee took the difficult task in hand with energy and tact worthy of their predecessor, and at

(264)

the end of twelve months had paid the debt, increased the number of children in the Home from fourteen to twenty-two, and had a balance in the bank to their credit, nearly as large as the debt with which they began.

The receipts that made all this possible, came from various, sometimes unexpected sources. But, " the chief support was due to the untiring exertions of Dr. Gould." Speaking of him, the Committee say :

But for his efforts it would have been necessary to close the Home last summer. In the month of July, when Rome was almost deserted by foreigners, the few members of the Committee remaining in the city, felt it was a grave responsibility to retain the charge of sixteen children, when but five francs remained in the treasury ; and they had a meeting called to consider seriously the duty of breaking up the Institution rather than incur the risk of getting into debt. Signor Prochet, the President of the Waldensian Mission Board, who was present at that meeting, urged the exercise of the patience of faith so long as there was property to represent the liabilities ; he felt assured that God would provide for these 'children, some of whom, but for the Home would be utterly destitute. In a few days a considerable sum arrived from Dr. Gould, and after this experience the Committee in all subsequent difficulties have been sustained by trust in the goodness and faithfulness of our Heavenly Father to overcome all difficulties in the way of this work of charity.

A temporary arrangement was made, very advantageous, for the time, to all parties, by which the Waldensian day-schools occupied the school-rooms of the Home; and ultimately the "Italo-American Schools" were amalgamated with those of the Waldensian Board, the Home and Schools being carried on in the house Mrs. Gould held on lease. But it was found difficult to observe the proper

12

discipline of the Home and day-schools together, whilst it was equally impossible to extend the industries beyond that of the printing-press, for want of room; so that, when the lease of the house expired, it was thought a fitting opportunity to separate the Home from the day-schools, and thus carry out more efficiently the work as an Industrial Institution, apart from any particular branch of the Christian Church.

Now that the institution had begun to depend, not on a single mind and voice and pen, but on the coöperation of an organized Board, a new difficulty appeared, the seriousness of which will not be fully appreciated except by those who have known the fluctuations of the colonies of English-speaking sojourners in European continental towns. Again and again, within the course of a few months, this cherished work, the fruit of such heroic sacrifice and such trustful prayer, seemed to be at the point of extinction. Before the perils of a Roman summer, its friends were driven in various directions, and grave emergencies would arise, demanding wisdom, courage, and pecuniary resources, when there were few or none to counsel or help, and when these few would be doubtful of the return of those on whom they had been wont to rely. Rarely has any "labor of love" been more emphatically a "work of faith."

Such an extreme emergency occurred during the summer of 1877. The President of the Committee, who had gone to the Tyrol for the hot season, was startled by a letter from Rome to the effect that the affairs of the Institution were such that it seemed necessary to break it up altogether. She wrote back entreating that the work might be continued until the Committee could be gathered again at Rome; and then, following her letter as far as Florence, she met the report that the Home was already broken up, and that steps were in progress to disperse the children. Consulting with such of her colleagues as she could find, she took measures to " redeem the time," with a deep feeling of responsibility in the position which she had reluctantly accepted. "I reflected," she says, " on the aspects of the work toward Italy, toward so many poor children in Rome—that it was a woman's work, so nobly begun, so energetically carried on, even to the sacrifice of its founder's life. I dared not assume the responsibility of being one to consent to the ruin of that which had cost so much labor, and which might so easily be destroyed; but at what cost, at what labor, could it be built up again?" She sketched a plan on which, if the immediate difficulties could be surmounted, the work could be carried on, and wrote to Dr. Gould in New York, submitting it for his approval and consent.

In the pending situation, the members of the Committee that were present shrank from making themselves severally and personally responsible as signers of a lease for a house. The lease for the old house had already expired, and the Home was remaining there from day to day on mere sufferance. It was evident that the Committee as a body would not take the grave responsibility required; and on motion a formal vote was passed by which the

Committee was dissolved. "At that very moment," says the President, "a telegram from Dr. Gould was put into my hands, approving my plans, promising his support, and appointing me his legal representative to secure the interests and carry on the work of the Home." Four ladies, two Americans and two English, agreed to stand by each other in the responsibility of the work, and the books and papers of the Home were transferred to their hands.

From this point the Gould Memorial Home seems to emerge into daylight. But even when these hesitations, difficulties and anxieties were perplexing the minds of those in charge of its interests, it must not be supposed that the useful labors of the institution were interrupted. On the contrary, while those responsible for its affairs were passing anxious days and nights, the work of the school was proceeding with unabated interest and usefulness. A few of the letters from the scholars, quoted *literatim*, will give an exact idea of the progress that was making:

DEAR MRS. EDWARDES:

On beginning this letter I must ask you excuse if I am been so long in writing you. We have had so much to do that sometimes we had not a moment to play. We have had our general examination, and therefore I have not write to you before. We had our examination during five days, on the first of which we had the examination in written, as composition, problem and other things to write. On the second day we had the Old and New Testament. On the third we had the French dictation and other things to write. On the fourth the national history, that is to say, pieces of history of Italy taken here and there, after the geography and our English examination. Mr. Burtchaell came to ask us questions upon it ; and we had to read, to translate, to answer in English at his Italian questions, and at last he asked us about the formation of plural in the words, where comes from the English language, how many letters are German and of strange tongues in 100 English words ; and other things. We answered as well as we could. On the fifth day we had the French grammar and some pieces of poetry to say. Every day came some person to hear us, but on Thursday and Friday the school was full of English and Italian ladies and gentlemen. Mrs. Gajani, Mr. Burtchaell and some others were also in the school, and when we had to go in the midst of them to speak, you can imagine if we were not afraid. But at last it is all passed, now we have two months to get rest. At the end of the examination, Mr. Especa arose and said : " I have the commission to tell you that one day of the next week all the boys and girls of the Home will go to Frascati," and he said to them of the School : " You can come, but you must have your voyage paid." I am not sure if we go on Monday ; but tomorrow we have our promotions in the Waldensian Church at 4 o'clock, and Mr. Garnieri will tell us the day in which we will go.

Dear Mrs. Edwardes, we are all afraid to forget what we know of English ; but I have the Pilgrim's Progress to translate into English from Italian. If it please God, I'll translate it into French.

We were very sorry when a person, I do not remind who was, came to tell us that you was gone, but we hope that you shall be soon among us.

On the next letter I'll tell you the result of my examination and how we have amuse ourselves to Frascati.

We are all well, as we hope you are ; Mark is better, now he can work very well in the Stamperia ; Beppino is better too. All salute you.

Your truly

ROME, 1st *July*, 1876.　　　　　　　　　　——— ———.

DEAR DR. GOULD :—By Mrs. Gajani's goodness my humble letter can rich you till there. All the others are well, as they

hope of you.   Although we are so far one another, by few words
we can communicate our thought and our love.   Our vacanzes
are finished, and since the 4th September the school is opened
again.   During the last two months I asked permission to Mr.
Garnieri to be absent from the Home for five days to go to my
birth-village, where I have so enjoyed myself that at the time
when I came home I returned with red chicks and with a coun-
try-man's color.

Dear Dr. Gould, what would I like more than Mrs. Gould's
photograph ?   I beg you, if you can to send me a copy of it.   We
are 17 in the Home, presently, and I hope that soon the number
will be augmented by my brother.

In this month I have gained francs 10.25, in the last 5.61, and
in July 4.52—so altogether I gained in the Printing-Office 20.38
in three months. . . . . I hope to see you again before we die,
and if we can not see, in this world, one another, we will see
each other in the eternal glory.   No more.   I will never forget
you, and I hope that you will never forget

Your humble servant

ROME, *6th September*, 1876.   —— ——.

ROME, *May 12th*, 1877.

DEAR DOCTOR GOULD :—I am very glad to write you to tell
you some of our news.

Now we go to the gymnasium at the Orto Bottanico where
we are very happy ; we play there, and there is the teacher that
teaches us, and we go there twice a week.

Every Sunday we go to the Sunday School and there we are
attentive to the word of Jesus Christ, and there we learn some
verses.   If we have twenty points at the end of the month we
receive a small card with a text of Scripture from the New or
Old Testament surrounded by pretty flowers.   Here is one :
"Jesus saith unto him, I am the Way, the Truth and the Life.
No man cometh unto the Father but by me." And then the teacher
tells us some thing about the missionaries, who go to announce
to the people the Gospel.

Now there are in Home eighteen boys and seven girls. There are five boys and one girl that have just come.

The printing-office now goes on well and we all work in the printing office.

All the children of the Home salute you.

I am
Your Humble Servant

——— ———.

ROME, *May* 12, 1877.

DEAR DOCTOR GOULD:—I am glad to be able to give you also this time some news about ourselves.

All the boys and girls now are in good health, save our little companion Beppino Bartoli of Venice who was ill in the hospital of "Bambino Gesù," but he is come back to the Home, but always ill.

Some days ago, we had fourteen boys and seven girls, while now the Home is increased by four other boys of Rome, and we are now in number of eighteen boys without the girls, who are seven. We hope that this number will be soon doubled, because some persons have told us that the number would be augmented to forty boys and girls. . . . .

Some days ago there come to visit our Schools the Rev'd Pastor Leopold Witte, a member of the Society Gustavo-Adolfo, who came to Italy some weeks ago to visit the Evangelical Italian churches, to write a book on this, which shall be read in all countries.

I hope that you will excuse the mistakes, which are many in this letter.

All the children of the Home in Rome salute you. . . . .

ROME, 7 *April*, 1878.

DEAR LADY :*—Miss Edwardes have said to me if I will write a letter to you, and I write to you how you see.

---

* This letter is addressed to one of the friends of the school by a boy who is sustained by her bounty. The total cost of supporting a scholar is $80 a year.

I am four years and three months that I am in this college.
I came here that I dont no nothing, no read, no write, not at all
of English, no France.   Now I have learn to read, to write, a
little of English and a little of France.   And I thank very much
that good person that have take me in this home.

The onomastic day of our new king Umberto di Savoia there
was a festival, and the Committee have let us to go and make a
walk.   That day there was very much of soldiers.

The day of the incoronation of our new king, there was also
very much of soldiers.

In this college we have three times a week the English lesson.

There is also a beautiful garden.   I have 14 years and I am
from Milan.   There is also the printing-office and I am one
of the boys that go there.   We are in the printing-office five
boys.   There is also the shous-man [shoemaker] and the boys
that go there are four.   The other boys learn their lesson.   And
the girls work at their work.   In the Printing-office we compose
a news-paper intitolated : *L'Educatore Evangelico.*

I salute you.   Receive my compliments ; and that God be with
you all the time of your years, and that God bless you and your
family.   Good-bye.   I am your
                                        Servant,
                                        ——— ———.

The work of the Editor of this book is now finished.
It has been little more than the work of putting together
the words of others so as to tell the story of a noble life,
and the results of it.   What remains to be said may best
be given in a letter of Mrs. Edgecumbe Edwardes, the
President of the new Committee, that all readers may see
not only how, in its new growth and expansion, the Home is
answering to the ideal and hope of its founder, but with
what love for Mrs. Gould's memory, and with a heart and
purpose how congenial to her own, the work of her life's toil
and of her dying prayers has been taken up and carried

forward. Those who have followed the story with any feeling of patriotic satisfaction, as it has recounted the noble deeds of an American woman in the metropolis of the ancient world, will feel the pulsation of a wider sympathy in seeing the charge of her twice-orphaned children devolved into the hands of an English lady, her kinswoman by family, her sister in the fellowship of the Universal Church, and her worthy and congenial associate in this work of Christian mercy.*

Pending all our perplexities and discussions, we had not been idle in our efforts to secure a house. Many difficulties, which at first seemed insurmountable, were thrown in our way, but at last, in the new quarter of Rome, on the Esquiline, a suitable house was found, as if it had been waiting for us—a villa standing in its own garden (making an excellent play-ground) with lofty rooms for dormitories and class-rooms, and with plenty of space on the ground floor for workshops.

A busy scene now began in the old Home. The children, who had been asking ceaseless questions and making many guesses as to what was to become of them, were told that a new home had been found for them, and immediately preparations began for removal. The active little people, like strings of ants, began

---

* Mrs. Edwardes is the widow of Major-General Edwardes, Surgeon-General of the British forces during the war of the Sepoy Rebellion, in which he was the companion-in-arms, and the near friend of General Sir Henry Havelock. With cordial and active interest, as a member of the Honorary Committee, Lady Havelock is now a fellow-laborer with Mrs. Edwardes in the Gould memorial work at Rome.

General Edwardes was cousin to Mr. R. M. Blatchford, uncle to Mrs. Gould, and some time American Minister Resident at Rome. A letter of thanks was sent to General Edwardes, by the American Board of Foreign Missions, for his services in saving the lives of American missionaries during the Sepoy war.

There can be no need of apology for these brief personal details.

12*

collecting their possessions, and were to be seen, at almost any time during these few days, tying or untying bundles, and consulting with each other how this or that peculiar treasure was to be carried. Many of the little ones were found guarding with jealous care some useless rag or broken toy. On the 2d of January, 1878, the final order was given, and the twenty-three children were marched up to take possession of the new Home.

Great was their delight to find such a magnificent *palazzo*, as they called it. Worn out with excitement, they dropped asleep that evening in the eager anticipation of a play in the garden the next morning.

In doing this, we thought we had accomplished a great deal;

but we had only begun our work. Everything had now to be arranged. Divisions had to be made for the different workshops; the printing-press to be set up; the laundry to be prepared; doors to be put up in some places, and taken down in others. I need not enter into the many delays through the unpunctuality of workmen, the endless disappointments, the constant changes to be made when first arrangements would not do. But even at the end of the first fortnight it was wonderful to see what perseverance had gradually done. Every one and everything seemed to fall into place.

Our first care was to obtain a good matron for the girls—a very difficult thing. Here, again, one was found who seemed to have been in training for the situation—an Englishwoman, the widow of an Italian, who has thus far proved like a mother to the girls.

It was impossible to hold an inaugural feast for the children in the new Home so soon after their arrival in it. I therefore asked them all to my house on the 6th of January, not only to give them a Christmas treat, but that I might have the opportunity of introducing them to many of our English and American friends whom I was anxious to interest in the work. Our rooms were crowded with guests coming and going, who not only waited on the children at their feast, but joined in the merry games that followed. It proved a very happy evening. The children's faces beamed with delight, and the visitors expressed astonishment and pleasure at their appearance and manners. Two English ladies who had a *protégé* among the children did not at first recognize, in a frank, open-faced boy, the dull, cowed-looking little fellow they had placed in the Home only six months before; and so pleased were they that they asked if, on the payment of a certain sum, we would receive his brother into the school. An American lady who sat the whole evening watching the children sent the next morning a handsome donation in proof of her interest in the work.

Our first meeting in the Committee-Room of the new house was held January 9th. The applications for admittance had by this time become so numerous that we scarcely knew how to choose, each case appearing more urgent than another. After strict inquiry, six of the most needy were passed. We were grieved to refuse any, but were compelled to administer the funds with the utmost prudence, as the removal had involved heavy expenses.

This 9th of January was a sad day for Rome. Almost the first words I heard on returning home were "*il re è morto!*" We strangers, English and American, felt the king's death almost as deeply as Italy's own children. So much was he loved among his subjects, that when it was announced in the school, little Mary, only four years old, clasped her tiny hands together exclaiming, "*Mama! il re galantuomo—morto!*" and burst into tears. We wish to encourage a loyal and national spirit among our boys, and at the afternoon service held at the Home the following Sunday, Signor Garnieri gave a little sketch of the late king—his bravery, his love of liberty, his great respect for his word—confirming each point by anecdotes well known among the Italians. The boys were much interested, and we could see big tears roll down their cheeks when instances of his heroism were narrated. At the public funeral all the children appeared in mourning, the girls watching the procession from our own "loggia." The national flag, draped in crape, was displayed from the terrace of the Villa. I must not omit to mention how fervently the young king was prayed for by our boys.

Strangers now began to find out where the new Home was situated, and visitors to come on the appointed days. A very busy scene was presented by the children in their classes or at their different trades. Great was the alacrity with which, at the ringing of a bell, the boys would drop their arithmetic or geography lesson, fall into marching order and proceed down-stairs, some to the shoemaking or mending, others to type-setting or the printing-press, while the girls would go up-stairs to their sewing or house-work.

Applications for admittance continued to increase. We were now obliged to limit the number and define what cases should be considered eligible. The applications did not always come from the very poor, but from all classes—from pastors of different denominations seeking a shelter and Christian education for some poor orphan of their flock; from ladies high in rank; and from professors in the Italian Government colleges. Many a sad tale of struggling poverty and sorrow has come to my knowledge through these petitions.

Our institution was rapidly filling up, so that contrivance was necessary to make room. The dining-tables were too crowded, and before long the little ones overflowed into another room, where additional tables had to be supplied.

The time when most of the visitors to Rome leave for the summer, and donations cease, was approaching. We dreaded crowding our dormitories in the hot months, or encountering anxieties in respect to funds. The Committee accordingly issued a notice that admissions to the Home would be discontinued until their return in the autumn. This brought a veritable avalanche of petitions upon us, as if no one had ever thought of it before, or had only realized the benefit of the Home for the first time.

During these few months I have noticed an increased willingness on the part of parents to send their girls to us. *Willingness* is scarcely the word—a manifest anxiety would best express the change of feeling. Formerly when a vacancy occurred in the girls' part of the house, and the applications were for boys, if we offered to take a girl instead, the answer generally was: " No, the boys are bread-winners ; the better they learn the more they earn ; we are too poor to let our girls go ; there is the baby to mind and the washing to do ; what good is learning to a girl ? " Sometimes it was : " She is too useful to me at home. Take the boy ; I can't manage him, but he's a bright fellow, and will make a good shoemaker in no time." Now the answer often is : " Signora, for the love of Heaven take my girl. She is a good girl, she loves her mother, and if she only knew how, she would help me ; and " (lowering the voice) " I know the children in the *Asilo* are taught to fear God, so that I would not be afraid for my girl if I had to leave her in this sad world."

We strive to keep the number of the girls equal with that of the boys, and to give them an equally good education. No part of the Home arouses more interest in visitors than the room where the girls are assembled. Here almost all the work of the house is carried on—the knitting of all the stockings, all the cutting-out, sewing, making, and mending of garments for the children, and of the house linen. A certain number are told off for house-work, and when the study hours are also counted, it is made clear that our girls, like the good woman of the Proverbs, " eat not the bread of idleness."

It is our aim to train these dark-eyed, interesting daughters of Italy to be good daughters and wives—to be virtuous and modest, *not because they are watched and spied upon*, but because they honor God and respect themselves. Early habits of order and industry are seldom wholly laid aside in after life ; and if these once come to be loved for their own sake, a great advance will be gained toward the improvement of society.

I have tried to give some idea of our progress and our encouragements. But it would be unjust to ourselves if I did not say something of our hindrances, trials, and disappointments. These are constantly arising, from the children themselves, from their parents and relations, and from the opposition of the priests.

This opposition, I regret to say, does not diminish. The Cardinal Vicar of Rome, in his late charge, condescends to aim a special blow at us, and threatens with the severest ecclesiastical penalties such as in future send their children to the Home, or leave them there after this warning. Even the Pope does not consider it beneath his dignity to add an anathema, and affirms that until Protestant congregations and schools are driven out of Rome, it is impossible for him to hold friendly relations with the Government. This has taken effect chiefly among the women, and has led to serious annoyances at the Home, resulting, in some instances, in the withdrawal of some of the children. Frequently, however, the very women who had clamored for the dismission of their children would return a day or two afterward entreating us to receive them again. Sometimes, out of compassion to the children, we have done this. With others, it was only too flagrant that money had been paid to induce them to withdraw their children ; and the most frivolous pretences are alleged to justify the withdrawal. But, for all these things, the Home prospers and increases in numbers and usefulness.

Our needs also increase. It is impossible to extend the industries without outlay. We want to start a laundry, which will be as great a help to the girls as printing is to the boys. I am convinced that it may be made not only self-supporting, but a source of income. . . . .

Another great need is our rent. If it were possible to buy a house, it would take a great burden off our mind. We scarcely dare hope for it, but as a step in that direction, I propose that we commence a fund by placing to its account any balance we may have at the close of the year.

Not to speak of other desirable things, we want a little gymnasium for the boys, and something of the same kind for the girls, to encourage them to outdoor games. But an urgent need we have felt all along has been to provide for the very little ones, and for those who, though not positively ill, need a little change, a little rest and care, which could not be given without withdrawing some of the elder children from their work, or overtasking the strength of matron or teachers.

Of course we shall be told that the answer to the first demand is easy—Don't take very young children. And this is what we had decided on—to receive none under seven years old. But this is the only institution of the kind in Rome, and it became very hard to enforce this rule arbitrarily. Six was very near to seven, and five was not much further; and little creatures of four and three, with sad, earnest eyes and old faces, delicate and under-fed, were brought with tears and entreaties that we would take them. And it was impossible not to see the advantage, both to the institution and to the children, if we could take them at an earlier age before bad habits were formed, and while yet tendencies to disease might be overcome by proper nourishment.

I thought it well over, and determined to make the venture and give my plan a fair trial before laying it formally before the Committee, or involving our fund in the expense. This I did by taking a house at Frascati, where rent is much less and the air so good, placing in it an English nurse, whose kindness and patience in sickness we knew, reserving the best and airiest room for such of the children of the institution as required change, and filling the other rooms with the dear little ones we had been obliged to reject because of age.

We began with some of the most touching cases of want and desertion I have ever known. One was recommended by the wife of your excellent Ambassador, whose praise I need not speak, she is so well known as foremost in all good works; but I may say how much her kind words helped me to make this beginning. "I am confident," she wrote to me at that time, "that this branch of the work will meet with the greatest sympathy from all, and a response in every mother's heart." An English lady at once gave me five pounds toward it, which enabled me to send the few articles of furniture required. So this off-shoot of the Home began, and, I rejoice to say, has succeeded beyond expectation. The expense has not exceeded what we formerly paid for nursing cases of serious illness in the Home. We now have a chance to ascertain what ailments children have, before sending them to the Home, and during this probation can test the truth of statements made concerning them. And above all we give the poor little people a better chance for a healthy life, and so for a happy and useful one. Sixteen or eighteen of our children at the Home have in this way had a change of air and scene. We are able to give them more freedom than is possible under the stricter discipline of the Home, so as to get more at individual disposition and character. The very breaking of the monotony of regular school life has been good. A more homelike feeling has grown up. Many are the little anecdotes stored up to tell, on their return, about work and walks when "in villeggiatura." It is their great delight, both boys and girls, to help with the house-work and then, each in charge of one or more of the little ones, to start for the Aldobrandini gardens, where they can sit by the fountains, or wander at sweet will. But the greatest of all treats was to make a *pique-nique*, taking their brown loaves, some figs and clusters of grapes, and away in the fresh morning air over the hills among the cyclamen and wild thyme to dear old Tusculum, still, as in the old days, pleasant and very beautiful in the eyes of all Romans.

Thus, then, the Junior Home is established at Frascati. Work is opening before us in all directions. The Institution will soon be better known among the Italians themselves; and among Christians of every name we may look for help, as its benefits are more and more felt and it is better understood that we love all and seek to help all, irrespective of party feeling.

Am I too ambitious when I look forward to seeing one day our own building, large enough to contain double our present number—boys on one side, girls on the other, with chapel and class-rooms in the centre? This, so far as I knew Mrs. Gould's plans, would just meet her wishes; and our aim should be to carry out her work as she would have done were she still with us. This is the best tribute to her memory.

Until I entered upon this portion of her work, I had no idea how extreme and unwearied her labors were. I am astonished at what one woman, by courage and energy, actually got through in a single day, while burdened with weakness and suffering which to most of us would have been an excuse for doing nothing. To her it was a reason for leaving nothing undone which it was possible to do.

Well do I remember meeting her at the foot of the Spanish steps a few days before we left Rome, in the summer of 1875. It was a very hot and trying afternoon. " Where are you going ? " said I ; " you look only fit for your bed."

" Please don't talk of bed," she replied ; " I dread being obliged to take to it more than I can tell. I was on my way to see you, but wondered how I was to get up those steps. See how good God is ! He knew I wanted terribly to see you, and as I could not get up, he just sent you down."

We stood on one side, near the fountain in the Piazza di Spagna, while she told me of her anxieties, her hopes and fears. Even then, she seemed to have an idea that her time was short. I urged her to form a Committee in Rome, that might aid her at least in obtaining funds. As we were saying good-bye, she grasped my hand and added: "You have promised to help me with those dear children. You will work with me when you come back. It takes a load off my mind and gives me fresh courage. Now, I know why I craved so to see you."

Soon after that, I called on her in the Via Babuino to say farewell. She was too ill to leave her room, and was lying on her bed looking pale and worn. She "could not forsake the poor children," she said ; and there, on each side of her couch, was a little cot with a sick child, and two other children were waiting on them and trying to amuse them. I could see, by the drawn look of pain, that she was in great suffering ; but even then, she seemed entirely to forget herself in trying to interest us in the children, and even sat up with a great effort in her eagerness to show some work and a drawing that the little ones had made.

" Does it not tire you too much to leave them with you ? "

" Oh, no, no !" she answered. "I should only be fretting for fear they would not get all they needed in their illness."

In reply to another question, she said : "I am in a loving Father's hands to raise me up, if he sees good, or—" hesitating as a look of deep sorrow passed over her face—" or carry on my work by other hands. Remember, dear friend," she added, "you have promised to help me, and it makes me happy, for I know you will do it."

" If I live," I said, " I will try." I felt that we were saying farewell for the last time, and with many warm expressions we parted. We had scarcely reached the outer door, when to our great surprise, she appeared on the landing, and throwing her arms around my neck, the great tears rolling down her cheeks, she murmured : "I could not part with you so. I must kiss you once more and say, *I trust you to care for those dear children.*"

When we returned to Rome, a few months later, she was at rest, wearied out with the heat and burden of the day. Her works do follow her, and I am thankful if in any measure I can fulfill my promise and help to carry them on.

Her life speaks for itself. It was one of unwearied benevolence, love, and self-devotion. It appeals especially to all Christian ladies among her own countrywomen, to sustain what she so nobly and courageously began. Another has labored, and ye have entered into her labors. One sows and others reap ; but the time is fast coming when the sower and the reapers shall rejoice together. Their work is wrought for the great Master who Himself when on earth took the little children in his arms and blessed them, and has promised, when he returns again, to "give to every man according as his work shall be." . . . .

I remain, with sincere respect,

Yours truly,

M. L. EDWARDES.